"Faith," Price said, "there must be something I can give you. Just name it."

A totally preposterous thought popped into Faith's head: *Make love to me.*

She flushed crimson. How could she even *think* such a thing?

She wanted real love. A lifetime commitment. A houseful of kids. Spending the night with Price Montgomery wouldn't move her one inch toward those goals.

But she did love him. And tomorrow she was leaving him and Montgomery House. Forever.

One night to remember. Was that such a bad going-away gift to want?

"Faith?" he repeated. He was looking at her piercingly now.

Faith had no idea where she got the nerve. But she heard herself saying, "If you really want to give me something—"

"What, Faith? Tell me."

She did. "Make love to me."

Dear Reader,

The skies won't be the only place to find fireworks this month. Special Edition has six wonderful, heartwarming books for your July.

Babies are fun in the summer, and this July we're highlighting "the little ones." We begin with RITA-award-winning author Cheryl Reavis, and our THAT SPECIAL WOMAN! title for the month, *Meggie's Baby*. You last saw Meg Baron in Cheryl's book, *One of Our Own*. Now Meg returns to the home she left—pregnant and seeking the man she's never been able to stop loving. In *The Bachelor and the Baby Wish*, by Kate Freiman, a handsome bachelor tries to help his best friend achieve her fondest wish—to have a child. And the always wonderful Susan Mallery gives us a man, his secret baby and the woman he's falling for in *Full-Time Father*.

And rounding out the month we've got the ever-popular JONES GANG—don't miss *No Less Than a Lifetime* from bestselling author Christine Rimmer. Also, it's time for another of those SWEET HOPE WEDDINGS from Amy Frazier in *A Good Groom Is Hard To Find*, and Sierra Rydell brings us a sizzling reunion in *The Road Back Home*.

A whole summer of love and romance has just begun from Special Edition! I hope you enjoy each and every story to come!

Sincerely,

Tara Gavin, Senior Editor

Please address questions and book requests to:
Silhouette Reader Service
U.S.: 3010 Walden Ave., P.O. Box 1325, Buffalo, NY 14269
Canadian: P.O. Box 609, Fort Erie, Ont. L2A 5X3

CHRISTINE RIMMER
NO LESS THAN A LIFETIME

SPECIAL EDITION®

Published by Silhouette Books
America's Publisher of Contemporary Romance

For my mother, Auralee Smith, former PTA prez, leader of my Brownie Troop, head of my Girl Scout Troop, cookie baker, Christmas maker. And we won't even get into later, when I was *supposed* to be a grown-up....
Thanks for all of it, Mom. I love you.

And thanks to Llewellyn Publications for the phases of the moon.

 SILHOUETTE BOOKS

ISBN 0-373-24040-6

NO LESS THAN A LIFETIME

Copyright © 1996 by Christine Rimmer

This edition published by arrangement with Harlequin Books S.A.

Printed in U.S.A.

Books by Christine Rimmer

CHRISTINE RIMMER

is a third-generation Californian who came to her profession the long way around. Before settling down to write about the magic of romance, she'd been an actress, a sales clerk, a janitor, a model, a phone sales representative, a teacher, a waitress, a playwright and an office manager. Now that she's finally found work that suits her perfectly, she insists she never had a problem keeping a job—she was merely gaining "life experience" for her future as a novelist. Those who know her best withhold comment when she makes such claims; they are grateful that she's at last found steady work. Christine is grateful, too—not only for the joy she finds in writing, but for what waits when the day's work is through: a man she loves who loves her right back and the privilege of watching their children grow and change day to day.

THE JONES GANG

Legend
Broken Lines indicate previous marriages
* One illegitimate son: Jack Roper
† One child by a previous marriage: Mark
ø Three children by a previous marriage

Ogden Bartholomew "Bart" Jones
Delilah St. James

* Ogden "Oggie" Elijah
Bathsheba Riley
Isaiah Michael

Nathaniel John

Gideon Ezekiel
Mary Keyes

Jared
Eden Parker

Patrick
Regina Black

Delilah
Sam Fletcher
Brendan

Amy Riggins

Nevada
Faith
Evangeline
ø Erik Riggins

Heather
† Lucas Drury
Cecilia

Sally Willis
Belle Daniels
Sally

Teresa
Marnie

Marybeth Lynch
Anthea

Bathsheba
Eliza

Chapter One

"Just what do you plan to do with yourself, Faith?"

Before he finished the sentence, Price Montgomery knew he sounded harsh. Faith Jones, his housekeeper of over a decade, apparently thought so, too. Her slender hands tightened in her lap and her wide brown eyes shifted away.

Regret at his own gruffness tugged at him—but not too hard. After all, she certainly couldn't expect him to be pleased with what she'd just told him.

Faith was still looking away, out the graceful Palladian window of the library, at the gray January sky and the dense tangle of greenery that clung to the hill on which Montgomery House towered. She held her chin very high. For a moment, Price almost believed that when she faced him again she would inform him that what she planned to do with herself was no concern of his.

But the moment passed. Price watched as she collected herself. When she spoke, it was in that gentle, reasonable tone she always used. "I'm going to run my own business."

"Oh?" This time Price was careful to sound interested, and nothing more. "What kind of business?"

"I've bought a motel. In North Magdalene." Her soft mouth curved in a slight smile. "You do remember my mentioning North Magdalene, don't you, Price?"

Price remembered. North Magdalene was a tiny town in the Sierra foothills. Faith had a sister who lived there. In the past year or so, Faith had visited the place a lot. Price hadn't thought much about the visits at the time—except to be vaguely irritated at the thousand and one little things that were never quite right at Montgomery House without Faith's skilled hand to keep them in line.

"Price? *Do* you remember North Magdalene?"

"Of course I do."

She was still smiling, a sort of musing, indulgent smile. "It's a beautiful little town."

"I'm sure. You've bought a motel, you said?" He stuck with the interested tone, though it wasn't easy.

"Yes. A motel. It's a little run-down. The former owner's kind of let it go. So I got a great price on it. I'm going to remodel it and manage it myself."

"Do you have the money for this?"

Her soft smile fled; she looked uncomfortable again. His question must have sounded curt. He had to watch himself. He wasn't taking this well at all.

Faith answered after drawing a long, slow breath. "Yes, Price. You've paid me generously over the years. I have enough money to carry out my plans."

She was right. He *had* paid her well; she'd earned every penny. And right now, he almost wished he'd kept her at minimum wage. Which wasn't like him at all. He had his failings, but he'd always treated his employees fairly, at least.

Right this minute, though, Price didn't feel like being fair. Or even reasonable.

The really strange truth was, he wanted to shout at her. He wanted to stand up from behind his massive semicircular mahogany desk and loom over her and tell her that she couldn't do this. He wouldn't allow it.

On his Quotron, which was one of the three computer screens before him, stock prices for companies all over the world scrolled in an endless chain. Price supported himself and his eccentric household by the effective management of a diverse stock portfolio. As a young man, he'd been driven by one goal: to gain and keep the financial stability he and his parents had never known when he was a child. He'd achieved that goal in his twenties, by patenting an invention of his father's and then effectively investing the income from the patent.

Price stared hard at the moving columns of numbers. But he hardly saw them, really. He was using the screen as a point of focus, to get himself under control.

When he felt that he could speak without shouting, Price rose from his leather chair. He came out from behind the bank of phones and computer screens. Slowly he circled the desk and sat on the outer rim of it, a few feet from where Faith perched so straight in her seat.

She seemed to stiffen even more, to pull into herself at his nearness. He leaned a little closer, feeling cruel—but somehow justified in his cruelty. "I thought you were happy here, Faith."

"I have been." She swallowed. "Happy."

"Then why?"

She looked into her lap at her tightly folded hands, then back up at him. "Why am I leaving Montgomery House?"

"Yes."

"I'm . . . ready to take a few chances, that's all. It's time for me to move on. And I do have a lot of family in North Magdalene." She looked at him hopefully, seemed to see he wasn't convinced, and so forged on with more explanations. "I have a wonderful uncle, Oggie Jones. He's old and lame and smokes cigars. And he's . . . magic." She smiled then, a pleased, secret smile. "Positively magic. And he has five children. All of them are grown and all of them live there, in North Magdalene, with their own families."

Her eyes were sparkling now, looking more gold than brown. "And then there's Evie, my sister. She married over a year ago, which you may remember, and she has three stepchildren. They're darling children. Two girls and a boy. I want to . . . get to know them. I want to watch them grow up."

All her chatter about her relatives reminded Price of his own mother and father, who inhabited a suite of rooms on the second floor. They weren't going to like losing Faith any more than he did. And he didn't even want to consider how his reclusive younger brother, Parker, was going to take the news. Parker lived on the third floor, off the ballroom, near Faith's rooms. Parker never went out. And Faith was the only person outside the family who was ever allowed in his room.

Faith was still talking about her dear old uncle and his children, about what a warm, welcoming place North Magdalene was, about how she couldn't wait to start her new life there.

Price had heard much more than enough by the time she paused for a breath. He spoke before she could ramble on. "You want to be with your family, is that what you're telling me?"

She sank back in her chair a little, her cheeks flushing, probably realizing that she'd let herself get carried away in her glowing descriptions of the Joneses of North Magdalene.

"Yes ." Her tone was clipped now. "And I want my own business." She lifted one pale hand and stroked her brown hair in its neat little bun. A few silky tendrils had come loose. They curled around her temples. Combined with the spots of color on her cheeks, the wayward strands made her look very young. Vulnerable. He watched as she dropped her hand to her lap once more, and folded it again with its mate.

"Don't laugh at me, Price."

He must have been smiling. He made his face a blank. "I'm not."

"I know you depend on me. That's why I plan to give you time to replace me. But I *am* going."

Price looked at the far wall, between two sets of ceiling-high bookcases, where a gilt-framed seventeenth-century drawing of the head of Hercules hung.

Give me strength, Price thought wryly.

He reminded himself that Faith's life was her own. He was only her employer, and he'd gone about as far as was reasonable toward trying to change her mind.

It was just damn hard to believe that she was really leaving after all these years.

Faith volunteered gently, "I'll be living in a beautiful little town, Price. With people I love. Be happy for me."

His first irrational anger was gone. Now he felt like a heel for trying to hold her back. "I am. Of course I am." The most reasonable thing to do right now would be to iron out the particulars.

He asked, "How much notice are you giving me?"

"Price." Her big eyes begged him not to be upset. "I know this is a surprise to you. But it's the best thing for me. Please try and understand."

Now she was trying to pacify him. Well, he didn't need pacifying. Just the facts. Just what she intended to do. "How much notice?"

She leaned forward in her chair, as if she were going to say something really important. But then she just sat back again and sighed. "I thought two weeks would be fair."

He felt another surge of senseless wrath. Two weeks was nothing. Not enough time at all.

He thought fast, then spoke evenly, "You're the one who created your position. Neither my parents nor I have the vaguest idea what to look for in a replacement. You're going to have to help us out a little here."

"Yes. Of course. I thought in two weeks I could—"

"How about if you find and train the person, however long that takes—and *then* go?"

Faith considered, then nodded. "All right. As long as the time frame is reasonable. I really don't want to leave you without someone competent."

Price hadn't realized how tense he'd become until he felt the tightness between his shoulder blades melt away. It could take a *long* time to find an acceptable replacement. And the longer it took, the more chance there was that she would rethink this idea of running a motel in some nowhere foothill town.

Casually Price suggested a condition. "Of course, the person would have to be approved by my father and mother—and myself."

Faith shifted uneasily in her chair. "Parker, too?"

Price knew he couldn't go quite that far. "No, we'll leave Parker out of it. Meeting your potential replacements would only upset him, anyway—assuming he'd do it in the first place."

Her uneasy look faded. She even smiled. "That's wise."

He smiled back. "All right. It's settled."

Her smile grew pensive. "Price. I want this clear. I'm not willing to stay on longer than a month or so."

"I understand."

For a moment, neither of them spoke. Then one of Price's phones rang.

Faith stood. "I know you want to get back to work."

"Yes. I should."

"I'll go now and speak with your parents. And then Parker, too, I suppose." She started for the door.

"Faith."

She turned back to him, her face bright and alert. "Um?"

How many times had she turned just that way, before leaving a room, to receive some final instruction he'd almost forgotten?

The phone went on ringing. He rose from the edge of the desk and went around to pick it up. "Montgomery here. Hold on." He put his hand over the mouthpiece and spoke to Faith again. "Let me talk to the family before you do, all right?"

"But why?"

"I'd just like to, that's all."

Her expression had become pensive again. But then she shrugged. "All right. If you want to. I won't mention it to them for a day or two. But I will begin making arrangements for the interviews."

"Great." He turned his back to her and spoke into the phone again. "Yes?"

Faith went out through the music room, which in turn opened onto the front parlor. Price hardly heard her go. Her crepe-soled shoes made no sound on the inlaid floors, and she was skilled at the silent closing of heavy doors.

Price finished on the phone and hung up. Then he went over to the big Palladian window, where he stood looking out. Here, on the first floor, the view was of dense greenery: oaks and palms and cypress trees, and the carpet of ivy and myrtle that spilled down the hillsides toward the Sausalito waterfront below. Far away, Price thought he heard the hollow sound of a boat's horn: a ferry boat or a river cruiser, carrying passengers back and forth from San Francisco, a few miles across the bay.

Price and his family had lived in Sausalito for fifteen years now, ever since he'd bought Montgomery House, when he was twenty-five and ready to put his first big profits into a real home. The then-derelict Queen Anne—style manse had looked all wrong, crammed onto its too-small, rock-terraced little plot of land high in the Sausalito hills. It had seemed to him an abandoned fortress, a neglected castle keep. Price had loved it on sight. He'd had it refurbished from basement to third-floor towers. Now it was everything he'd ever dreamed it might be.

And Faith made it all work. When she started running things, the house had finally acquired what had been missing: ease and grace. Faith made the place livable day to day. Under her expert hand, Montgomery House was a home, as well as a castle.

Price just didn't want to deal with the difficulty of getting along without her. Which was why he had to see to it that she changed her mind about this move.

The first thing Faith looked for, once she was safely in the music room, on the other side of the sliding library doors, was a place to sit down. A channel-backed wing chair near the grand piano presented itself. She dropped gratefully into it.

Once seated, she stared blankly out the bay window behind the piano as she waited for her heart to stop pounding so hard and her knees to stop shaking.

After a few moments of long, deep breaths, she began to feel better.

It was done now; she had given her notice. There was no going back. Within a month, she would leave Montgomery House—and Price—for good and all.

Faith knew she'd done the right thing. She'd worked for Price for eleven years. And for the last five of those years, he had owned her heart.

But Price had no idea of her feelings. He thought of her as an extension of his precious house. It was true that she loved the house almost as much as he did. However, a mutual passion for an imposing pile of brick and stone wasn't enough for her anymore.

She had to get out. She had to move on.

Since her legs felt as if they just might hold her up now, Faith pushed herself from the chair. She glanced at her watch. Twenty-five minutes from now, she had to be in the kitchen, to meet with Balthazar, the cook. They would go over the menus for next week.

Until then, she decided, she would retire to her rooms and put her feet up. By the time she came down again, her composure would be completely restored.

"Oh, but she can't leave us!" Ariel Montgomery cried. Price's mother lifted a slim hand and smoothed back the shoulder-length white hair that was always falling in her eyes.

"Price." Regis, Price's father, coughed in distress, then shot the cuffs of his velvet house jacket. "Surely you're joking. We can't get along without Faith."

"I'm not joking," Price said.

They were sitting in the living room of his parents' suite. Price always felt agitated here. His mother had insisted that the suite be completely redone when she and Regis claimed it. She'd cheerfully ordered all the wainscoting ripped out and the molded ceilings dragged down.

Ariel's passion for bold colors and simple lines now ruled. She'd bought fat, amorphous-shaped couches and had them upholstered in purples and yellows, bright greens and oranges. The walls glowed a deep salmon. The throw pillows were alive with chartreuse lizards and lemon-yellow giraffes.

Ariel erupted from the fuchsia chaise longue where she'd been reclining. "But *why* is she leaving?"

"She said she wants to be near her family, to watch her nieces and nephew grow up."

Ariel began to pace the room, trailing the scent of Tabu, her signature perfume. "She *can't* leave. You remember what the house was like before we found her. A disaster. We lived in *hell*. I can't live like that anymore, Price. I'm an artist. I have my priorities, and they have nothing to do with seeing that the chandeliers are properly cleaned. And think of your father." She flung out a hand toward Regis, whose still-handsome face wore a worried frown. "He has his inventions to consider." Regis had a workshop in the basement. No one but Faith was ever allowed to enter there. Regis claimed no one else showed the proper respect for his tools and equipment.

Ariel went on, "We can't let some stranger come in this house and disrupt everything. We simply can't deal with that. We aren't as young as we used to be. And what about Parker? Has anyone considered my poor baby?"

Though far from a baby, Parker was a full nineteen years younger than Price. Ariel, who'd been forty-six when Parker was born, often referred to him tenderly as "living proof that passion never dies."

"Parker isn't going to like this," Ariel predicted grimly. "You know how he counts on Faith to take care of him."

Through an arch several feet away, Price could see his mother's studio, where she painted the dazzling watercolors that had brought her modest fame in recent years. The walls in there were eggshell white. Ariel required neutral surroundings while she worked. Price wished they'd chosen the studio for this discussion, instead of the suffocatingly vivid living room.

"Are you listening to me, Price?" Ariel had planted her fists on her slender hips. That errant lock of white hair fell across her eyes again. She blew it out of the way.

"I'm listening, Mother. And as soon as you're through yelling and stomping around, I'll tell you the rest of what I have to say."

"I do *not* yell and stomp!" Ariel hit her chest with a fist, right on the floppy lemon-yellow bow tie of her bright coral painter's smock.

Regis chose that moment to rise from the chartreuse sectional in the corner and stride over to his wife. He draped an arm across her shoulders and placed a light kiss on her temple, right over the hair that never would stay out of her eyes. "Darling. Ease off. Price has more to say. Let's hear him out."

Ariel's sigh was long and dramatic. But she did relax a little. She leaned into her husband's embrace. "I suppose you're right." She and Regis exchanged fond smiles. "I sometimes do get carried away." She looked at her son again. "I'm sorry, dear."

Price nodded and restrained a sigh of his own. He loved his mother, but the more successful her watercolors became, the more she seemed to think that every discussion was a perfect opportunity for an expansive display of artistic temperament.

Regis led his wife back to her chaise and guided her down in it, then sat at her feet.

Ariel fiddled with the floppy bow at her neck for a moment, then looked up and met her husband's eyes. She smiled. Regis smiled back. There might have been no one else in the world at that moment but the two of them.

Feeling like an intruder, Price glanced away. After over forty years of marriage, his parents still adored each other. They enjoyed the kind of relationship Price himself had once thought to have with the woman he married. But it hadn't worked out that way for him. His marriage had ended in tragedy and divorce.

"All right, dearest," Ariel said to Price a moment later. "I'm calm now. Tell us the rest."

Price found he was staring at a fifties-style lamp with a two-tiered shade and a turquoise ceramic mermaid for a base. When he was a child and his mother was required to run their household, he had often eaten mashed potatoes colored the exact aqua-blue of that mermaid lamp base. Ariel had found the natural color of potatoes too bland for her tastes, so she had doused them with food coloring to brighten them up. Fortunately for everyone involved, there had been no need for Ariel to prepare a meal in over fifteen years.

"Price?" Ariel said, prompting him. "Tell us the rest. About Faith."

Price blinked and looked at his mother and father once more. "Yes. All right. Faith has agreed to hire and train her replacement before she leaves us."

Ariel looked at Regis. "Is that good?" Regis only frowned and gave his wife an I-don't-know shake of his head. She turned to Price again. "Well? Is that good?"

"It will take *time* to find a replacement."

"Time." Ariel stroked her bow. "Yes. Time is good." Regis made a low sound of agreement.

Price added, "She also understands that any applicant would have to be approved by the three of us before being hired."

Regis sat up straighter on the end of the chaise. "Hmm..." he said. He and Ariel looked at each other. Matching smiles bloomed on gracefully aging faces.

Ariel grinned at her older son. "I get it. Of course. *We* approve the new housekeeper—or there'll *be* no new housekeeper."

Price nodded. "Exactly."

"And Faith would *never* leave us without someone to take care of us. The dear girl is much too tenderhearted to do something like that."

"Right."

"And, eventually, if we hold out long enough, she just might change her mind altogether about going away."

"It seems possible, at least."

Ariel delicately smoothed back her wayward hair. "Oh, my dears. It's a shame, isn't it, how truly *impossible* it is to find good help these days? Especially for a family as exacting as the Montgomerys."

Chapter Two

After letting out the fifth and final applicant of the day, Faith returned to the morning room, where the interviews had taken place.

The bottom half of a two-story addition off the kitchen, the morning room had lots of windows and was furnished in what Faith always thought of as "classic Victorian porch." It boasted a good deal of white wicker furniture, as well as an abundance of potted palms and hanging ferns. There was even a talking mynah bird, Sir Winston Churchill, who lived in a wrought-iron cage in a corner between a parlor palm and a ficus tree.

In the center of the morning room stood a long table with a jointed maple top and sturdy white-painted turned legs. Around the table were ten mismatched Windsor chairs.

When Faith emerged from the kitchen, Regis, Ariel and Price were waiting at one end of the table, right where she'd left them a few minutes before. Regis and Ariel were whispering together. They stopped immediately when they caught sight of Faith—which probably should have warned her that all was not as it should be.

Gripping a clipboard that held the applications, Faith moved toward the foot of the table opposite the rest of them. Just before she sank into the chair there, Ariel gestured expansively. "Oh, come on, dear. Don't sit ten miles away from us. Let's get *together* on this thing."

Price, who was lounging at the head of the table, pulled out the chair next to him, on his left. He smiled at her, inviting her to take the seat he offered.

Faith looked from his enticing smile to his lean hand, which still rested on the back of the chair he'd pulled out for her. If she sat there, she would be less than two feet from him.

Though the morning room was no more than pleasantly warm, Faith felt a dew of moisture break out on her upper lip. She didn't want to sit that close to Price. Whenever she was forced to be too near him, she had terrible trouble concentrating. Sometimes, when he came near, she could smell the expensive after-shave he wore—the after-shave that she herself regularly ordered by phone from a world-famous house of design. She loved the smell of that after-shave; it was subtle and clean and undeniably masculine.

"Faith, dear?" Ariel said. All three Montgomerys were watching her expectantly.

Faith gripped her clipboard more tightly and marched down the table to take the chair Price held out for her.

His hand was still resting on the back of the chair when she sat in it, which caused her to experience a swift and stunningly seductive vision. She saw herself leaning back in the chair—and Price laying his hand on her shoulder. She imagined his fingers rubbing idly, in an absentminded caress.

Of course, that was something he would never, ever do. Nonetheless, she couldn't help envisioning it.

She breathed a little easier when he took his hand away. Quickly she scooted her chair even closer to the table—and marginally farther away from him. Then she busied herself with her clipboard, lifting the clamp to release the applications that the prospective housekeepers had filled out. She set the applications on the table, within easy reach of everyone.

That done, she cleared her throat. "Now," she began. "I think we—"

Sir Winston chose that moment to interrupt. The mynah bird shrieked, "What's going on here? What's the haps? What's the story?"

A musical trill of laughter escaped Ariel. She smoothed her white hair away from her eyes and turned toward the bird. "Winnie, you naughty boy." She followed the comment with several loud kissing noises, which the bird ardently returned.

Faith shuffled the applications some more as she waited politely for Ariel to stop throwing kisses at the bird.

At last Ariel seemed to realize that she was holding up the proceedings. "Oh. Sorry. Carry on." She smiled sweetly and folded her hands on the table.

Faith removed the pen she'd hooked on the top of the clipboard and straightened the plain piece of paper she'd left under the clip for note-taking. She pointed at the applications with the pen. "Well, all I was saying was that I think we have some really good possibilities here."

No one said a word. Faith looked from Ariel to Regis and back to Ariel again, waiting for one of them to say something. At last, Ariel broke the silence with a long drawn-out sigh.

Puzzled, Faith shifted her gaze to Regis, who was rolling up the sleeve of his chambray work shirt. Regis had been called from the basement for the interviews. He always wore a chambray shirt and loose khaki pants when he worked on his inventions. Regis looked up from his sleeve and into Faith's eyes. He sighed, too.

"What? What is it?" Faith glanced at Price, though the tingle all through her body when she did that almost made her wish she hadn't.

"Faith." Price said, and nothing more. He sounded hopelessly grim.

"What?"

Ariel spoke up at last. "We're sorry, dear." Her voice seemed to drip regret. "But not one of those women will do."

"Bad news, boys!" cawed Sir Winston.

"They're not for us at all," Regis solemnly declared.

Bewildered, Faith could only sputter, "B-but...why not? They all have excellent references and related work experience. And they'd all be willing to live in."

Ariel sniffed. "References aren't everything."

"And nothing relates to working at Montgomery House," Regis chided as he rolled up his other sleeve.

Faith was inclined to agree with Regis on that particular point; there really was nothing like working at Montgomery House. But they needed a new housekeeper. So *someone* would have to tackle the job.

"And we don't want some *stranger* living here, anyway," Ariel added.

"What are you telling me?" Faith asked. "Have you changed your mind about needing someone available at all times? Would you prefer that the new housekeeper live off the premises?"

"No," Ariel replied. "We need someone here. Just not some stranger."

"Well, Ariel." Faith kept her voice reasonable only because she'd had so many years of experience in dealing with Montgomerys. "Everyone's a stranger at first."

"Not everyone."

To Faith's right, Price made a sound that closely resembled a stifled laugh. Faith shot him a glance. His face was alert and interested and impossible to read.

Faith frowned at him. He lifted a brow, as if he were wondering, in all innocence, why she had frowned at him.

Faith gave up on him and faced Ariel again. "I'm not going to argue with you about the definition of the word *stranger*," she told her.

"Well, of course you're not, dear." Ariel's face bloomed in a gracious lady-of-the manor smile.

Faith mentally counted to ten. "Let's go over your choices, then." She snared up one of the applications. "Look at this one. Ms. Annabella Fenton. She's run a successful bed-and-breakfast for five years in a row."

"So why did she stop?" Regis wanted to know.

Faith patiently explained, "She told us. You remember. The B-and-B was sold, and the new owners wanted to run it themselves."

"So she *said*," Ariel grumbled. "Did you notice how she never smiled? I could not tolerate a housekeeper who never smiled."

"You are so right, my angel," Regis concurred. "That Ms. Fenton was much too glum."

Refusing to be daunted, Faith held up a second application. "How about this one? She's run a twenty-room estate in Bel Air. And she seemed very friendly."

"Too friendly," Ariel muttered. "I can't stand a woman who smiles all the time. It's almost as bad as a woman who *never* smiles."

Over in his ficus-and-palm bower, Sir Winston squawked out what sounded like enthusiastic agreement.

Regis picked up a third application himself. "Remember this one? Too quiet by half. I'd never know what she was thinking. I couldn't live with that."

Ariel leaned over and planted a light kiss on her husband's cheek. "Precisely, my darling." She shivered. "Creepy. Too quiet is creepy. We don't need creepiness around here." She laughed, a throaty sound. "No more creepiness than we've already got, anyway."

"Oh, my sweet," Regis said tenderly. "You do have a way...with words, among other things." They stared into each other's eyes.

"Je t'adore," Ariel whispered.

"Te amo," said Regis.

Faith wanted to strangle them both. She knew what was coming next—what always occurred when Price's parents started talking to each other in foreign languages.

"If we could just..." Faith began.

But now Regis was whispering in his wife's ear. Ariel sucked in one quick little gasp. She was blushing.

The two aging lovebirds stood at the same time. "We'll be retiring now," Ariel said with a girlish giggle.

"But what about the applicants?" Faith pleaded.

Ariel blew in her husband's ear before answering. "Dear. None of them will do. We told you. You'll have to tell that agency to send some more people over. Not tomorrow, though. We'll be busy tomorrow."

"But I..."

Ariel and Regis were already at the arch that led to the kitchen. Ariel giggled again. Regis made a low growling sound. And then they were gone, on their way up the back stairs to their suite on the second floor.

Sir Winston cawed after them, "Go to it, baby!"

Faith put her head down on the table and let out a groan.

"Sorry. You know how they are," said a deep, indulgent voice beside her.

Faith snapped upright. She'd been so frustrated with the elder Montgomerys, she'd actually forgotten for a moment that Price was still sitting at her side.

Faith took a calming few seconds to close her eyes and rub the tension from her temples. Then she made herself face him, though, as always, she had to steel herself against the flood of hopeless yearning that swept through her when her eyes met his.

Price gestured casually at the discarded applications. "In spite of their thoughtless behavior, I have to agree with my parents about the women we interviewed today. None of them would have worked out."

"I disagree."

"Yes, I know that." His voice was gentle, infuriatingly so. "But you aren't the one with the choice."

"We don't have forever on this, Price."

He shrugged. "This was only the first day we've interviewed. Call the agency. Have them send over another group on Friday—after one, of course." The stock market was open until four on the East Coast, which meant one o'clock their time. If possible, Price never handled household business until after the day's trading was through.

Faith busied herself gathering up the applications and sticking them back in the clipboard. By the time she had it all in order, she had thoroughly quelled her annoyance. There was nothing she could do if the Montgomerys chose to turn down perfectly good people. Friday, she'd bring on the next group and hope that her employers had sense enough to make a choice.

Clipboard in hand, she stood. "All right, then. We'll try again Friday."

"Faith?"

She looked down at him. It wasn't easy. She got all fluttery inside. She wanted to reach out and caress his silky black hair, to get lost in his deep blue eyes, to stroke his healthy bronze skin, and to trace the perfect blade that was his nose.

But she'd been hiding her love for a long time. She kept her back straight, her expression remote. "Yes?"

"You've never really told me anything about that motel you bought."

She clutched the clipboard against her breasts. Under it, her heart was pounding so hard she actually feared he might hear it. "Well, I...um..."

"Come on." He put his hand on the back of her chair again. "Sit with me. You can spare a few minutes, can't you?"

She gulped. "Mary's up in the ballroom." Mary was one of the two part-time day maids. "She's oiling the woodwork. I should—"

"Mary can get along on her own for a few minutes more, don't you think?"

"Well..."

He patted the back of her vacated chair. "Come on."

Unable to think of more excuses—and as thrilled as she was terrified at the prospect of talking to Price about something other than the running of Montgomery House—Faith sat down once more. For a split second, as she settled back in the chair, she leaned close to him. That wonderful aftershave taunted her. Her stomach lurched in a dangerous, and thoroughly marvelous, way.

As before, Price removed his hand as soon as she dropped into the chair. Grateful for small favors, Faith set the clipboard on the table again and turned the chair so that she was facing him. Facing him was better. She wasn't quite so close that way, and it was easier to think.

Price leaned back in his own chair, getting comfortable, as if he had all day to talk to her. "What made you buy a motel?"

Her lips felt dry, but he was watching her so closely, she didn't want to lick them. She settled for pressing them together, then realized that was a nervous-looking action. She ordered her mouth to relax and forced herself to explain. "Well, for the last several months I've been really thinking of moving closer to my sister and her family. I've been on the lookout, I guess, for a business opportunity in North Magdalene that might be right for me."

He was watching her lips, as if every word she said really mattered to him. "I see."

She forged on, trying not to sound as breathless as she felt. "The motel's been on the market for a while now. The former owner was gone a lot. She really wanted to get rid of it. So the price was low."

"Have you actually closed escrow yet?"

"A week ago."

He was smiling now. He had the most wonderful mouth, sculpted on top, slightly fuller below. "So it really is all yours."

"Yes. It is. All mine. Well, after I pay off the loan, of course."

"Of course. How many units?"

"Twelve."

"That's not very big."

"I'm going to add onto it. Eventually."

"I see." Today he wore dark twill trousers and a midnight-blue cashmere sweater. He'd pushed the sleeves of the sweater up to the elbows, revealing lean, corded arms. His shoulders looked hard and broad beneath the incredibly soft wool.

Price's left hand rested on the wooden arm of his chair. There was no wedding band on that hand; there hadn't been for over five years now.

It occurred to Faith, as she gazed at that ringless hand, that she knew a great deal about Price. Too much, really.

She had lived in his house and cared for him and his family during some very rocky years. She had heard most, if not all, of his deepest secrets. She knew what Price had suffered, and the dark vows he'd made to himself.

She knew that he would never wear a wedding band again.

"What are your immediate plans?"

Faith realized she'd stared too long at his hand. She looked up and put on a bright smile. "You mean for the motel?"

"Yes."

"Well, I'm going to spend the rest of the winter taking stock, I think. Getting a real handle on everything that needs to be done. And then, when spring comes, I'll start the renovations, two or three units at a time. It's a one-motel town, and in the summer they get a lot of tourists. So even though the place is run-down, there should still be a demand for rooms. I'll keep the rates nice and low at first. And then, when it's all fixed up, I'll be able to charge a little more."

"You've thought it out carefully, then?"

"Oh, yes."

"Could you use an investor?"

For a moment, she wondered if she'd heard him correctly. "Excuse me?"

He chuckled, and the sound sang along her nerve endings. "I said, could you use an investor?"

"You mean *you?*"

"Who else?"

"But I don't—"

He lifted that ringless left hand and leaned forward a little in his chair. "Wait. It's just an idea. Hear me out."

"I ... All right."

"Who's running the motel now?"

"Chuck Swan, the uncle of the former owner."

"Well, then. Let Chuck Swan continue to run it for a while. Or close it down, if you want. But you could stay on here and keep your job. Take a few days off a week, whatever you think you need, to visit your property and take stock, as you put it. Then, when spring comes, hire a builder and see that the work gets done all at once. Since you have so many family members in North Magdalene, I'm sure one of them would be happy to keep an eye on things for you. And, as I said, I'd be willing to let you have as much time off as you need. And lend you the money so you can get things done quickly. You could probably reopen by autumn." He sat back again. "What do you think?"

She thought that she loved him, that it was very possible she would always love him. Still, if she was ever going to have the life she dreamed of, she had to do everything in her power to get away from him.

"Well?"

"Oh, Price."

Now he was frowning. "What's the matter? It's a sound proposal. And, of course, I would expect to get my money back with interest."

"I'm sure you would."

"So what do you say?"

"I say I'm flattered that you'd do all that just to keep me around for a few extra months."

"Good. Accept my offer."

"Thank you, but no."

"Why not?"

"Price. I know you believe that no one can take my place here."

"I don't *believe* it. I *know* it. We Montgomerys are not your average family."

Amen to that, she thought.

He went on. "My parents are eccentric, and my brother hasn't been himself for two years now. You understand them. You respect their individuality. You're exacting in the way you take care of the house—and totally indulgent of my family. They adore you. And they won't do well without you. You are ideally suited to Montgomery House. No one else will do.''

Faith's head was swimming. She would drown in such high praise, if she didn't watch out. She made herself look at Price steadily. "I will find you someone. Someone perfect.''

"*You're* perfect.''

"I'm pleased that you think so. But I'm no longer available. I'm moving to North Magdalene as soon as I possibly can.''

The ringless hand was gripping the chair arm now. "Why? When you can live here and continue working, bringing in a good income, while your new business is being fixed up just the way you want it?''

"I want to fix up my new business myself.''

"You *will* be doing it yourself." He was leaning close again, too close. She smelled that seductive scent of his, felt the strength of his indomitable will. "Agree to my offer.''

She looked at him pleadingly. "Price.''

"Agree.''

"Please don't—''

He reached out and laid that ringless hand over hers.

Faith gasped. The touch seemed to send sparks shooting through her whole body—out to the tips of her fingers and down into her toes. They stared at each other.

Sir Winston chose that moment to let out a protracted wolf whistle.

Price blinked at the sound. Then he removed his hand and shifted back in his chair, away from her. "Sorry. Of course. You'll do what you think is best." His voice was cold.

Faith knew she had to get out of there. She snatched up the clipboard again and clutched it to her pounding heart. "I have to go. To check on Mary..."

He shrugged. "Right."

She stood too quickly, upsetting the chair.

He caught it before it toppled. "Watch out."

"Yes. Thank you. I will."

Faith drew up her shoulders and turned for the kitchen. She prayed with all her heart that he couldn't see her knees shaking as she strode toward the door to the back stairs.

That night, Price went out for dinner. Regis and Ariel never emerged from their rooms, so Faith had Balthazar leave some delicacies in plain view in the big subzero refrigerator.

Faith carried a tray up for Parker, and discreetly knocked on the door of his room. She heard shuffling inside, and then a wary voice asked, "Faith?"

"Yes, Parker. I have your dinner."

The door slowly opened. Faith entered the small, dark room and set the tray down where she always put it, on the battered chest of drawers near the door. Parker had retreated to stand by his desk in the corner, where the screen of the computer he never turned off cast an eerie glow over the room.

Faith smiled at him. "Just leave it outside the door when you're finished."

"I always do."

"Good."

She turned to go.

"Faith?"

She paused halfway out the door. "Yes?"

"Mom says you're moving out."

"Yes, Parker. I am."

"Why?"

"I want . . . a new life."

"A new life." Parker said the words with a sigh.

Faith turned to him again. The computer screen gave off enough light that she could see that he was wearing a threadbare T-shirt with the logo of some rock group on the front. Old jeans and Converse high-tops completed his ensemble. The headphones to his stereo hung around his neck. She ached for him, as she always did. He was twenty-one now. And yet he seemed younger. A teenager, frozen in time.

"I wish you'd stay with us," Parker said.

Faith thought of Price, of the feel of his hand on hers a few hours before. She wished she could stay, too. But she couldn't. It simply wasn't enough anymore to live on dreams that would never come true.

She told Parker, "Well, I *won't* stay. But I'll find someone terrific to replace me before I go."

He was quiet. Then he muttered, "It won't be the same."

"No. But you never know. It might be better."

"I don't think so. I'll miss you, Faith."

"And I'll miss you, too."

Friday, in the morning room, they saw six more applicants. After Faith had shown the last one out, the Montgomerys told her that not a single one of them would do.

Faith made the mistake of asking why. And the Montgomerys told her.

Regis started with the first applicant of the afternoon. He claimed she was shifty-eyed.

"And how can we bear having some shifty-eyed woman taking care of the house?" Ariel demanded, then complained that the second applicant to be interviewed had been dressed entirely in beige. "I simply never have been able to trust a person who isn't willing to show a little color here and there," Ariel proclaimed.

"And this one." Regis waved the third application, to make sure he had everyone's attention. "Remember this one? She let out a little squeak of alarm every single time Sir Winston squawked or whistled. Not a good sign, I'm telling you. She's got something she's guilty about, mark my words."

Ariel held up another application. "This one was a cold fish. Did you see the way she stared? Zap. Right through a person. Narrow-eyed and narrow-minded, I feel it in my bones."

"And this Miss Fidgely." Regis pointed to the fifth application. "How can I say this? She *smelled* odd. Did you notice? Like moldy ironing...."

"And this fellow." Ariel frowned at the sixth and final application, from the single male applicant so far. "I've seen that face before, I'm positive. In the post office. On a Wanted poster."

"No," Regis declared, "none of that group will do."

Ariel chimed in. "They're each and every one all wrong."

"And now," Regis said, "I have to get moving." He stood. "I've got to get back down to the basement. I can't explain what I'm working on, but I will say this—it is destined to *blow the lid* off the jar industry."

Ariel stood. "And I must go, too. It's only a week until my new show. Where does the time go, I ask you? I'm working at *white heat,* and it's still not fast enough."

"Tallyho," Regis said.

They turned together and exited through the kitchen.

As on Wednesday, Faith and Price were left alone at the big table.

Faith dared a quick glance at Price. He smiled at her—rather ruefully, she thought. She decided it was time to confront him about this little game he and his parents seemed to be playing with her.

She folded her hands on the table and spoke in clipped tones. "The agency is running out of suitable applicants, Price."

Price lifted his broad shoulders in an unconcerned shrug. "Maybe you'll have to try another agency."

She saw that she was going to have to be more direct. "What good is another agency going to do, if you and your parents refuse to take this interview process seriously?"

Price picked up one of the discarded applications, frowned at it, and dropped it again. "We're taking the process seriously, Faith. *You* just haven't found anyone we want to hire yet."

She breathed deeply—twice—before she pressed on. "I know what the three of you are up to. And it isn't going to work."

He didn't look guilty in the least. "I don't know what you're talking about."

"You and your parents are purposely finding something wrong with every person who applies for my job."

"I'm sorry you think that."

"No, you're not. You don't care if I think that. You have some idea that I'll stay here indefinitely if you don't make a choice. You are mistaken."

He waved a hand. "Call another agency. That's all I can suggest."

Though his gesture and his tone were casual, his eyes had grown hard as sapphires. She let the subject drop. Really, there wasn't much more to say. She'd told him she knew what he was doing; if he continued to do it, he'd be the one to lose out.

And besides, though she was exasperated with the Montgomerys, she couldn't help but be touched that they were willing to go to such lengths to try to keep her around.

Price was smiling again, this time in a teasing way. Her heart did a silly little flip-flop. And suddenly even her exasperation was gone. She really was utterly defenseless when it came to him.

She gathered up the applications. When they were all in her clipboard, she pushed back her chair.

"Stay," he said when she was halfway on her feet. "Tell me about your family. In North Magdalene."

She stood the rest of the way and looked down at him, longing to remain with him for a few minutes, yet determined to hold her own. "Price. If this is some new angle on getting me to change my mind—"

He shook his head. "I swear. I'd just like to talk for a while, that's all."

And, somehow, she was sinking into her chair once more. They ended up sitting there for a good twenty minutes, talking about her family and North Magdalene and why she thought it was the right place for her to make a new life.

They were interrupted by the ringing of the cellular phone that Price had brought in from the library with him. When he answered, he found it was something he needed one of his computers to handle, so he left her. But he actually seemed reluctant to go.

Faith sat alone at the table for several minutes after he departed, thinking about how comfortably they'd been talking. It had seemed almost as if they were friends; the words and glances, smiles and laughter, had flowed so naturally between them.

"Love hurts!" cawed Sir Winston.

Faith jumped. And then she laughed.

A few days before, Faith would have agreed with the mouthy black bird. But just lately she wasn't so sure. Since she'd given her notice, Price really did seem different. He had grown more attentive, she would have sworn to it, more *aware* of her.

But then she shook her head. She had to be careful not to get her hopes up over a couple of friendly conversations and a teasing glance or two.

Still, as one day became the next, Faith couldn't help thinking that perhaps she'd been hasty in giving up on Price. It began to seem to her as if every time they spoke he wanted to prolong the conversation. If she entered the morning room when he was there, he'd insist she sit down, have a cup of coffee and tell him how her day was going. Or he'd wander into the butler's pantry while she was arranging the vases of fresh flowers that she kept in all the major rooms of the house. He'd pull out a chair and sit down. He'd laugh and roll his eyes as he talked about his mother, who seemed to become more and more temperamental as the night of her big watercolor show approached.

They saw three more groups of applicants, on Monday, Wednesday and Thursday of the second week after Faith had given her notice. Each and every applicant was found wanting, for reasons only a Montgomery could have dreamed up.

By then, Faith had exhausted all the possibilities at several Bay Area domestic employment agencies. She really was running out of prospective housekeepers to parade before her finicky employers. And she wasn't even sure she cared.

Thursday, Price once again sat with her for a while after his parents retreated to their rooms. They talked about Parker, who had been living the life of a recluse for the past two years.

Parker Montgomery was a very talented young man, who'd played the piano like a virtuoso from around the age of seven. After high school, he'd been accepted at Juilliard. But then something had gone wrong. He'd flunked out in the first year there. Then he'd decided to volunteer for active military duty. But since he'd been born missing two toes on his right foot, he'd been classified 4-F. Depressed, he'd taken to hitchhiking around the country. Unfortunately, after a few months on the road, he'd been beaten and robbed by an unknown assailant and ended up in a coma for two weeks.

Though Parker had eventually recovered physically, it seemed as if the light had gone out inside him. Price had hired the finest psychiatrists to try to get through to him. But Parker wouldn't talk to any of them. He'd taken over the tiny, dark room on the third floor, with its minuscule bath, and he'd never once ventured down to the music room, where the grand piano waited in silence for his loving touch.

Price asked, "Does he seem any better to you?"

Faith sighed. "I don't know. Sometimes it seems as if he's not quite as withdrawn as he used to be. But maybe that's only wishful thinking on my part."

"Mother says she told him that you're leaving."

"Yes. He said he'd be sorry to see me go."

"And that's all?"

"Pretty much."

"It sounds like he took it well."

"I think so."

From his cage, Sir Winston crowed out something rude.

Faith and Price both turned toward the sound, then smiled at each other.

"Has my father told you about his latest invention?" Price asked.

"The one that's got something to do with the jar industry?"

"That's it."

"No, he hasn't said much about it."

"Consider yourself lucky."

"I like to hear about your father's inventions."

"You don't want to hear about this one."

"Yes, I do."

"You're sure?"

"Tell me."

"Well, all right. But remember, you asked for it." Price leaned a little closer, and pitched his voice low, as if imparting state secrets. "He's calling it the Lid-No-More. It's a small tube with a bulb on one end. You stick the tube end under the lip of a jar and then depress the bulb at the other end."

"And then?"

"There's a surge of air that breaks the seal so that the lid screws right off." He shifted away from her and glanced at the ceiling fan overhead, as if seeking help from above. "Dad wants me to patent the thing immediately, before someone else beats us to it."

"So why do you seem so reluctant?"

Price leaned close again, causing her pulse to accelerate deliciously. "Faith. Have you got any idea how many devices there are already for screwing the lids off jars?"

She wrinkled her nose at him. "Lots?"

He nodded. "More than lots."

"So you're saying this won't be a big money-maker."

"Right."

She shrugged. "Well, in a week Regis will be working on something else. The Lid-No-More will be nothing but a vague memory to him."

"It's what I'm counting on, believe me."

A moment later, Price said he was hungry. They wandered into the kitchen to pester Balthazar, who threatened them with a rolling pin and then gave in and let them sample his latest masterpiece, a puff pastry with some sort of spicy meat filling that was so delicious both Faith and Price begged for seconds.

Soon after they'd eaten their fill, Price's phone rang. He had to return to the library.

Faith went upstairs to get her coat and purse. She had errands to run. Wearing a wide, silly grin, she strolled out to the three-car garage, a hundred yards up a ramplike drive from the house. The garage sat on a flat space that had been scooped out of the hillside and terraced with natural stone, in the same manner as the plot on which the house itself sat.

Faith climbed into her efficient little Isuzu Trooper, which Price allowed her to park between his Jaguar and Ariel's Range Rover. She started up her car and backed out, thinking that life was wonderful. Humming a little tune to herself, she drove down the twisting, narrow streets on her way to Caledonia Street, where all the locals shopped.

A misty rain was falling when she finally found a parking space. She put her money in the meter and marched off down the sidewalk, getting wet and not caring in the least. Nothing could bother her today, because she really was starting to believe that Price had noticed her at last. She could see that she was becoming more to him than just the trusted employee who made his house a pleasant place to live. He was starting to see her as a person in her own right.

It took her a little longer than she'd expected to visit the deli and the cleaners, the art-supply store, the hardware store and the record store where Parker had asked her to pick up a couple of CDs he wanted. Each time she emerged from a shop with a purchase, she ran to the Trooper to stow it safely inside. But she forgot to watch the meter, and the time got away from her. When she returned to her car for the last time, she found that the meter had run out and a soggy slip of paper was stuck under the windshield wiper. But even a parking ticket couldn't put a damper on her good mood. She slid back behind the wheel, dripping-wet and grinning.

For the rest of that day and the next, Faith walked around with her feet several inches above the inlaid floors. She found herself thinking that Chuck Swan could probably handle things at the motel indefinitely, until the right applicant to fill her shoes at Montgomery House finally came along. Which might take a long, long time. Who could tell about something like that? And, really, what was her hurry? She had a wonderful job here. She loved the Montgomerys.

And she'd waited so long for Price to pay her a little attention. And now he was. Why should she be in such a rush to get away from him?

The next evening was Friday, the night of Ariel's big watercolor show. Price drove his parents to the event. They left a little before eight, all three of them looking splendid in full evening dress.

Faith went up to her rooms shortly after they departed, feeling just a tiny bit like Cinderella—not invited to the ball. But then she laughed at herself. She and Price were growing closer. That was enough for her right now.

She called Chuck Swan in North Magdalene, and he told her that a section of the roof had sprung a few leaks. But she wasn't to worry, he had some experience as a roofer. He'd patch things up just fine, as soon as the weather cleared for a day or two.

Next, she called her sister, Evie. Evie asked how things were going and how soon she'd be ready to move. Evie's husband, Erik, would bring an able-bodied cousin or two, and a couple of pickups, and haul all of her personal belongings to her new home.

Faith answered vaguely. "I have a lot to tie up here, Evie. I'm working at it, I really am."

With her natural intuitiveness, Evie sensed what was really going on. "Has something happened, then? Between you and Price?"

Evie knew about Faith's hopeless love for Price, of course. Perhaps Faith's sensitive younger sister had always known. But Faith had actually confided in her sister last spring, during one of Faith's frequent visits to North Mag-dalene. At the time, Faith had been sure that Price would never look twice at her. So she'd told Evie that she really thought she had to start a new kind of life. Evie had urged her to try North Magdalene. And Faith had said yes, she'd been thinking of doing just that.

"Faith," Evie asked softly, "what's going on?"

Faith longed to tell all. But this thing between herself and Price was so fragile and new. It seemed too soon to talk about it.

"Nothing's going on," she lied. "Really. It's just ... turned out to be a longer process than I antici-pated."

"What has?"

"Finding my replacement."

"You're all right, then?"

"Oh, yes." She allowed just a little of her excitement to vibrate in her voice. "Never better."

"Well, you certainly *sound* fine."

"I am. I truly am."

When she was through on the phone, Faith watched tele-vision for a while, then climbed into bed with a big, juicy romance. She fell asleep smiling, and dreamed of Price, bending close to her, devotion in his eyes.

A bleating sound awakened her. Price's adoring image began to fade. The sound came again. Faith's foggy mind identified it: a ringing phone. Faith forced her eyes open and saw that the red light was blinking on the house line.

She punched the button and picked up the phone. "This is Faith."

"Dear, I'm so sorry to wake you." It was Ariel, her voice charged and buoyant. The show must have been a success.

Faith squinted at her bedside clock: a little after 1:00 a.m.

"Faith? Are you still there?"

"Um. Yes. How did it go?"

"Wonderful. It was wonderful. They said such lovely things about me."

Faith rolled over and smiled sleepily into the darkness. "Such as?"

"Well, that I've redefined the form."

"And they're right. You have."

"Several of the pieces have already been sold."

"Great."

"I'm so excited. Giddy. Foolish. We all came home for a nice little drink...."

Faith yawned and sat up. "All right. What can't you find?"

"Dear, you truly do take care of us. We never could survive without you."

"Thank you, Ariel. But we both know you'll manage just fine without me. Now, what do you need?"

"Cassis. We've looked all through the liquor cabinet. Not a sign of it."

"Did you look way in back?"

"Yes, dear. All the way. It simply is not there."

Most likely, Faith thought, Balthazar had used it in one of his exotic desserts and left it in the kitchen cupboard, next to the cooking sherry. Faith swung her feet over the edge of the bed. "Give me five minutes. I'll be down."

"We're terribly selfish, aren't we?"

They were, of course. And Faith adored them. "It's all right. Five minutes."

Quickly, Faith pulled on her clothes and slid her feet into her soft-soled shoes. She hurried down the back stairs and right to the kitchen, where she found the cassis in the cupboard, exactly where she'd thought it might be. Then, bottle in hand, she went out through the central hall, the dining room and the music room, and finally through the second set of sliding double doors, which stood wide-open on the huge front parlor.

The first thing she saw when she went through those double doors was Price, holding a crystal glass with amber liquid in it, leaning lazily on the back of a maroon velvet wing chair. In the chair sat Annette Leclaire, a woman Price had dated on and off for the past couple of years.

Annette lived a little farther down the hillside. It occurred to Faith that the Montgomerys had probably swung by Annette's house to pick her up on the way to the opening—a very logical thing for them to have done. And, really, Faith should have assumed that Price would be taking a date.

But she hadn't. She'd thought he'd gone on his own.

Because she'd imagined that something was happening between the two of them. Something special. Something . . . new and delicate and important to both of them.

Fool that she was. At that moment, Price became aware of Faith. He looked up from whatever he was saying to his date, and right into her eyes. Faith felt the bottle of cassis slipping from her hands.

Chapter Three

"Watch out!" warned Annette Leclaire.

Faith grabbed for the bottle and caught it before it fell and shattered on the antique rug beneath her feet.

Annette Leclaire chuckled in relief. "Good catch." Faith tried not to look at her. She looked so beautiful and sophisticated, dressed in teal-blue silk, with diamonds winking at her ears and throat.

Regis materialized at Faith's side. "You are a lifesaver." He took the bottle from her numb hands and trotted with it over to the wet bar on the east wall.

"Yes, dear. You are priceless," Ariel declared.

"No problem," Faith heard her own voice say. She turned, thinking only of getting out of that room, of retracing her steps to the third floor and gaining the lonely sanctuary of her own bed.

"Faith. Wait."

It was Price. She froze.

"Faith?"

Slowly, she turned. "Yes?"

"Stay. Share a toast with us." He was smiling. Friendly. He had no idea what he'd just done to all her frail, stupid little hopes.

"Yes, please," Ariel put in. "Stay for just one little drink." She gestured at Regis, who was already busy mixing cassis and soda—which would be for Annette. Faith remembered now; Annette Leclaire drank cassis and soda. "Regis is doing the honors tonight," Ariel was saying. "Put in your order with him."

"No," Faith said, rallying all her will into sounding offhand. "Thank you, but it really is late." She smiled at each face in turn, a quick, distant smile, then spun on her heel and made for the double doors once more.

"Faith." Price's voice again.

Oh, what was the matter with him? Why wouldn't he just let her escape?

She turned once more. "Yes?"

He looked puzzled. "Is everything all right?"

She went on smiling, though the smile felt as false as all her ridiculous hopes had been. "Yes. Of course." Annette Leclaire was looking at her, strangely, Faith thought. She backed toward the music room. "Now, if you'll excuse me..."

Price shrugged. "Good night, then."

"Good night." Faith turned. She put one foot in front of the other, back the way she had come, through the music room and the dining room to the central hall and the blessed back stairs.

Once she'd reached the safety of her two small rooms, she stripped off her clothes and yanked her nightgown down over her head. She slid under the covers, turned off the lamp and lay there, curled in a ball in the dark, shivering though she wasn't really cold.

After a while, her shivering eased. She uncurled a little. She took deep breaths.

She was calm. The pain and mortification were passing. It had been a lesson in reality, that was all. Yes, she'd made a fool of herself. But only in her heart. Price remained utterly ignorant of her feelings for him. She had seen that in his face when he asked her if everything was all right.

Once more she relived that awful moment when she'd walked into the front parlor and caught sight of him, leaning close to Annette Leclaire. The memory had her shivering all over again, curling into herself like a wounded thing.

Faith really did know too much about Price's personal life. She knew all the tiny, damning details. Once Mary had found a diamond earring tangled in the sheets of Price's king-size bed. Mary had brought the earring to Faith, and Faith had given it to Price, who had smiled and thanked her for being so conscientious. The earring had looked very much like one of the pair that Annette Leclaire was wearing tonight.

Faith simply had to get real here. Price Montgomery was a complicated man who'd been burned badly when it came to love. There would always be beautiful, charming women willing to share his bed. But he was never going to let any woman get too close again. And he certainly wouldn't be giving marriage another try—especially not with his lackluster, sexually inexperienced housekeeper.

"More than ten years," Faith whispered tightly to herself. She had worked at Montgomery House for over a decade. And Price had been a single man for just about half that time. If something was going to happen between the two of them, it would have happened by now.

The truth, faced so directly, had a calming affect. The shivering stopped. Faith uncurled once more.

From now on, she was going to concentrate on her future, on the new life she would create for herself in North

Magdalene. And she was putting her dreamy-eyed fantasies about Price behind her for good.

Annette's house was a classic Sausalito brown shingle, which stood on stilts overlooking the bay. Price eased the Jag into the house's tiny driveway.

Annette glanced at him from the passenger seat and smiled invitingly. He smiled back, then got out and went around to open the car door for her. When she stood from the leather seat, her skirt fell away, exposing a fair amount of satiny thigh.

She gathered her evening wrap closer around her. "Chilly tonight." She shivered a little.

"Yes."

Together, they walked around the back of the car and up to her door. There, she turned to him. "Come in with me."

The idea held absolutely no appeal. "Annette..."

She chuckled, a low, rueful sound. "Oh, Price."

He studied her attractive, fine-boned face. She was a good lover. Yet tonight, looking at her, he felt no urge at all to take her in his arms. Her earrings sparkled, white fire in the darkness. Once, she'd left an earring in his bed. One of the maids had found it the next day and given it to Faith, who brought it to him.

Faith.

Every time Price thought of Faith lately, he was reminded that he could be losing her.

But still, things had looked better the past few days. She'd seemed less and less perturbed that no new housekeeper had been chosen. Price had dared to imagine that his scheme to keep her at Montgomery House was working.

But then, tonight, when his mother called her down to find that bottle of cassis, she'd acted so strangely. She'd seemed withdrawn. He couldn't help wondering if she was becoming impatient all over again to get away to the mountains and that damn motel of hers.

Annette was sighing. "I have thoroughly enjoyed the time we've spent together, Price."

Price put Faith out of his mind and looked at Annette more closely. "Are you telling me goodbye?"

"Well." Annette tossed her head; the earrings danced. "You tell me. I saw the way you looked at your housekeeper tonight."

Price backed up a little. It was odd that Annette should mention Faith, when he'd just been thinking of her. "What are you saying? You believe that Faith and I—?" He let the thought finish itself.

Annette smiled knowingly. Price felt a vague stab of irritation at her. Where could she have come up with an idea like that?

He shook his head. "I'm afraid you're imagining things. Faith is an invaluable employee, but there's nothing going on between the two of us."

Annette sighed again.

Price's annoyance with her increased. "Annette. If you have something to say, then say it."

Now she looked a little wistful. "Oh, Price. All I'm telling you is that we've shared a mature, responsible—and basically casual—relationship. And now it looks to me as if you're ready for more than that—with someone else."

Price frowned. She was wrong, of course. He had no interest in any relationship beyond the type she'd first described. But he saw nothing to be gained by arguing the point.

Annette shrugged. "Look. Never mind. I can see you don't want to talk about it, and I'm not really sure that I want to, either. Let's just leave it as it is." She leaned toward him and placed a light kiss on his cheek.

Relieved that this uncomfortable conversation was over, he murmured a good-night.

Annette let a beat elapse before she replied, with finality, "Goodbye, Price."

The next day was Saturday. Faith found Price in the morning room, where he was lingering over his newspaper. He looked up, smiling, thinking that he'd coax her to sit with him for a while.

But the second he saw her face, he changed his mind. Her eyes were stormy, and her mouth was set in a grim line.

"Price, I must speak with you."

He heard it all in the tone of her voice; she *was* stirred up again about leaving. She was going to start nagging him about it, start pushing him to hire her replacement right away.

He folded his paper and stood. "I can't talk now. I have some calls to make."

"But, Price..."

"Later, Faith." He turned and walked away without a backward glance.

She came at him again the next morning, but he was ready for her. He stood from the table before she reached his side.

"Price, I—"

"I'm late, Faith. I'll be gone all day." He was out the front door in twenty minutes flat. He spent most of the day at his health club, pumping iron like a man possessed and beating all comers at racquetball. He didn't return until evening.

She tried twice on Monday. He put her off both times.

But then, on Tuesday morning, when he was still locked in the library for the early hours of trading, she materialized from the central hall.

Price had one phone in each ear. He asked both parties to hold on and pressed the mute buttons on the phones. Then he cast her a frostbitten glare. "Faith. I have work to do. I'm really too busy right now to—"

She pulled the doors firmly closed behind her, then turned and cut him off. "It's been two weeks and a day since I gave my notice, Price. I told you from the first that I wouldn't be willing to let this drag on too long."

Price stared at her. Her soft oval face was flushed, and her eyes were bright. She was leaning back against the doors, as if she'd keep him there bodily if he tried to escape her again.

She went on, "I'll be leaving this house in just under two weeks from now, on the third of February—whether I've found a replacement that satisfies you and your parents or not."

Without saying a word to either of his callers, Price quietly hung up both phones.

"The third of February. Do you understand?"

His gaze wandered downward. She was wearing a fuzzy little sweater with a lace collar. The sweater was buttoned all the way up the front. Beneath the sweater, her soft breasts rose and fell with each agitated breath she took. From what he could see of them, they appeared to be very nice, round, high breasts.

Faith licked her lips, leaving them shiny and full-looking. "Price?"

Outside, it was raining. Far off, Price heard the rumble of thunder. The air seemed electric. Was it just from the storm?

"Did you hear me?"

He had, of course. He was just having trouble processing incoming information at the moment. Both the phones he'd just hung up started ringing. He felt around the sides of them until he found the ringer switches and turned them off. The third phone, the fold-up one that he carried around the house with him when he was waiting for a call, bleated like a lost lamb. He silenced it, too. Now the only sound was the rain outside.

And Faith's voice. "Price, are you listening to me?"

I saw the way you looked at your housekeeper, Annette had said.

He'd told her she was wrong, that she was imagining things.

But Annette was a bright woman.

Faith's smooth brows had drawn together. "Price. Are you feeling all right?"

"Yes. Yes, I'm fine." He stood. He wanted to get a little closer to her. Had he ever really let himself get a good look at her?

Well, it was damn sure time he did. He came around the desk toward her, his mind spinning. Outside, the gray sky lightened, and then thunder boomed and rolled away.

"Price. Will you please *talk* to me about this?"

"Of course." He took another step toward her.

She blinked and seemed to press herself back against the tall doors, as if she didn't want him to come closer.

He stopped where he was and gestured toward the chair she'd taken that day two weeks ago, when she first told him she was leaving. "Have a seat."

She turned her head, eyeing him sideways, a portrait of suspicion. One of those silky tendrils of hair that was always getting out of the plain bun she wore kissed her cheek. He wanted to rub that wisp of hair between his thumb and forefinger. He wanted to caress that cheek; it looked so soft and white.

She would not come away from the door. The rain drummed harder against the windows.

"Come on, Faith. Sit down."

"I don't—"

"What's the matter? I won't bite you, I promise."

She stood taller then. "Well, of course you won't."

"Then sit down."

She peeled herself off the door and approached him. Just as she reached the chair, he slipped around behind her and held it for her. Her head whipped around. "What are you doing?"

Sweet Lord, he could *smell* her. A fresh scent. Like tea roses and morning mist.

"Price?"

"What?"

"You're acting so strangely."

"No, I'm not. I'm holding the chair for you."

"But why?"

"I don't know. Don't ask, all right? Just please sit down."

Slowly, she did. Once she was seated, he knew he should move out from behind her. But he didn't. She bowed her head a little, as if displaying for him the nape of her neck, so pale and vulnerable. He wanted to put his hand there, on that softness.

He wanted . . . By God. He wanted *her*. He wanted Faith. Imagine. *Faith*. After all these years.

She coughed; it was a frightened, nervous sound.

He realized that he couldn't stand behind her forever. He came around and swung a leg up on the outer edge of his desk, as he'd done that other time.

"All right." He thought he sounded pretty damn casual, considering that for him the world seemed to have suddenly stopped on its axis and started spinning the other way. "What can I do for you?"

Her lips became a thin line. "You know what. You and your parents are going to have to settle on someone, or you'll be stuck without anyone to take care of this house."

He realized she had a slight overbite. He found it adorable.

"I said you need to hire someone to take care of your house, Price."

"*And* us," he said softly. He felt himself smiling. He felt so damn *alive* all of a sudden.

She swallowed. "Excuse me?"

He leaned forward and rested a forearm on his knee. "I was only pointing out that it's not just the house you take care of. You take care of *us*, too." He spoke even more softly. "Who's going to take care of us, when you're gone?"

She pressed herself back into the chair, the way she'd done at the door, as if she were trying to squeeze every last centimeter out of the distance between them. "Um. I'm sorry. I really am. But I can't be responsible for—"

He leaned even closer, got another whiff of her captivating scent. "No, I mean it, Faith. You really have become almost like one of the family over the years. And the brutal truth is that I'm having a hell of a time imagining how we're going to get along without you."

She was blushing, the color creeping up from underneath her prim little collar, turning her pale cheeks an enchanting pink.

"Price." She was trying to look stern. "I am not a part of your family. The truth is, I'm the housekeeper, and *only* the housekeeper. And if you will only allow me to find you someone effective to replace me, you will manage just fine when I'm gone." She stood then, swiftly, and slid around behind the chair, as if she needed the reassurance of a solid object between herself and him.

He said, very reasonably, "See, there? You called me Price. You always call me Price. No one else on the staff calls me by my first name."

She gripped the back of the chair. "Whether I call you by your first name or not, I am a paid employee. And nothing more."

Her breathing, he noticed, was even more ragged than before. And he could see the little pulse beating in her white throat. "I am leaving for North Magdalene on the third of

February," she insisted in a shaky voice. "You and your parents had better choose one of the applicants I keep proposing, or I will have no time to train my replacement before I go."

Price stood, though it caused him some discomfort to do it. He found he was thoroughly aroused right then—in that hot, intense, overwhelming way he hadn't been since he was very young.

Every cell in his body screamed at him to get closer to her.

It was insane.

He had to be careful here.

The logical part of his mind started shouting demands of its own: *Get rid of her. Now. Before you do something totally unacceptable.*

He made himself turn away from her and retrace his steps to the other side of his desk. He looked toward the window for a moment, where the rain beat hard on the glass. Then he turned and sat in his big chair. Once settled, he tried to tell himself that he had the distance he needed now. He had put his desk and a mountain of electronic equipment between them. She had contributed her chair. He leaned back, trying to look as if he had everything under control.

She started in on him again. "Price. I mean this. I have three people for you to see tomorrow. Choose one. For your own good, and the good of your family." He watched her mouth, wondered what her lips would taste like...

"Price. What is the matter with you?"

"Nothing." With a massive effort of will, he managed to stop looking at her mouth. "Is that all?"

She regarded him apprehensively. "*Will* you choose someone? Please?"

For some reason, that *please* almost undid him. He swallowed. "I suppose I'd better, hadn't I?"

She lifted her chin high. "Yes."

For a moment, there was silence. They watched each other. The rain outside seemed to beat harder than ever against the windowpanes. To Price, the air literally vibrated with sexual tension.

"Is there anything else?" He sounded harsh as hell, and didn't care one bit.

"I . . . No. That's all."

"Good. Now, if you'll excuse me, I have a lot of work to do."

With a tight little nod, she turned and left.

When she was gone, Price sat at his desk for a long time, staring blankly at one of his computer screens, paying no attention to his frantically blinking phones. The rain outside kept drumming like impatient fingers against the glass.

He was appalled at himself. He'd come very damn close to making a move on Faith. It was inexcusable. She was an *employee,* for God's sake. He had responsibilities toward her.

And beyond his responsibilities toward her, there was an . . . innocence about her. She wasn't the type of woman for him at all. Faith was the kind of woman a man married, settled down with, had kids with.

Kids. The word got stuck in his head.

And it happened. He thought of Danny.

As clearly as if it were yesterday, he saw Danny as he'd been not long before his death.

Danny at three, with his plump face and pug nose. Danny laughing, holding up his chubby arms.

"Hold me, Daddy. Hug me tight. . . ."

Price closed his eyes. He pressed his temples between his thumb and his middle finger. He *willed* the image of his lost son away.

The memory faded. He leaned back and rubbed his eyes.

His mind turned to Faith again. To what he had *almost* done.

He wondered if he was suffering from some sort of chemical imbalance. He was only forty, but maybe he'd been struck by some early midlife crisis. A few days ago, he'd turned down Annette's invitation to spend the night with her. The thought of making love with her had left him cold.

But then, today with Faith, he'd been like some hormone-crazed teenager. All he could think of was the shape of her breasts beneath that fuzzy little sweater, how pink her tongue looked when she nervously licked her lips, the wisps of hair that kept coming out of her bun.

He could imagine in detail the act of seducing her, could see it in his mind's eye, as if it were happening.

Instead of coaxing her away from the library doors, he'd back her up against them. Her eyes would be so wide—a little fearful, but soft, full of a longing she didn't understand. One by one, he'd unbutton those little pink buttons. Taking forever, he'd peel the sweater open.

Did she wear a slip? Surely there would be a bra. A white bra. With a back clasp. He would pull the straps of the slip down her soft, slender arms. He would reach behind her and undo the clasp of the bra.

And her breasts would fill his hands . . .

Price groaned at his computer screens.

He *had* to stop thinking about her.

It was crazy. And disorienting. And it had come on him so suddenly.

Or had it?

That thought stopped him. He swiveled his chair away from his desk and looked out the streaming window at a sky full of roiling clouds. The wind whipped the fronds of the palms around as Price took slow, deep breaths and accepted the fact that Faith really did have to go.

They would just have to choose one of the applicants who would be showing up tomorrow. Faith would train the person. And Price would stay away from Faith until the third of February, when she'd leave for her precious motel in the Sierra foothills and he would never have to see her again.

Price met with his parents that evening.

"She's determined to go," he told them. "It's what she really wants. So the game's over. We're going to have to choose someone to take her place."

Regis and Ariel tried to argue with him, but he kept reminding them that Faith was sure about the move and wanted to be on her way.

They gave in soon enough. They were crazy about Faith and didn't want to see her unhappy. Also, neither of them had ever been a match for Price once he made up his mind.

And Price *had* made up his mind.

Faith was going—the sooner the better. And he would stay clear of her until then.

Chapter Four

Justine Clary was the last to be interviewed the following day. She had excellent references. She'd started out in food service and spent the past four years as a housekeeper in a fine old house in San Rafael whose aged owner had recently died. She asked intelligent questions about Montgomery House, about the size of the staff, the daily routines, the special requirements of the individual members of the family.

And, more important than that, Justine Clary chuckled when Sir Winston whistled at her. She was fascinated by Regis's work in the basement and seemed to understand what he meant when he said she was never to touch anything down there—but that he liked a clean shop, which would be her responsibility. Justine also told Ariel that she was an admirer of her work. She'd actually been to the local gallery where Ariel showed her watercolors. And she seemed neither judgmental nor put off when they explained about Parker, only eager to understand how he wished to be treated.

Faith sat at the far end of the table—today, there had been no urging that she sit close to the others—and grew more certain by the moment that her replacement had been found. There was real warmth in Ariel's voice as she and Justine chatted about local artists. Regis was leaning forward in his chair, listening attentively to the talk between his wife and this particular applicant.

Faith told herself she was happy. She could get on with her new life at last.

But then Price spoke. "You're a widow, it says here." He held up Justine's application.

"Yes. My husband was a fire fighter. He died five years ago. On the job."

"I'm sorry to hear that."

Justine looked down at her lap, then up with a sad smile.

Price said, "You have a child, I see."

Justine nodded. "Yes. His name's Eli. He's six."

"Where does he live?"

"With me."

"You would expect him to live here, then? Is that what you're saying?"

"Yes." Justine smiled her serene smile. "I would. He's a very well-behaved child. And he's in school for several hours of the day now. I don't see him as a problem. Mrs. Curry, my last employer, was actually quite fond of him. But if you don't want to deal with him, please don't worry. I'll keep him out of your way, I promise you."

"I see," Price said flatly.

Faith's spirits sank. It had been going so well. But she knew Price. She could read his closed look as if he'd spoken aloud.

Price was going to veto Justine. Because of the child. He couldn't bear having a child around, to remind him of all that he'd once had and lost.

The interview ended soon after that. Faith saw Justine out, explaining that they'd be in touch through the agency within twenty-four hours.

The Montgomerys were already going at it when she returned to the morning room.

Ariel let out a big puff of air, which blew the hair away from her eyes. "If we have to lose Faith, then Justine is the one." She folded her arms across her chest.

"Yes. I liked her," said Regis.

"No children," said Price.

Faith stopped in the arch to the kitchen. Ariel looked up and saw her. "Faith. Tell him. Justine is just what we need around here—I mean, if we can't have you, of course."

"Yes," urged Regis. "Help us. If you really are determined to leave us, make sure our pigheaded son chooses the right person to take your place."

Though Faith had been avoiding eye contact with Price all through the interviews, she made herself look at him now. He met her gaze. The force of his stare was like something reaching out and touching her.

Goose bumps rose on her skin, and her heart kicked against her breastbone. It was worse than it had ever been, this pull she felt toward him. Yesterday, in the library, she'd thought she'd imagined this—that the force of her longing had doubled somehow. But now, here, today, it was the same as it had been then. As if the energy of desire had multiplied on itself. Now, it was so powerful, she feared she was becoming a little deluded.

Because it had started to seem as if *his* yearning matched hers . . .

She had to leave here, that was all. As soon as possible. Or she feared that she wouldn't get out with her poor heart intact.

Price's gaze flickered down. Faith could have sworn he cast a quick glance at her breasts. She was wearing a long-sleeved white blouse and a buttoned vest over that. Surely he couldn't see anything beneath both the shirt and the vest. He couldn't detect that her nipples were hard—achy against the cups of her bra. There was simply no way he could see that.

She longed to look down, just to check. But, somehow, she stopped herself.

"Faith, don't just stand there," Ariel pleaded. "Tell him. Justine is the one."

"Yes, tell him," said Regis.

Sir Winston cawed and cackled.

Faith and Price went on staring at each other. Price was smiling now. It wasn't a very nice smile. "Well, Faith. Come on. Tell me. I'm listening."

Faith felt caught in the middle. She thought the world of Regis and Ariel. But they rarely managed to hold their own in the face of their older son's steely will. They almost always counted on Faith to come to their rescue at moments like this. She wished they'd tackle the job themselves this time. Perhaps even do the forbidden and bring up Danny. Confront Price with how unhealthy it was for him to turn away from all children just because he'd lost his own.

But they would never do that. They'd seen Price's suffering after his son died. Nobody could bear to remind him of that.

So they waited for Faith to take charge.

From someplace deep inside, Faith found her own calm, reasonable voice. "Your parents are right. Hire her. She'll do very well here. She's the perfect housekeeper for Montgomery House—and the Montgomerys."

"Yes," said Regis.

"Exactly," added Ariel.

Sir Winston, for once, kept his peace.

Price looked from his mother to his father—and finally back at Faith. His mean smile had faded. Suddenly he looked tired. And not quite so determined to have his way.

Faith could hardly believe the evidence of her own eyes. Price Montgomery was weakening.

She added another argument to the list. "And at this point, you're about out of alternatives."

"She's right," said Ariel.

"There really is no other choice," Regis intoned.

Price was looking off toward a Boston fern near Sir Winston's cage. His mouth was a grim line. "She'd have to keep the child out of my way."

Ariel and Regis exchanged gleeful glances. They couldn't believe it, either. But it was happening. Price was actually going to allow a woman with a child to live in his house.

Ariel piped up eagerly. "I'll tell Justine how you feel. She seems a very capable woman. And she's already said she can keep the boy from bothering you."

Price rose to his feet. "Fine. Do it, then. Let's get her ready to take over. Then Faith can get out of here."

His words were like a slap in the face. All at once it was achingly clear why he had decided to let them hire Justine.

He was fed up and furious. With Faith. She'd caused too much upheaval. He'd finally reached the point where he wanted her out of his house—and his life.

Price moved then, toward the exit through the kitchen. Faith was still standing there, so he had to go by her to get out. He brushed past without so much as a sideways glance.

Faith stared straight ahead as he left, despising herself for the foolish tears that pushed at the back of her throat. He was behaving like a jerk about this, and she should be angry at him. The last thing she should want to do was cry.

"Faith," Ariel said.

Faith swallowed down the tears. "Um?"

"Don't take it so hard," Ariel advised gently. "My older son is a good man, but he's also a bit of a despot. He hates being outvoted, because secretly he thinks all decisions should be his alone. Give him time. He'll get over the bad attitude. Just wait and see."

But as the days passed and Justine slowly began assuming the duties that had once been Faith's, Price didn't get over his bad attitude at all.

He hardly spoke to Faith. If she entered the morning room when he was there, he'd get up and leave. If she passed him in the foyer or on the stairs, he'd nod curtly and move on.

Faith told herself it was for the best. The day of her departure was fast approaching. As long as Price treated her coldly, there was no chance under heaven that she'd slip up and reveal what was in her heart. She'd leave with her pride intact, if nothing else.

Justine caught on quickly to her new job. Faith kept a system of file cards for all the routine cleaning and maintenance tasks of the big house. Justine had to assign the jobs to the maids when they came up on the cards and understand enough about how to do the work that she could supervise effectively. And, of course, she had to plan menus with Balthazar. And arrange the flowers and run the errands. And cater to each slightest whim of every Montgomery.

Justine's son, Eli, turned out to be a little charmer. A very nice boy, as his mother had promised he would be, he had Justine's pale hair and soft hazel eyes. Ariel and Regis fell in love with him on sight; he had the run of their suite from the first day he moved in.

And either someone had warned the boy to avoid Price, or he did it naturally. It seemed to Faith that whenever Price appeared, Eli, who always seemed to be underfoot the rest of the time, was nowhere to be found.

All told, Faith thought, the transition seemed to be going smoothly. Yes, she spent a few sleepless nights longing for what would never be. But that was nothing new to her. And since Price continued to treat her so coldly, it became easier and easier to tell herself that she wasn't going to miss him at all when she left. She thought she was handling things surprisingly well.

Price, on the other hand, was living in hell.

It seemed to him that wanting Faith was like a fresh, deep wound. He'd been cut. And cut bad. And every time he saw her—setting a vase of long-stemmed roses on the piano, or opening the curtains in the front parlor—he wanted to scream out his agony. He wanted to grab her. To caress her. To taste those lips that he didn't even dare to look at, for fear he'd go over the line.

He hardly slept at all. He lay in his big bed at night, wondering how he was going to get through the last few days. Until she was gone. Until he could enter a room in his own house again without fearing—and praying—that she'd be there.

He didn't want to want her. He didn't want to let any woman become too important to him.

And yet, as the day she would leave his house forever approached, Price began to realize that he couldn't just allow her to go this way—with so much cold distance between them. He couldn't let her walk out of his life without another word, when she'd meant so much to him.

And she *had* meant a lot. Maybe he hadn't let himself really consider how much until now, when he was losing her.

More and more, as her departure approached, the sleepless nights became a time when he recalled the past.

Like that first day he'd noticed her, a waif with a long brown braid down her back, trying to reset the ormolu clock that crouched on the Eastlake mantel in the front parlor.

She'd turned, her eyes wide, when she heard him cough behind her.

"That thing's never on time," he told her.

She thought for a moment. "Maybe it should be taken apart and cleaned."

"Why don't you take care of it?"

"All right. I will."

Faith had only been a part-time maid, like Mary, at first. But then another in the endless chain of housekeepers had quit, and they hadn't known what to do. They'd never known what to do, actually. And they'd always hired someone new, who left soon after she started.

Faith had asked for an interview with him and Marisa, his wife. They'd talked in the library. And Faith had said she'd like to be their housekeeper.

Marisa had been all for it. "Let her try it," she'd said, after Faith left them alone. "I've watched her. She's bright and conscientious. And somehow, she's both quiet and fun, too. She's exactly what we need to run things around here." Marisa, like Ariel, was an artist. She'd had no interest at all in taking care of a house.

Price had agreed to try Faith out. And slowly, over that first year, she'd taken his chaotic household, where nothing ever went right, and made it into a place of comfort, warmth and beauty.

And she'd been incredible when Danny died. The rest of them had been immobilized by grief, but Faith had done what had to be done. She'd seen to all the arrangements, though Price knew damn well that she'd loved Danny too, and must have grieved, also.

And there was more. The hardest part to admit.

His own worst hours.

His marriage to Marisa, which he'd once thought would last a lifetime, hadn't survived the awful loss of their only child.

After Danny died, Marisa had turned away from him—and into the arms of a series of other men. Price had tried his damnedest to care that his wife was sleeping around. But it hadn't mattered to him, not really; nothing had. They'd had some ugly battles; there had been a lot of shouting and slamming of doors. But on his part, at least, those fights had been all noise and bluster. He'd raged at Marisa—but it had been a counterfeit rage. Inside, he'd been numb. His heart was in the grave with his son.

At last, Marisa had left. She'd filed for divorce. That had reached him, when she filed on him. He'd understood then that he'd lost it all.

More than once, in those two years between Danny's death and the final disintegration of his marriage, Faith had found Price passed out drunk at his desk in the library. She would put her cool hand on his brow and help him to bed.

One time, when he felt her soft hand on him, the awful, ugly tears had come, welling up from that deep, dark hole that losing Danny—and Marisa—had left in him.

"Oh, Price. Oh, I know," she had whispered. He'd clutched at her, laid his head against her belly. And she'd wrapped her arms around him, just stood there, holding him so tight and yet so gently as the sobs tore out his insides.

And then, when he had no tears left, she'd patiently helped him to stand. She'd anchored his arm around her slender shoulders. They'd started for the back stairs.

He didn't really remember the grim trip to his room. But she must have dragged him up the stairs somehow, because the next morning he woke in his own bed, his head pounding as if all of hell's demons were loose in there.

That had been rock bottom. Five years ago. And after that, he'd slowly pulled it together again. He'd stopped drinking himself into oblivion every night. He'd gotten on with his life.

Over time, he supposed, he had even started to tell himself that none of those nights when Faith put him to bed had actually occurred.

But now, with her leaving, he had to face the truth about how it had been. And Danny's death and the loss of Marisa weren't all of it. There was all she'd done for Parker, as well.

At first, when Parker took over the room upstairs, Faith had been the only person he would even speak to. He'd locked himself in at all times, and he'd open the door only if Faith knocked and gently called to him.

The truth was, Faith was one of the best things that had ever happened to the Montgomerys. And they were losing big, now that she was moving on.

After a week of treating Faith as if she didn't exist, Price finally admitted to himself how cruelly he was behaving. More than once, he'd snubbed Faith outright.

It had been for a good cause, of course. If he pretended she wasn't in the room, he was less likely to grab her and try to make love with her.

But now he could see that he'd been wrong to behave so coldly. And grossly ungrateful. He had to do something to make it all up to her.

The next day he drove across the Golden Gate to San Francisco. He visited a jeweler he knew and he purchased a delicate gold watch with good-quality diamonds encircling the face.

Back at home, he called a certain restaurant he liked, one with fabulous bay and city views, since it occupied the top floor of a five-star hotel. He made reservations for that Saturday night. The maître d' knew him, so he was able to get just the table he wanted, a secluded one that overlooked the bay. Next, he wrote out a big check: a severance bonus.

As soon as he tore the check from his checkbook, he realized he felt better. He'd take Faith to the restaurant and present her with the watch and the check. Then he'd tell her that he hoped she'd accept those small tokens as proof of his gratitude for all the years she'd given to him and his family. He'd wish her the best and thank her from the bottom of his heart.

And then, knowing that he'd done right by her and that she was going where she wanted to be, he'd be able to put her out of his mind.

Second thoughts assailed him at that point. What if she was so angry at him for the way he'd treated her recently that she wouldn't have dinner with him? Well, he'd grovel a little. He deserved to grovel. He had been cruel.

And what if she said she'd go to dinner with him, and then he couldn't keep his hands off of her? He'd stayed away from her for good reason, after all.

But surely he could get through one evening in her company without forcing himself on her. He was a man, after all, not some wild animal.

Price rang for the housekeeper.

A few minutes later, Justine walked in. "What can I do for you, Mr. Montgomery?"

He stared at her for a moment, caught completely off guard. He was going to have to get used to this. When he rang for the housekeeper, Faith would no longer come.

He coughed. "Actually, I wanted to talk to Faith."

"Shall I tell her to come here to the library?"

"Uh, yes. That would be fine. Thank you, Justine."

With a polite little nod, Justine went out. After what seemed like forever—but was in fact five minutes and fifty-four seconds—there was a discreet tap on the inner door, which opened onto the central hall.

Price picked up a pen and began drawing scowling faces on the yellow legal pad he always kept at his elbow. "Come in, Faith."

Her heart racing and her palms moist, Faith pushed open the door and stepped over the threshold into Price's sanctuary.

He looked up—and smiled.

Faith was barely over her shock at such a blatant display of congeniality when he said, in a perfectly friendly voice, "Close the door, why don't you?" He gestured toward the chair she always seemed to end up in lately, whenever she entered this room. "Make yourself comfortable."

Though comfortable was the last thing she was capable of being right then, she did scoot across the room and plunk herself into the chair.

He'd been writing something on a yellow legal pad. Now he set his pen aside. "Well. How is Justine working out?" He was still smiling.

She wondered what he could be up to now. "Just fine."

He nodded and made a serious face, as if she'd said something of great depth and import. "Good. Very good." He rested his elbows on the arms of his big chair and templed his fingers. "So. You're getting all ready to leave us, I suppose."

"Yes."

"We *will* miss you, you know."

You could have fooled me, she thought. "Thank you," she said. "I'll . . . miss you, too."

He was quiet, just looking at her through the gap between two of his computer screens. She had that *feeling* again, of something crackling in the air, coming as much from him as from her.

"Faith, I . . ."

She realized she was sitting forward in the chair. "Yes?" She sounded ridiculously eager. She made herself sit back again.

"I've behaved badly for the past week or so. And I want to apologize."

Was this real? Should she pinch herself? "You do?"

"I do. Will you . . . forgive me, for being such a rat?"

She said nothing, though her foolish heart felt about ten pounds lighter suddenly.

"Faith? Will you please accept my apology?"

She couldn't let him off the hook too easily. "You *have* been pretty terrible to me, Price."

"I know. And I *am* sorry. I just didn't want you to go. I've come to count on you. More than I realized, I'm afraid. And when I saw that nothing was going to keep you here, I was angry. And I took it out on you."

She sighed.

"Faith? Come on."

"Oh, all right. Let's forget it."

He looked genuinely humble and grateful. She drank in the sight; it was so rare. Then he coughed. "I've made reservations. At Tower on the Bay. For this Saturday night."

She tried to keep looking alert and interested. But she couldn't help wondering what in the world his having dinner at the best restaurant in San Francisco could have to do with her? Did he hope she'd go out and choose some little gift for his date?

If so, she was going to bluntly inform him that requests like that must now be addressed to Justine.

Price went on. "I was really hoping you might go with me."

Faith opened her mouth. And closed it. "Excuse me?" she murmured faintly.

"I said, would you go out to dinner with me? Saturday night."

It took her a moment more to really believe what he was asking her.

And then, as her stunned surprise faded a little, she began to understand what he was up to.

He'd finally forgiven her for leaving. His basically generous nature had surfaced again at last. He really did feel rotten about how badly he'd treated her, and he was going to be wonderful to her from now on.

Oh, she knew him. She knew exactly what he was planning. She would be getting the farewell dinner, the gold watch and the severance bonus—as well as a big fat thank-you-very-much-for-all-you've-done.

"Faith? Will you?"

Loving him as she did, could she bear such a thing?

"Faith?"

She smiled. You bet she could. So what if he was just being kind? She would be able to leave Montgomery House with one lovely memory to treasure for the rest of her life: her dream date with Price Montgomery.

"Thank you, Price," Faith said. "I'd love to go."

Chapter Five

That Saturday evening, Price was nursing a Chivas and soda in the front parlor, waiting for Faith to appear, when a small figure shot past the entrance to the music room. Price took another sip of his drink and pretended he hadn't noticed a thing.

Having the boy in the house was working out all right after all. And as long as the child gave Price a wide berth, it would continue to work out all right.

Price heard the faint tattoo of small feet across the wood floor in the dining room. Then quiet descended as the child retreated to the central hall—probably on his way up the back stairs to the temporary quarters he shared with his mother. When Faith left, Justine and the boy would take over her third-floor suite.

Price wandered over to the tower window alcove, which was tucked between the east and north walls. Outside, it was already dark, so there wasn't much to see in the glass but his own reflection and the grand room behind him. Nervously he patted an inner pocket of his jacket. The velvet box was there, of course, with the watch and the folded check tucked safely inside.

"Price?"

He jumped at the sound of his name, then settled down a little when he realized it was his mother's voice. He turned and smiled at Ariel and Regis, who were just coming in from the front foyer, where the main staircase led up to the second floor and their suite of rooms.

"Mind if we join you, dear?"

He went to the nearby wet bar and opened the beveled glass cabinet. "What can I get for you?"

Ariel asked for a martini, and Regis said he'd like a Glenlivet over ice. Price was happy to make the drinks. It took his mind off how idiotically edgy he felt. His father appeared at his elbow just as he finished pouring out the Scotch. Regis took the drinks from him and carried them to the brocade sofa in the middle of the room, where Ariel had already found a seat.

Price resisted the urge to freshen his own drink. He wandered over to a wing chair near his parents, but couldn't quite make himself sit down.

Ariel had just started to tell him how lovely she thought it was that he was taking Faith out somewhere nice when they all heard the tapping of high heels through the arch that led to the music room. Ariel stopped in midsentence.

The three of them looked expectantly toward the entrance to the room where the grand piano stood. Price heard his father's indrawn breath at precisely the same moment he himself forgot how to breathe altogether.

Faith was there. In the archway, looking like he'd never seen her before.

She wore black. Black velvet. With a high neck and long, clinging sleeves that accentuated her slim, pale hands. The dress clung to her body, flaring out a little as it got past the soft curves of her hips. It had some shiny stuff wrapped around it at the waist, like satin, only stiffer. The skirt ended just above her shapely knees. He looked at those knees and then lower, all the way to her high-heeled black shoes.

And then up again, to her white throat and her hair, which seemed to fall like sable water, over her shoulders and down her back. Her earrings were like teardrops. Ruby-red teardrops. Her lips were redder than usual, with some kind of gloss. Her pretty white teeth were worrying them just a little.

Ariel found her voice first. "Dear. You look fabulous." She set her martini aside and jumped to her feet, dancing lightly over to the archway, where Faith stood so still and wary.

Ariel took Faith's arm. "Come on. Sit with us. Just for a moment before you and Price take off." She glanced over at Price. "Price. This girl deserves a drink, don't you think?"

He dragged a breath into starving lungs. "Absolutely. What will it be?"

Faith shifted her black wrap and her beaded evening bag from one hand to the other. "Just some tonic water."

"Whatever you want." Price returned to the bar area.

"Come, dear. Sit down," Ariel said to Faith.

Price hardly recalled what happened in the next few minutes. Somehow, he dropped some ice cubes in a tumbler, filled the thing with tonic and threw in a wedge of lime. He carried the drink to Faith—and then nearly dropped it in her lap when he saw that damn dress from the side. The back was cut to the waist in a deep vee. A big bow of that stiff, satiny material perched right below where the vee ended. And her hair was tied loosely in the middle of her bare back with a strip of black velvet.

His hands itched to trace the shape of that vee, to pull on the end of that strip of black velvet until her hair came totally free.

He wondered if he'd lost his mind, to have even imagined that he could make it through a whole evening with her. He would disgrace himself; he had no doubt now. He would end up begging her for a caress, on his knees in the hope of a single kiss.

She murmured a sweet, demure thank-you when he handed her the drink.

He stood above her, by her chair, as she and his parents made small talk, about how adorable Justine's kid was, and how well Justine was doing at taking over Faith's job. Once in a while, one of them would turn to him.

"Don't you think so, Price?"

"Price, isn't that right?"

He managed, somehow, to formulate a brief answer to each question, as if he had some idea what they were all babbling about.

At last, it was time to go. He took Faith's drink and set it on the bar, and then helped her into the little velvet evening jacket that matched the dress. The jacket, he decided, was a real lifesaver; it covered her silky-looking bare back and made it marginally easier for him to concentrate on getting them out the door.

They moved out of the parlor and into the foyer. Ariel kissed Faith on the cheek and told her to have a wonderful time. Faith promised that she would. Regis opened the door.

Price dared to put his hand on the small of Faith's back, right above that black bow. She stiffened, but then seemed to relax under his touch. He guided her gently over the threshold.

* * *

Regis shut the door quietly. Then he turned to his wife.

"Oh, my darling," she said. "How could we not have seen it?"

Regis shook his head. "We've been blind, my love."

Ariel brushed the hair from her face. "Price is fighting it. He's been hurt so much. And Faith is . . . so tender, so inexperienced. It breaks my heart to watch them." Regis heard the sadness in her voice, saw it in her violet eyes. "How will they ever find their way to each other?"

Regis closed the distance between them and gathered her into his arms. "Let's not worry, all right? I'm sure everything will work out as it should."

"But, Regis . . ."

"Shh . . ." He kissed the tip of her beautiful nose. *"Te quiero."*

Her eyes widened. She drew in a sharp little breath. *"Sagapo."*

They turned for the stairs with their arms around each other.

Beyond the window beside their table for two, a layer of clouds obscured the stars, as well as the waning moon.

Far below them lay the bay. If Faith turned her head slightly, she could see Angel Island. Before her, beyond Price's left shoulder, the Golden Gate Bridge, studded with its double string of lights, glittered through the darkness. A yacht and a river cruiser traveled the shadowed waters, white, foamy wakes spinning out behind them.

Their table itself was an invitation to romance, complete with a glowing candle and a single red rose in a crystal bud vase. Faith sighed as she took it all in. She shouldn't get carried away, of course. But in a setting like this, how could she help herself?

The wine steward appeared at Price's elbow. Price ordered a vintage Dom Perignon, then grinned across the table at Faith. "Don't say it. This is a special night. And *almost* isn't good enough."

Faith put on a patient look, which was always her response when Price insisted on having the best, no matter the cost. Years ago, for Danny's christening, Price and Marisa had thrown a big party. Price had expressly ordered Dom Perignon for his guests. Faith had argued with him; she knew of another champagne that was much less expensive and almost as good.

Price had insisted, *Almost isn't good enough.*

Faith rested her elbows on the table, on either side of her gold-rimmed plate and gleaming silverware. "You're an extravagant man."

"No. I like the best—and I'm willing to pay for it."

Faith let her glance slide away, and knew that he went on looking at her, his eyes warm and full of admiration.

She loved it, to have him look at her like that.

She'd spent a small fortune on her dress, running out and buying it even though she couldn't really afford it, because she was determined that this would be a night she'd remember all her life.

And she'd been right to do it. The dress made her feel like someone else, someone sophisticated and knowing, someone who always dined on gold-rimmed china and casually sipped Dom Perignon.

She looked at Price. He smiled at her.

She really did have to watch it. She had to keep reminding herself that this wasn't a *real* date.

But keeping a grip on reality wasn't easy. How could it be? Right now she felt as if she'd stepped out of her ordinary, hum-drum life and into an honest-to-goodness dream come true.

The champagne arrived. The waiter poured.

Price offered a toast. "To your new life."

Faith raised her glass and drank, feeling the bubbles go down and laughing just a little at the wonderful way they tickled her throat.

He set his glass on the snowy tablecloth and leaned toward her. "You know, I just realized . . ."

"What?"

"You've lived in my house for all these years, and yet I don't know where you grew up, what high school you went to, none of that stuff."

Out the window now, Faith could actually see a star or two. The high clouds must have cleared just a little.

"Faith?"

She looked at him. "You don't want to hear all that."

His gaze didn't waver. "Yes, I do."

He seemed so honestly interested that she found herself explaining, "I had an . . . unsettled life during my school years. To tell you the truth, I took night classes to finish high school."

"So you missed all the high school things, is that what you're saying? The homecoming games and the proms and the big graduation night?"

She nodded.

"I missed them, too," Price said. "Or at least most of them. We moved around a lot."

Faith felt suddenly closer to him, thinking that his childhood might have been just a little like hers. But not in the way that really mattered, of course. Price had always had two parents who loved him with all their hearts.

He looked at the candle between them, then back up at her. "You were, what—in your early twenties when you came to work for me?"

She sipped more champagne; a small sip. "Twenty-four. Almost twenty-five."

"Okay, *almost* twenty-five. I seem to recall you'd had a year or two of college."

"I did." She set the glass down; it wouldn't do to get tipsy. "But only one year. At Chico State."

"Why Chico State?"

"My sisters and I lived together in Chico for a few years, after we struck out on our own."

"You have two sisters, right? Evie, and . . ."

"Nevada." She volunteered, "Nevada lives in Phoenix."

"What does she do? I don't think you've ever said."

"Price. Why all these questions?"

"Because I want to know. Hell. This may be my last chance to find out about you."

It seemed a reasonable enough answer. And yet all this interest in her life made her nervous. The champagne glass seemed to beckon. She picked it up and sipped some more. "Nevada hosts a talk radio show. She gives advice to the lovelorn."

"All of a sudden, you're grinning."

"I am?"

"You are. Why?"

Dom Perignon really was an excellent champagne. "You'd have to know Nevada. She'll never marry. She rarely even dates. And yet she has a talent for telling other people how to handle their love lives."

The flame of the candle between them gleamed in Price's eyes. "What about you, Faith? Will you ever marry?"

The question seemed awfully personal. But that was okay, wasn't it? She held out her glass. He refilled it. "I hope to get married someday. And have children. I've seen what Evie has with Erik. And I'd like to have that myself. If I meet the right guy." The bubbles tickled her nose as she drank again.

He was watching her. "But you're more like your other sister, aren't you?"

"Why do you say that?"

"I mean, you don't date much."

Faith set her glass down and told herself not to pick it up until she'd eaten something. She leaned back in her chair and studied the planes and angles of Price's face. She felt...bold. And capable of a certain degree of honesty. She went with it. "My sisters and I had a difficult childhood. Our mother died when we were all pretty young. We were raised by our father...well, it was more like we *grew up* with our father. He never really raised us. He did what he wanted, traveled around all the time, and he dragged us around with him."

"You resent him?"

"I used to. But I think I've gotten over that, as the years have gone by. My father never could hold a job. And he was...cruel at heart. Until Evie met Erik, we all three believed we'd never marry. We just had too many bad memories of what a man can be like." She gave him a sheepish look. "No offense intended."

He chuckled at that. "None taken." And then his expression turned more serious. "And I know, from what happened over a year ago, that your father has serious problems."

Price was putting it mildly. Fifteen months before, Evie had been kidnapped by their father, whose unstable mind had finally snapped.

"Your father's in Oregon now, is that right?"

Faith straightened the silverware. "An institution for the criminally insane." She looked out at the Golden Gate again. On the other side of it was Sausalito. And, though of course she couldn't see it from here, she knew that high in the hills, Montgomery House stood tall and proud. Something deep and painful moved inside her. She would miss that house—and the people who lived in it. "I've been happy, Price. In your house."

He raised his glass again. Faith broke her promise to herself and picked up her own glass. This time the toast was a silent one. They drank at the same time.

Then a waiter appeared with appetizers: steamed mussels drowned in herbs, prosciutto-wrapped bread sticks and fried shrimp and cucumbers with a spicy peanut sauce for dipping.

Price took one of the shrimp and dipped it in the sauce.

"Good?" Faith asked, after he'd popped the shrimp into his mouth.

He nodded. She tried one, too, then sipped more of the bubbly wine.

He said, "I'm glad you've been happy. You are so good at . . . what you do."

She made a small noise of mock disgust.

"What?" He looked a little abashed. "Did I say something wrong?"

"No. It's just the *way* you said it. *What you do.* Like there wasn't really a name for . . . a talent for taking care of people. And I guess there isn't." She took a bread stick and nibbled the end of it. "*Nurturer,* maybe. But is that a job?" She laughed, then answered her own question. "If it is, I don't believe it pays well, as a general rule."

"Hey." He looked wounded.

"All right. *You* have paid me well," she confessed.

"Thank you."

"And you know, I've always been the type of person who takes care of other people. Even when I was little. I was always the one who worried about whether we were eating right. I took care of what clothes we had, mending them and washing them." She tried a mussel. It was sublime. Then she heard herself musing aloud, "We were each so different, my sisters and I."

He ate a mussel, too. "How so?"

"Well, Evie was . . . the special one. She had a talent for reading the future, for seeing things no one else could see."

"You mean like a psychic?"

"Exactly. My father exploited her. He made a lot of money off of what he called her 'gifts.' "

Price was looking at her sideways. "Is this true?"

Faith lifted a hand, palm up. "Scout's honor." She giggled. "Not that I was ever a scout." She leaned a little closer to him, across the table. "Do you want to hear all this? Really?"

He looked at her with what she dared to imagine was affection. "Yes. I do."

"Well, all right." She held out her glass. He filled it. "Anyway, Evie, the youngest, was the special one. And Nevada, who's the oldest, was the strong one. She fought my father tooth and nail. She . . . protected us from him as best she could."

"And you were—?"

"The caregiver. The *nurturer.* I tried to make sure we got balanced meals, and I scoured the Goodwill stores for bargains. And I put my father to bed when he drank too much."

Price was watching her so closely. "Just like you did for me."

Faith bit her lower lip and looked down at the inviting plates of appetizers. It was the first time in five years that Price had referred, even obliquely, to that dark period immediately after he had lost Danny and then his wife.

Price said, "When I was little, we moved all over, too. There was plenty of love, but no financial security. And no place to call home. I always wanted that, a real home."

She teased, "But you settled for a castle. Montgomery House."

He wasn't laughing. "More like a fortress. That's what it looked like to me, the first time I saw it. Stone and brick, three stories high. It looked . . . impossible. Like something from hundreds of years ago. It even had towers. It seemed like a place where my family would always be safe.''

But even stone walls couldn't keep death out, Faith thought. It came to her again that there were similarities between them. She said as much. ''Maybe we're a little alike, Price.''

''What do you mean?''

''Oh, I don't know . . .''

''No. I'm serious. Tell me.''

''Well, it just seems as if we've looked for the same things. Peace. Security. I loved Montgomery House, too, the first time I saw it.''

''You did?''

''Yes. I thought, *Here, I'll be safe.*''

Price's expression changed. He looked out the window, over her shoulder, in the direction of Alcatraz. She knew he wanted to ask, *Then why don't you stay?* But he didn't.

He forced a smile and raised his champagne glass. ''But now, you're ready to move to the mountains and go into business for yourself. Here's to your success.''

They drank again. The half-finished appetizers were whisked away. Soon enough, there was shrimp and scallop soup. And then the main course. Faith chose seared quail with leeks and star anise. Price had prime rib. They talked easily throughout the meal. Price was funny and warm and attentive; he really seemed to hang on every word she said. Faith felt like a queen.

No, not like a queen at all. Like a desirable woman out with a man who set her pulse racing. She tried to be careful with the champagne, slowing down a little as the meal progressed, so that she wouldn't get thoroughly intoxicated and make a fool of herself.

But intoxicated she was. As the waiter cleared the plates away, Faith realized she'd given up all attempts to stay grounded in reality. This evening, in this elegant place, with the bay spread out below and her forbidden love across from her, was her most outrageous, impossible fantasy made real.

Was it any wonder that her heart was singing?

Price ordered espresso and something utterly decadent called black-bottom cappuccino mousse cake for dessert.

Then he opened his suit jacket and slipped a hand in an inside pocket. He brought out a blue velvet box, which he set on the table between the candle and the crystal bud vase with the single red rose in it.

He cleared his throat. "Faith, I..."

She knew what was coming; she'd expected what was coming. But it didn't matter that she knew.

The evening was ruined. As far as Faith was concerned, he might as well have taken the silver ice bucket with the upended champagne bottle in it and tossed the whole thing in her face.

Faith's stomach knotted; she feared, for a split second, that she was going to be sick. Her face burned.

Price was frowning. "Faith?"

Oh, how could she have let herself be sucked in like this? How could she have done what she'd warned herself that, above all, she mustn't do? How could she have put aside the basic truth: that this was not a real date at all.

It was only a nice farewell dinner for a trusted employee. And now was the big moment; time for the gold watch and the thank-you-very-much.

Price was leaning toward her, his beautiful eyes full of worry and bewilderment. "Faith? Are you ill?"

She clenched her teeth together, fisted her hands in her lap. She willed all the emotions away, into hiding, down to the deepest part of her, where she'd kept them prisoner for years.

But they just wouldn't go.

"Faith." He reached toward her.

"No!" She shoved her chair back and stood.

"Faith, I don't—"

She put up a hand. "No. Stop. I can't... I'm sorry."

"But, Faith..."

Ugly, traitorous tears scalded the back of her throat. She had to get out of there. Fast. Somehow, she managed to squeeze out the words, "Excuse me, please."

And then she fled, almost mowing down the waiter with their twin espressos and matching plates of black-bottom cappuccino mousse cake.

The waiter let out an exclamation of distress.

The tears at the back of her throat pushed harder. They rose in her eyes, making everything blurry as she blundered through the linen-clad tables of well-dressed diners, praying that she'd make it to the ladies' room before she could no longer contain her sobs.

Behind her, she heard Price calling, "Faith, wait! Faith!"

She moved faster, bumping the side of a table and sending glassware toppling and clinking together.

"My goodness!" someone said.

"Look out!" another warned.

"Faith!" called Price.

At last, she made it clear of all the tables. She shot past the reservation podium and out into a hallway. A sign straight ahead said Rest Rooms and, below that, Telephone. Faith ran for the sign.

When she reached it, she turned the corner and there it was, at the end of a short hall: the ladies' room.

Just then, Price caught up to her.

"Faith..."

She turned on him. "No. I have to.... You have to..." She had no words. She whirled for the ladies' room once more.

He caught her arm. "Faith, what is it? What did I do?"

She shook him off and shrank back, toward the phone kiosks not far away. "Just leave me alone, Price. Just...go away."

"No, I can't do that. You know I can't let you run off like this when you—"

"You using that phone, ma'am?"

Both of them turned and gaped at the man who was gesturing toward the kiosk Faith was standing in front of.

"Uh, no. You go ahead...." Faith backed the other way— and pretty much right into Price.

He grabbed her hand.

She tried to jerk away. "Don't. Please . . ."

"Come with me." His face was set.

"But I . . ."

He turned and retreated the way they'd come, towing her with him out of the phone area. They were halfway back to the reservation podium when he stopped.

"We can't talk here," he said distractedly.

"Price, I don't—"

He pulled her down another hallway, to the banks of gleaming brass elevators. One was open and empty.

"Come on."

They were inside and the elevator door was sliding closed before she could even squeak out a protest. He turned to her. "Now—what is it? What's wrong?"

She looked away. This was like a bad dream. A small, strangled laugh escaped her. Her ultimate fantasy had turned into the worst nightmare of her life.

"Faith." He touched her shoulder. She jerked away.

The elevator stopped and the doors slid open. A man and a woman got on.

"Great," Price muttered, and grabbed her hand again.

"Let me go."

He ignored her, yanking her out the doors just before they slid shut again. "We're going to find somewhere we can talk,'' he muttered under his breath. They were on the twentieth floor.

Price set off again. Doors with room numbers on them fled back behind them. Faith staggered along at his side, still managing, the Lord above knew how, to hold back the hot, humiliating tears.

They turned a corner, then another. Every once in a while, Price would pause to try a random door. None of them opened.

''Price, this is hopeless.''

''Shh... Just wait.'' They came to a door that said Housekeeping on it. Price tried the handle. It gave. ''Here.''

He pushed the door back, found the light switch on the inside wall and flicked it on. Then he pulled her in among the mops, buckets and cleaning supplies.

Once they were both inside, he shut the door and closed them in there together.

Faith backed up, away from him.

''Hell,'' he said. ''Faith...''

She was shaking her head. And those stupid tears were rising. They stared at each other. Faith thought that, just possibly, this was the worst moment of her life.

A tear spilled over and trailed down her cheek.

''Faith. What's wrong?''

She opened her mouth—and nothing came out.

She wished she could melt backward through the cans of cleanser and bottles of spray cleaner. She longed to disappear. But that was not to be, so she let her knees buckle. She crumpled onto the cold concrete floor, crushing the black taffeta bow at the back of her spectacular dress.

Her misery claimed her. She buried her face in her hands and burst into sobs.

Price covered the distance between them. He dropped down in front of her.

And then he was touching her, lifting her, gathering her into his strong arms.

"Hey, hey," he whispered, stroking her hair, her tear-streaked face, her shaking shoulders. "It's okay. It's all right."

He rocked her. He actually *rocked* her, as if she were a baby, someone frail and precious and terribly needy. And he whispered comforting things. He stroked her hair and cradled her close.

And Faith *was* comforted. His tenderness right then meant more than she ever could have told him. And he didn't stint. He went on, stroking and whispering and rocking her gently, until the torrent of weeping crested and finally subsided.

Once she was down to a random hiccup or two and an occasional involuntary sob, he took her by the shoulders and carefully held her away. He pulled a snowy handkerchief from his breast pocket, then cupped her chin in his right hand and blotted her eyes with his left. For some reason, that struck her as funny. She giggled, and then hiccuped.

"What's so funny?" he asked.

"You. A southpaw."

"Didn't you know that?"

She nodded. "It just hit me all over again, because you dried my eyes backward."

He put the handkerchief over her nose. "Blow," he instructed tenderly.

She blew, then took the handkerchief herself and finished drying her foolish tears. That done, she slumped back, against a big drum of some cleaning fluid or other.

She knew those blue eyes were on her. She made herself meet them.

Price said, "Now, talk. What happened? Tell me."

She went on looking at him, part of her longing to just give him those terrible, wonderful words....

I love you. I've loved you for years.

But, in spite of all that had happened tonight, she found she couldn't do it. All this time she'd feared she'd betray her heart to him, and now the moment was here.

And she couldn't do it.

She knew he never intended to let a woman get really close to him again. If she declared her feelings, she'd only embarrass him, not to mention humiliate herself. And she'd had quite enough humiliation for one night, thank you.

No. Price was not the man for her. She knew that. She only prayed that someday her poor heart would get the message and let her find someone else.

"Come on," Price coaxed, when she'd been quiet for too long. "You can tell me."

She blotted beneath her eyes with the soggy handkerchief, just knowing that her nose must be as red as a circus clown's and her eye makeup smeared all over her face.

"Faith. Please."

She managed a wavery smile—and a little of the truth. "It was the watch, Price."

He stiffened. "The watch? How did you—?"

"There was a watch in that little velvet box, wasn't there?"

He looked flummoxed. "Well, yeah."

"I knew it."

"How?"

"I just did. It was...so like you, to come up with the gold watch for your trusty housekeeper. And I know you had it engraved with something like 'To Faith. Thanks.' Am I right?"

His gaze slid away for a moment, telling her she'd hit the mark. Then he gave her a wounded look. "It's a damn good watch."

"I have no doubt."

He'd been crouched in front of her. Now he dropped to a sitting position on the bare floor and raked his hair back with a hand. "So what are you saying? You don't want the watch?"

She wiped at her eyes again and blew her nose one more time. "That is exactly what I'm saying. I do not want the watch."

"But why not?"

She gestured weakly with his handkerchief. "Oh, Price."

"Just tell me. Why not?"

She sighed. "Remember when you tried to tell me that I was a little like a member of the Montgomery family?"

"Yeah. You said I was wrong. In no uncertain terms."

"I lied."

His brows drew together. "You did?"

"Yes. You and your family mean the world to me. And I'll miss you. And I don't want any gold watch to remember you by. You give a gold watch to an employee. I know that's what I am. But still, it feels like more. For a long time, it's felt like more."

He looked at her for a moment, his eyes shadowed in the harsh light of the single metal-caged overhead bulb. Then he said, "Well, all right, if you really—"

She spoke firmly. "I mean it. No watch. And no generous severance bonus, either."

"God. How do you know all this?"

Because I know *you,* she thought, though all she did was shrug and sigh.

He scooted over, so that he could lean against the rows of shelves perpendicular to the ones she was leaning on. He rested his head against a shelf and then blinked when the light from above blinded him. He rubbed his eyes. "But I want to do *something.*"

A totally preposterous thought popped into her head: *If you want to do something, then make love to me....*

Her face flushed crimson; she could feel it. Hoping he wouldn't notice her sudden blush, she turned her head away from him and stared hard at a plumber's friend that was propped up in the corner.

How could she even be *thinking* such a thing? She wanted real love. A lifetime commitment. A houseful of kids. Spending the night with Price Montgomery wouldn't move her one inch toward those goals.

But she did love him. And the day after tomorrow, she was leaving him. Forever.

One night to remember. Was that such a bad going-away gift to long for?

"Faith, I mean it. There must be something you want. Name it. If I possibly can, I'll give it to you."

Above the plumber's friend was a shelf stacked with fluffy white towels. Faith stared at them for a while.

"Faith, look at me. Talk to me."

Slowly, she turned to face him again. And she heard herself asking, "Do you mean that? Whatever I want?"

His gaze didn't waver. "I meant it. Just name it."

She couldn't believe she was keeping on with this. But she was. "Well, um, if you want to, you could give me..." And that was it. As far as she could go. It was too impossible. Her throat closed off the words.

But he was looking at her piercingly now. "What? Faith, *what?*"

She had no idea where she was getting all this nerve. But she heard herself starting that last sentence again. "If you really want to give me something, you can..."

"What? Tell me."

She did. "...make love to me tonight...."

Chapter Six

Price was looking at her as if she'd lost her mind. He shook his head. "This is crazy. Faith, you can't mean—"

She couldn't bear his stunned expression, so she turned to face the plumber's friend again. "Oh, don't say that."

"But, Faith, I—"

She spoke through clenched teeth. "Don't tell me what I mean. Just tell me if you will or not."

"But, I—"

"Don't."

He was silent. She stared at the fluffy towels, then higher, at a shelf laden with complimentary toilet supplies in clear plastic tubs: bars of scented soap, shampoo, conditioner, tiny mending kits....

"Where?" she heard him ask in a rough whisper.

"What?"

"Where? You mean here, in the hotel?"

She couldn't believe that they were talking about this, as if they would actually do it, as if it were truly an option. She kept her eyes on the tub of mending kits. "Um, yes. Here. We could get a room. Just one night. You and me . . ."

"But this is—"

She whipped her head around and pinned him with a glare. "Will you? This one night. And that's all. That's what I want."

He blinked. "But why?"

Her nerve deserted her. She slumped back against the big drum of whatever-it-was again. The metal felt cold against her bare back. "Oh, I'm being a fool. It's the champagne. And my going away. That's all." She tried a conciliatory smile. "Never mind, all right? Let's just forget that I—"

But Price wasn't smiling. "No. Let's not forget. Why? Why would you want to do this?"

Because I love you, her heart cried. "I told you. Forget it. It was all that champagne." She looked at him pleadingly, begging him with her eyes to forget the whole thing.

But Price had spent too many nights lying awake imagining her in his bed. Her suggestion wasn't something he could easily dismiss.

On the one hand, he knew she was right; they *should* forget it. Her shocking suggestion was not a wise idea.

On the other hand, though, what the hell was wisdom worth, in a situation like this? He didn't know what had hit him since she'd said she was leaving his house. Over the past few weeks, his well-ordered life had gone to hell. He'd been living on an emotional roller coaster. Damn it, he wanted her like he'd never wanted any other woman. And soon she would be gone. He might never see her again.

Just one night . . . The words echoed in his brain. He'd been a fool to muddle around asking *why.* Life was short and cruel. A man should take whatever precious gifts were offered and be grateful for them.

He scooted closer to her along the cold concrete. "Faith, maybe I . . ." He didn't know how to go on.

"What?" Her voice was small and full of misery, and her head was turned away once more.

He moved again, until they were side by side, their shoulders touching. Then he reached across and guided her chin around with two fingers of his right hand.

Her pretty brows drew together. She sighed. "What, Price?"

He looked at her mouth. Something hot and hungry pulsed through him. It would happen; he would taste her mouth.

"I know we shouldn't," he murmured.

"So do I." She sniffed and tried to turn her head again. "You're right."

He didn't allow her to look away. He cupped her chin, holding it firm.

"Price?" She said it on a little hitch of a breath. Her eyes were so wide, a little wondering. She was starting to understand.

"I want to make love with you, Faith."

Her eyes widened even more. They took over her face. He could fall into those eyes, be enveloped by them. "Y-you do?"

"I do." He shifted a little, so that he could get his arm behind her, and then he gathered her close.

He ran his hand down her bare, smooth back, under the veil of her silky hair, which swung free now, the little strip of black velvet having completely disappeared. He breathed in that wonderful, seductive, sweet scent of her.

"Lord," he said, "you can't know how much I . . ."

"What?"

"How I . . ."

"Yes?"

He had no idea how to finish that sentence. And right then, words seemed superfluous, anyway. Action was called for.

So he simply leaned a little closer and settled his mouth on hers.

"Oh!" she said, the word a breath against his lips. And then he felt her smile.

He whispered her name.

"Price," she whispered back, her slender arms lifting to curl around his neck.

Price could hardly believe it. The moment he'd dreamed of through two weeks of sleepless nights had actually come to pass. He savored the sweet taste of her, kissing her lightly at first, not wanting to startle her, or make her pull away.

That bow of hers rustled, an unbearably arousing sound. He heard himself moan.

He cupped her head, turning her. She came willingly—eagerly, even—to lie across his lap. Wanting more, unable to completely hold back, Price deepened the kiss, urging her lips to open.

After a brief moment of resistance, she gave up her mouth. Her lips softened and parted like some moist, tender flower before the probing of his hungry tongue.

His tongue slid inside her mouth. She stiffened. He pulled back. She relaxed, went soft and pliant once more. He tried again, another stroke. This time she only sighed, her lips moving a little, as if she knew him now and welcomed him.

Already, inside his trousers, he was aching for her. One of his hands was behind her, cradling her bare back, tangled in the long skeins of her hair. His other hand, crossed over the front of her, clutched her shoulder. Against that arm, he could feel the soft swell of her breasts. He wanted to caress them. To peel back the black velvet and taste them.

He wanted to undress her. And this was not the place to do that.

Reluctantly he raised his head. She sighed. He looked down at her as her eyes drifted open. Her mouth was full, moist, kissed-looking. He wanted to take it again.

But he didn't. "We have to go."

"I...um..."

There it was, that innocence. That total vulnerability.

His arousal intensified. It occurred to him that he could ease his need right here and now if he wanted. She wouldn't say no.

But he wouldn't do that to her.

She deserved better.

Better than me, he thought. *More than I can ever give her.*

Hell. He should do the right thing. Call this off right now.

But he wanted her too damn much to stop now. And she wanted him, too. She'd said so.

He'd get them out of this closet and into a decent bed. And that was as far as his scruples would force him to go.

She murmured hesitantly, "I...suppose we have to see about a room."

"Yes."

"Okay." She sat up and pulled away from him. He resisted the urge to hold her there. She held out his handkerchief. "Um. Here. Thanks."

He took it and shoved it in a pocket. Then he watched for a moment, bemused, as she started fiddling with her hair, which looked a little wild now, hanging free, clinging to the black velvet dress.

Realizing they couldn't sit on the floor of that closet forever, he gathered his feet under him and stood. She looked up at him, clearly a little afraid, her white teeth worrying her full bottom lip. He reached down a hand.

With his help, she rose to stand beside him.

Her hand felt warm and soft in his. He wanted to touch it with his lips. But she didn't give him the chance. She pulled away and started tugging on her dress, straightening it. And then she glanced down at her legs. A small sound of distress escaped her at the sight of her now ruined stockings.

Price watched her little attempts to put herself in order, wanting to smile as much as he wanted to reach for her and ruin what little progress toward tidiness she'd made.

She gave him a nervous glance. "I, um, suppose we have to go back up to the restaurant. I left my purse and my jacket."

His sigh was rueful. "And I forgot to pay the bill."

She was pulling at the bow on the back of her dress, not looking at him. But then the humor of the situation seemed to reach her. She met his eyes. They shared a smile.

Damn. He did *like* her. He had always liked her. It was this *wanting* that was new, that made him do things he shouldn't—like take advantage of her, the woman who'd made his house a home for so long he couldn't picture how he was going to get along when she was gone.

He reached out, grasped her waist and turned her around. "Let me help."

"Thank you." She pulled her hair out of his way over one shoulder, exposing the side of her neck, so white and pure. The earring dangling there was red as blood against her snowy skin.

He wanted to put his lips there. Right beneath the earring...

"Price?" She sent him a questioning glance over the shoulder she'd bared.

"Oh. Sorry." He shook himself and straightened the bow. "There."

She started to pull away. He held her still, unable to resist brushing a kiss on that shoulder, right at the place where the black velvet started. She shuddered a little when his lips touched her skin. His own body caught fire.

Suppressing a groan, he pulled her back against him, grateful for the slightly crumpled black bow that would keep her from realizing just how ready he was to finish what they'd started.

He kissed her ear, right over the top of that dangling earring; his teeth grazed the red stone. She stiffened, then sighed.

"Are you afraid?"

Her head bobbed up and down.

While his body screamed, *Don't say it!* he made himself ask, "Do you want to back out?"

Her head went back and forth.

He let himself breathe again. "Something *is* wrong, though. What is it?"

"Oh, Price."

"Tell me."

"It's just..."

"Yes?"

"I'm a mcss."

"No..."

"Yes. My dress is all wrinkled. I have several huge runs in my nylons."

"It's all right...."

"No, it's not. I'm...embarrassed. I don't want to go back there, to the restaurant. One look at me, and all those people will know what we've been doing. And I'm scared to death about going down to the lobby and checking into the room."

Her scent was driving him crazy. It was as sweet as ever, but faintly musky now, a woman's scent. He nuzzled her hair, loving the feel of it against his mouth. The strands felt so warm and smooth and alive.

"Tell you what," he whispered.

"What?"

"You take the elevator down to the lobby. Find a rest room there and freshen up a little. There's a row of gift shops around the corner from the registration desk. You know the ones I mean?"

"I'm sure I could find them."

"There's a fountain, in front of the gift shops. Wait for me there. I'll take care of everything."

She turned in his arms and looked up at him solemnly. "But it's not fair, that you should have to be responsible for all of it. I should—"

He kissed the tip of her nose. "I think I can handle it. Honestly."

"Ready?"

Faith jumped. She'd been waiting at the fountain for about ten minutes—ten minutes that had seemed like forever and a day.

She turned. Her heart was bouncing around like a paddleball inside her chest.

Price held out her little black bolero jacket and her evening bag. She took them. "Thank you." She shivered a little.

"Here." He took the jacket back and helped her to put it on. "Better?"

She nodded. "Did you—?"

"Everything's handled. Are you ready to go to the room?"

She had to swallow before she answered, "Yes."

He was looking at her; it was a stunningly intimate look, his eyes like blue velvet. He reached out slowly and touched the side of her face, catching and lifting a section of her hair that had caught beneath the collar of her jacket. He pulled it free and smoothed it over her shoulder.

Faith stood transfixed throughout the whole process. Something had happened to him. He was so different with her, since those forbidden moments in the tiny housekeeper's room upstairs. He seemed...possessive. And tender. As if he really did desire her.

And he had said as much: *I want to make love with you....*

Right then, his expression changed. His face was closed, suddenly. He stepped back. "Wait here. Just for a moment, okay?"

He turned, leaving her before she could ask what he was doing. He didn't go far, into one of the gift shops nearby. He came back minutes later, having bought nothing that she could see. "Let's go." He took her arm.

She wondered vaguely what that was all about. But she didn't ask. The room upstairs was waiting. Thoughts of what would happen there drove everything else from her mind.

"This way." He took her to the elevators again. They got on a car that was nearly full. Faith had taken off her hopelessly laddered panty hose in the rest room. She just knew everyone was staring at her bare, pale legs. She kept her chin high and her eyes straight ahead.

The elevator moved upward, stopping every few floors to drop someone off or to pick up new passengers. By the time they reached the twenty-fifth floor, the elevator was carrying more people than when they'd started. Faith and Price had gradually worked their way toward the back.

Price murmured, "This is us." The car stopped, the doors whooshed open. Price guided her out through the press of people into a hallway. The doors slid shut, and Faith was grateful. She'd felt that everyone was staring at her, wondering what that disheveled, stockingless woman could be doing on the arm of such a handsome, self-assured man.

Price took her hand again and led her off down a hallway. Soon enough, he stopped before a room. He stuck the card-key in the lock, and a little green light went on.

He turned the handle and pushed the door inward and moved back for her to enter first.

Her absolute certainty that this was all a dream redoubling with each second, Faith stepped into a small entranceway. To her left was a bathroom; straight ahead, a large living area. She moved forward into the living area, which was furnished with soft mauve-colored leather sofas and bleached oak tables. The room was seductively dim, lit only by the faint light that glowed in the bases of a few table lamps. A huge picture window took up most of the far wall. The filmy curtains were drawn back to reveal another spectacular view of the bay.

Having no idea what to do with herself, Faith dropped her evening bag on one of the sofas, then went to the window and stared out. The clouds had cleared off even more. The brightest stars winked at her, and the crescent moon dangled high in the sky.

Faith could hear Price moving behind her, opening doors, looking around. And then he materialized at her back. She felt the warmth of him.

He put his hands on her shoulders and began peeling her jacket away.

Once he'd slid the jacket down her arms, he tossed it lightly on a nearby chair. That done, he grasped her waist and pulled her against him, the way he had in that little closet, not too long ago. He kissed the top of her head, and then wrapped his arms around her.

Faith settled back into his embrace. He felt so solid and good. She could have leaned on him forever, if such a thing was possible. Which it was not.

"You're so quiet," he said into her ear. His breath was warm; it felt good against her cheek.

"What do you want me to say?"

He seemed to ponder her question, then told her, "Nothing, I guess." He nuzzled the shape of her ear. She cuddled closer, liking the way it felt to have him caress her.

She turned her head. Their lips met. She felt his tongue, probing, seeking. With a tiny gasp, she opened for him, turning in his arms at the same time, so that they were face-to-face. As her hands felt their way up the front of his silk shirt, she realized he'd already removed his jacket and taken off his tie.

The kiss lasted an eternity. Once or twice, Price raised his head, but only to slant his mouth the other way and kiss her some more.

When at last he actually pulled back and looked down at her, she was holding on to him, as much for support as because it felt so good to touch him. He traced the side of her face with a finger, smoothing her hair back and then letting his hand trail down to her black velvet neckline. He traced the neckline, idly, his finger moving back and forth against her skin. She felt goose bumps rise in the wake of each stroke, a delicious sensation.

"Such a pretty dress," he said, grasping her shoulders, holding her away a little, admiring her.

"Thank you."

He chuckled. "You are so well behaved."

She looked down, a bit flustered by his teasing.

He caught her chin. "No. Look at me. Always. I love to watch your eyes."

"You do?"

He nodded. "Such wide, wondering eyes." His hand slid down over the velvet. It covered one breast.

"Oh!" she said, and blinked.

"Oh, yes," he whispered, as if in reply.

He rubbed his palm against her breast, where it crested beneath the velvet. She felt her nipple rising, drawing tighter. She knew he could feel it, too.

His eyes looked darker, midnight blue. He went on, brushing his hand back and forth over the crest of her breast. "How do you get out of this pretty dress?"

Her eyelids felt so heavy, like the rest of her, heavy and liquid and melting away....

"Faith?"

She gathered her scattered wits and managed to tell him, "Little hooks and a zipper. In back, beneath the bow."

His hands slid around her, bringing her close against him once more. He looked down at her and she looked up at him as he worked at the big bow behind her.

"Ah." He found his way beneath the bow. One by one, the hooks gave way. And then the zipper slowly parted. He was smiling now. Into her eyes.

He took the sides of the dress and pulled them wide. She felt the air of the room slip along her ribs. He took the dress down and away, exposing her breasts as he did it, because her bra was sewn into the bodice. Instinctively she crossed her arms over herself.

He was kneeling then, not looking at her, helping her to step out of the dress. When she had stepped clear, he rose and tossed it onto the big leather chair behind her, where her jacket already lay. She turned around to look as she heard it land in a rustling of velvet and silk.

"Faith."

She made herself face him again, though she couldn't quite let her arms down. He helped her, taking her wrists and pulling them away from her body.

"In my eyes," he said again, so tenderly.

She didn't look away, though she knew that all her skin was flushed pink. He whispered that she was beautiful. She blushed pinker still.

"Let's go to bed."

She swallowed and nodded.

He still held one of her wrists. He turned, leading her behind him, and went to a pair of open louvered doors on the inside wall. Beyond them was a wide bed with a quilted spread in swirling gray and mauve and salmon pink. The night tables, on either side, bore lamps with soft lights glowing in the bases, like the ones in the outer room. She saw that his jacket and tie were thrown across a chair, not far from the bed. And on one of the night tables was a small box.

Faith knew enough to realize that the box held contraceptives. Now she understood what Price had bought in that gift shop downstairs.

He led her to the bed, took her shoulders and guided her to sit on the edge. He smiled. She smiled tremulously back.

And then he turned from her. He undressed quickly, tossing the rest of his clothes toward the chair, where they landed haphazardly on top of his jacket and tie.

She didn't feel quite so naked when he turned to her again. She still had on her half-slip and her panties and her shoes. But he was completely bare.

She dared to look her fill at him: her secret love, who by some miracle would spend the night with her. She saw a tall, dark man, with eyes like a mountain sky at night, indigo blue. His body was hard and muscular, in a lean, efficient way. His shoulders were broad, and his chest was wide, tapering down to a tight waist. Dark hair whorled out over masculine nipples and then down in a trail to the juncture of hard thighs.

He seemed very large—not that she was really any judge of such things—and very ready to make love to her. She looked away.

"In my eyes," he said again.

She met the tender challenge. He came and knelt before her, taking each of her feet in turn and slowly sliding her black shoes away. Then he laid his hands lightly on her thighs, over the silky fabric of her half-slip. He rubbed, with a breath of a caress. His eyes continued to hold hers captive.

Slowly, he pushed up the slip. At his urging, she lifted a little when he reached her hips. The slip bunched at her waist. He left it there, as his hands strayed upward. She gasped when he cupped her breasts.

She felt all weak inside. With a moan, she gave in to the weakness, reaching her hands behind her to grasp the bedspread, resting on them, letting her head fall back. She closed her eyes, expecting him to tell her again that she must look at him.

But he didn't. He was silent. She moaned again, in excitement at the heat that was spreading down inside her.

His hands were moving again, downward, over the bunched silk at her waist, and then lower still. He put a hand on either thigh, there, at the juncture of her legs. His thumbs delved inward.

She gasped again. He made a soothing sound as he rubbed the cleft that her panties still covered. She knew she was becoming very wet down there. She could feel the moisture, dampening the silk, betraying her longing in such an embarrassing way.

His hands slid up again. His fingers curled over the top of her panties. He peeled them down.

Faith kept her eyes closed, her head thrown back. And she lifted her hips so that he could take the panties away. Now she had no protection from him.

He made a sound then, a hungry sort of sound. She didn't look. She couldn't. She was so...hot. So weak. She wanted him to...

His hands, warm and sure and strong, took hold of her, one on each thigh. He guided her legs slowly apart. She resisted, just a little, but the inexorable pressure of his will was so delicious. Her resistance was token; they both knew that.

And then, when at last the most intimate secrets of her body were his alone, he touched her there once again. He caressed her slowly, gently at first, then with deeper, more demanding strokes.

She tossed her head. She felt the fire inside building, reaching to be something greater, an explosion, a... completion.

And then his mouth was there.

Faith was too overwhelmed to be shocked. Was this not what she had dreamed of, imagined, made happen in her mind through all the lonely nights, for too many years to admit?

His intimate kiss went on and on. She pushed herself toward him, frantic and needful and utterly without shame.

The explosion occurred. A hot flower of pure fire, it opened outward, shattering her completely as it bloomed.

She fell back against the bed.

But he had only started. He rose above her. She lay limp, totally open to him. There was a brief moment when he dealt with the box by the bed. And then he was urging her upward among the pillows, stripping away the rumpled half slip she still wore, settling himself between her thighs.

"Now," he said.

She opened her eyes. His were so blue. Was this happening? Was this real? All her sad and hopeless little dreams, real for this night, for this brief moment of erotic splendor in a tower by the Bay?

He pressed into her. She bit her lower lip.

"Faith!" His face contorted. He knew for sure right then that she had never done this thing before.

She lifted her legs, wrapped them tight around him and surged upward, pulling him down at the same time. Her innocence broke.

He made a strangled sound. "You . . . didn't tell me . . ."

She pulled him tighter, rocked herself against him. He moaned and surrendered, pushing deep into her. She stroked his powerful back through an eternity of breath-held stillness.

At last, he raised up on his forearms and looked down at her.

He pulled back—and pushed in. His eyes were cruel. And full of need.

"Does it hurt?" The question seemed ground out of him. "Do you want me to stop?"

It did hurt. But not as much as it pleasured. She shook her head against the pillows.

"Good." He did it again, a strong thrust of powerful hips.

She cried out then. But he didn't stop. He moved faster, deeper, and his eyes never let go of hers—until the end, when he allowed her to pull him down and hold him.

"Tighter," he whispered hoarsely into her ear. "Your legs and your arms. Tight around me. Before you go away forever."

She held him tighter. As tight as she could. And at last she felt him, pulsing deep within her. He cried out.

Her cry answered his. White light pulsed from the center of her, blinding, overwhelming. She went over the edge of the world for the second time that night.

Afterward, she stroked his back. He rubbed his head against her shoulder, in a gesture that spoke to her of infinite tenderness, of loving affection.

Right then, he seemed hers, as he had never been.

And would never be again . . .

He raised his head, looked at her. "What is it?"

She lied with a smile. "Nothing. Kiss me."

His mouth settled on hers once more, stealing all thought away. He began to caress her again.

Faith surrendered completely to his touch. This was the only night they'd ever share. She refused to waste a moment of it in pointless regret.

Chapter Seven

Faith woke from a dream of water and stillness. Slowly she floated up to consciousness.

She was lying on her back, with a hand thrown over her eyes. There was a weight across her stomach. Before she even moved, it all came back to her. The beautiful dinner. Her humiliating flight. The absurdity and wonder of those moments in the housekeeping closet on the twentieth floor.

And later. In the room. In *this* room...

Carefully she lowered the arm over her eyes. Daylight.

She turned her head.

Price. He slept on his stomach, facing the other way. His right arm was flung out over her, creating that weight across her middle that she hadn't quite understood as she was waking.

She raised her head a little, so that she could see out into the other room. Morning. Definitely. The light looked gray; an overcast day.

She glanced at the bedside clock. Not morning at all. Noon. A little past noon.

Beside her, Price groaned in his sleep. He shifted, moving the arm that pinned her down. Then he rolled onto his right side, so that now his whole body was facing away from her.

Everything that he'd done to her flooded through her mind. Everything they'd done together. Everything *she'd* done to him.

She had surprised herself, actually. She'd become extremely inventive in a very short period of time.

Faith closed her eyes and sighed—but it was a quiet sigh. She didn't want to wake him. She didn't want him to turn to her and look at her as if he weren't quite sure what she was doing in this bed with him.

She wanted—out. Now. Before she had to meet his eyes, lying here next to him, naked as the day she was born.

Faith waited, absolutely still, listening. His breath came evenly, shallow and slow.

Good. If she was quiet, she could probably make her escape without disturbing him.

With excruciating slowness, Faith eased back the spread. She slipped a leg over the side of the bed, and then slid the other one after it. She landed soundlessly on her feet. Her slip, panties and shoes were right there beside the bed. She snatched everything up and tiptoed into the other room.

There, she allowed herself to breathe again. She stopped by the big window and looked out. She saw a wall of gray mist. Fog had crept in during the night.

Faith yanked on her rumpled clothes—except for her shoes, which she decided to carry until she was safely out of the room. The zipper under the bow of her dress gave her trouble. She struggled with it, and let out a tiny moan of relief when she finally succeeded in pulling it up. She grabbed her little jacket and shoved her arms into it. At last, her shoes in one hand and her beaded purse in the other, she headed for the door.

Once in the hallway, she paused to slip into the shoes. Then she hurried for the elevators, looking straight ahead, not daring so much as a glance at the maid who approached and then trundled on by, pushing a cleaning cart.

At the elevators, she had to wait for a car. Each second was a year. And then, when one set of doors finally opened, there were two couples inside.

Faith knew what she looked like: the unmade bed she'd just slithered out of. She longed to race for the stairs. But she was on the twenty-fifth floor. It would be a long walk down.

No. She would ride. She clutched her purse tightly to the wrinkled bodice of her dress and boarded the elevator.

A lifetime later, she emerged on the lobby floor. She forced herself to walk at a sedate pace to the rest room.

Once safely inside, she used the facilities, washed her face and hands and then spent a good five minutes trying to coax the tangles from her flyaway hair. At last, she gave up on getting out all the snarls. She rolled the mess at the back of her head, anchoring it on itself in a loose knot.

As tidy as she could make herself in a crushed velvet dress with no stockings, Faith left the bathroom and headed for the main doors to the street.

Outside, the fog lay like a gray blanket over everything. But luck was with her. A cab materialized out of the mist.

Price woke smiling, facing the far wall, in complete awareness of where he was and how he'd arrived there. Memories of the night just past came to him, curling through his mind like the haunting strains of some lush, romantic song.

Price's smile deepened. He was aroused all over again. Damn difficult to believe. He wasn't any kid. After all that had gone on last night, sex should have been the last thing on his mind.

Price wondered about the time, but only distantly. The time didn't really matter. He wasn't letting Faith out of this bed until they'd made love again. Thoroughly.

He rolled over to reach for her.

When he saw that the other side of the bed was empty, his belly knotted in sudden apprehension. But then he relaxed. She was probably just in the shower.

He levered himself up on an elbow, listening. The suite seemed too quiet. On the nightstand by Faith's side of the bed, something gleamed: her earrings. She had removed them not too long before they finally dropped off to sleep last night.

A flash of memory revealed her to him. She'd been sitting up, her head tipped to the side as she fiddled with the posts. Her bare skin had looked creamy against the sheets. Her hair had fallen like a veil over her round breasts.

"These were my mother's. They're about the only thing I have left that was hers."

"They're beautiful. *You're* beautiful."

"No, I'm not."

"Yes, you are. Come here."

She'd set them on the nightstand and turned into his waiting arms. . . .

Eager to find her, Price threw back the covers and jumped from the bed. Naked, he stalked through the rooms. In short order, he discovered that Faith's clothes were gone—and so was she. While he lay sleeping, she had dressed and left, leaving nothing but her mother's earrings behind.

A seething, anxious anger moving through him, Price stood before the big window in the living area and stared out at a wall of grayness. A pigeon materialized out of the mist and landed against the outside sill, its wings fluttering as it tried to find a perch. Price watched its futile struggles until it gave up and flew away, disappearing into the swirling murk as if it had never been.

What the hell was she up to, running off like this? She'd left him without a word. Left him to wake up alone and wonder where she'd gotten herself off to. To pray she was all right.

Price sank to a nearby chair. He stared blindly at the gray nothingness beyond the glass. Slowly, his anger faded.

He and Faith had shared one night. That gave him no hold over her. She was free to go whenever—and wherever—she pleased. She had no responsibility to inform him of her plans.

And besides, what kind of *hold* was he thinking of, anyway? He wanted no *hold* over any woman, no matter how lovely, sensitive, warm and caring she was—not to mention incredibly responsive in bed.

And a virgin, on top of everything.

A virgin. Yes, that probably explained a lot, now that he thought about it. She'd been innocent. And in the cold light of morning, when she woke beside him, it had all been too much for her. She'd fled.

Price stood. He went looking for his clothes. He had to get home right away. To make certain she was there. And to see for himself that she was okay.

He dressed swiftly. Just before he left the suite, he scooped up her earrings from the nightstand and shoved them into a pocket of his slacks.

Because of the fog, the ride home took forever. But at last, an hour after she'd hailed the cab in front of the hotel, Faith arrived at the side door off the kitchen of Montgomery House.

She paid the cabbie and then ran up the steps to the door. She had no key. She'd had sense enough to bring some cash, but it had never occurred to her when they left last night that she'd be returning without Price—or that she'd have any reason at all to want to slip into the house unnoticed.

So Faith was forced to ring the bell. Then she had to wait for Justine to come, since it was Sunday and neither Balthazar nor the maids worked Sundays. The foggy air was cold enough to chill the bones. Her rumpled velvet jacket provided little warmth. Faith wrapped her arms around herself to control her shivering and waited to be let in.

At last, Justine pulled back the door.

Faith had to hand it to the new housekeeper. Justine knew how to deal with an awkward situation; she defused it by ignoring it.

"Hello, Faith." Justine stepped back, and Faith moved beyond the threshold, into the welcome warmth of the big kitchen. "I'm sorry it took me so long to get here. I was upstairs."

Faith forced a smile. "No problem. Where are Regis and Ariel?"

"In the morning room."

It was the answer that Faith had feared she'd get. To reach the back stairs, she'd have to walk right past them.

Faith looked closely at Justine and thought she saw sympathy in her hazel eyes. She decided she'd rather be frank with the new housekeeper than have to deal with Price's parents right then. "I don't want them to see me."

"Okay," Justine said, without missing a beat. "What do you want me to do?"

But Faith had no time to answer, because right then Ariel appeared from the morning room. "Justine, who—?" Violet eyes went wide. "Oh, my dear." Her hot-pink chiffon lounging pajamas fluttering with each step, Ariel rushed to Faith's side. "Are you all right?"

Faith clutched her evening bag so tightly that the beading dug into her fingers. Oh, why hadn't she considered what this morning would be like before she threw caution to the winds last night?

"Faith, are you ill?"

"No, I'm not. Really. I'm fine."

Ariel shoved her hair out of her eyes. "Oh, my. What's happened? Where's Price?"

"He'll, um, be along in a little while."

"But—"

Faith hastened to reassure the older woman. "He's fine. Truly. I just....decided to come home a little ahead of him."

"But, dear, I don't—"

"Listen. I've had a long night. I need a hot bath."

"Well, of course. But if you'd only—"

"Ariel. I'm just not up to going into any details right now. Please understand. Price will be along soon. I promise you."

Justine stepped in. "Yes, Ariel. Faith needs a little time to herself. Come on back to the morning room." She already had the older woman by the arm.

Casting Justine a look of abject gratitude, Faith scooted around the two women and headed for the door to the central hall. Behind her, Ariel was still sputtering and Justine was making soothing sounds. Faith tuned them out. All she wanted right then was to attain the privacy of her rooms.

She met little Eli on the second-floor landing.

"Hi, Faith." He held up a book. "I just read *The Berenstain Bears Get the Gimmies* all the way through. Wanna hear it?"

Faith paused, one hand clutching the rail. "I do, Eli. I honestly do. Just not right this minute, okay?"

He tipped his head and studied her. "When?"

She thought fast. "Bedtime. Tonight. I promise."

"But you're moving away."

"Not until tomorrow. Tonight, I'm all yours."

He considered, then nodded. "All right." His smile was wide, and it warmed her heart. "It's a deal." The boy turned and started down again, pausing after two steps to grin up at her one more time. "You're gonna love it. I'm really a super reader."

"I know you are."

She watched him go down the steps, thinking through the haze of her own misery that he was just about the sweetest six-year-old she'd ever met. Then she shook herself and climbed on to the top floor.

She would have been wiser to have removed her high heels first. But it had never occurred to her that Parker would emerge from his hideout of his own accord when he heard her tap-tapping past his door.

"Faith. Wait."

Faith froze. She sucked in a long, slow breath, frustration warring with amazement. Could this be. happening? Had Parker Montgomery really spoken from behind her?

"Faith?"

He certainly had.

Slowly, she turned.

He stood in his own doorway, looking pale, as always, and much too thin. His high-tops were untied, and his T-shirt said Megadeth. "Mom knocked on my door this morning. She asked if I'd heard you come in last night. She said you'd gone out to dinner with Price."

Faith had no idea what to say. She settled for "I see."

"Are you all right?"

"Of course. And I just, um, spoke with your mother. Downstairs." She tried a reassuring smile. "So you don't have to worry. She knows I'm just fine."

Parker wasn't buying. "You did go out with Price, didn't you?"

"I..."

"And you stayed with him. All night."

Faith felt herself weaving on her feet. "Parker, I'm just not up to dealing with..."

He was at her side immediately. Wiry arms supported her. "Come on. I'll help you."

"No, really. I'm okay...."

But he was already leading her toward her door, and pushing it open onto her small sitting room, which was cluttered with stacks of boxes now, all packed and ready for the move tomorrow. Guiding her gently around each obstacle, Parker took her to the sofa beneath the miniature bay window.

"Come on," he said. "Stretch out and kick off those shoes." She did as he instructed. He stuck a pillow beneath her head and fussed with it until he was sure she was comfortable. Then he stood and looked down at her. "I take it he was still asleep when you left?"

Faith closed her eyes.

"Never mind. I know already. I know you. And I know him."

Faith didn't want to hear any more in that vein. She turned her head away from him.

Parker went on anyway. "He'll be up to see you. As soon as he gets home."

"Look," she said to the back of the sofa, "could you just stop talking about it?"

Parker's answer was gentle. "Sure."

Faith rolled her head and looked at him once more. He was still staring down at her, his eyes full of concern. In spite of her own unhappy circumstances, Faith thought that it was wonderful to see him like this. He really was coming out of his shell at last.

"Listen," he said. "Just one more question. Do you think that now, after...whatever happened between you and Price, you might change your mind and stay?"

She rubbed her eyes. "No, Parker. I don't think so."

He shook his head. "I just can't picture this place without you."

Faith sighed and struggled to provide the reassurance he needed. "Justine will do wonderfully. Just wait and see."

"I know she will. I've been watching her. I see more than you know."

She gave him a wobbly smile. "I'm beginning to understand that."

"But Justine's not you. If I'd ever had a big sister, I'd have wanted her to be you. Someone who understands everything, but never pushes a guy."

Dejected as she felt right then, Faith couldn't help but be moved by such heartfelt words.

Parker wasn't finished. "There was a girl. When I was at Juilliard. I really loved her."

Faith took that in, then nodded. "I thought maybe there had been."

"She dumped me. I went to pieces. She was why I flunked out. Why I tried to join the army. How all this mess I've made of my life got started."

Faith absorbed what he'd just told her, thinking how much like Price he really was. Losing someone they loved had almost destroyed both of them. The Montgomery sons were the children of an artist and a visionary. Somehow, nothing in their upbringing had prepared them for the heartbreak life could bring.

She suggested what they both already knew. "Maybe it's time you got over that girl."

"Yeah. I've been thinking the same thing lately."

Faith let a moment pass before she softly suggested, "Come visit me sometime, why don't you? In North Magdalene. I think you'd like it there."

Parker raked a hand back through his ragged, shoulder-length hair. "I can't believe it. I'm actually tempted to say that I'll think about it."

"It's a start."

"I gotta go."

"I know. Lock the door on the way out, will you?"

"It won't keep him away from you, if he wants to get to you."

"I'll worry about that. Just lock it."

"Okay."

Ariel and Regis were waiting in the front parlor when Price let himself in the main door. They rushed to meet him.

"Price. At last!" Ariel cried. "We've been so terribly worried...."

He pushed the door shut behind him. "Is Faith home?"

Ariel blew her hair out of her eyes and put a hand to her throat. "Yes. She arrived about twenty-five minutes ago."

"Where is she?"

"Up in her rooms, I believe. But I—"

Price stepped around his parents and headed for the stairs, which he took two at a time. On the second floor, he strode down the hall between his own room and his parents' private living room, to the back stairs, which were the only ones that went all the way to the third floor.

At last he was standing before her door. Just as he lifted his hand to knock, his brother spoke from behind him.

"She doesn't want to see you, Price."

He whirled. *"Parker?"* He couldn't mask the disbelief in his voice. His younger brother so rarely emerged from his room. And Parker was totally wrapped up in his own problems. How could he have any idea what Faith wanted?

Parker folded his skinny arms over his narrow chest. "I said, she doesn't want to see you. Leave her alone. Unless you've got something worth having to offer her."

Price struggled to put aside his shock at being challenged—and by Parker, of all people. He cleared his throat and spoke carefully. "Are you...feeling all right?"

"I'm fine. Faith isn't. As I've said twice now, she doesn't want to see you."

"Did she tell you that?"

"More or less."

"Is she—?"

"She's exhausted and upset. And she wants to be alone. Unless—"

"Unless what?"

Some trick of the light made Parker's eyes look very old right then, old and infinitely wise. "I think you know."

Price stared at his brother. He knew, all right. Parker had said it already: unless Price had something worth having to offer her.

And he didn't. Nothing that would matter to a good and innocent woman who had told him last night that someday she hoped to find a man who would love her and marry her and give her children.

The silence stretched out. Then Price muttered, "She's okay, you said?"

Parker nodded.

"All right, then. I won't bother her. Tell her I picked up her earrings."

"Give them to me. I'll see that she gets them."

Price shook his head. "No, thanks. Just pass on the message."

Now Parker looked sullen. "Fine."

Price headed for the stairs again, but he turned to his brother one more time before descending. "It's good to see you outside your room. Even in this situation."

Parker looked away, then met Price's gaze once more. His lip curled in defiance. "Don't get any ideas."

"Ideas about what?"

"Bringing in the shrinks again. I won't talk to them."

"All right. No more shrinks."

"Good."

For another long moment, the brothers stared at each other. Then Price started down. When he reached the second floor, he paused. But he could hear nothing above. Either his brother was still standing in the same place, guarding Faith, or he'd slipped back inside his room and soundlessly shut the door.

For the rest of the day, Faith kept to her rooms. Justine brought her a late lunch on a tray, then asked if she wanted dinner in her room, as well. Faith said she'd really appreciate that.

Around two in the afternoon, Parker paid Faith another visit. He told her that Price had come to see her, but had decided not to bother her when Parker said she wanted to be left alone. He also gave her the message about the earrings.

Faith didn't know whether to thank Parker for looking out for her—or ask him to mind his own business. So she did neither. She gave him a tired smile and said she had more packing to do.

At seven on the dot, Eli knocked on Faith's door. When she answered, he held up his Berenstain Bears book. The boy read her the story with a great deal of vocal expression, then stayed to watch some TV. He told her he would miss her.

"You're almost as nice as my mom," he said. Faith took that for the high praise it was.

After Eli left, Faith packed the last of her things into a big suitcase and an overnight bag. Everything else was stacked in boxes, ready to go.

Faith was in bed by ten. Her dreams were troubled ones. When she looked in the mirror the next morning, there were dark circles under her eyes.

And yet outside, yesterday's fog had melted away. The birds were singing, and the winter sun shone down. The first day of her new life would be a bright one.

* * *

Faith's brother-in-law, Erik, arrived in his truck at a few minutes past nine. Following right behind him in a pickup were her cousin Jared and her uncle Oggie.

They parked by the kitchen entrance, as per Faith's instructions. Faith was waiting for them. She ran down the short steps to greet them.

Erik, a huge man with bronze-colored hair and a gentle demeanor, enfolded her in a hug of greeting.

"Hey, cousin," Jared said when Erik let her go. Jared was lean as a whip. The look in his slate-gray eyes warned all comers that he wasn't a man to be crossed, though he was happily married and, in Faith's experience, had always been a pussycat. "Ready for the big move?"

Faith smiled at Jared. "You bet."

"Where's the stuff?" Jared asked.

"On the third floor, I'm afraid."

Erik and Jared glanced up at the house together, then exchanged looks of great patience. Erik sighed and said, "I suppose we'd better get to work."

"Yep," Jared agreed. He called to Oggie, "You comin', Dad?"

Faith's uncle was still climbing down from the passenger seat of the pickup. "I'm comin', I'm comin'," Oggie grumbled. He shut the pickup door and hobbled toward them on his cane, favoring the foot he'd once shot accidentally with his own hunting rifle.

Faith watched the old sweetheart approach, wondering affectionately if he ever changed his clothes. Every time she saw him, he looked the same. He wore a rumpled, threadbare white shirt, grimy red suspenders, a battered pair of tan trousers and lace-up leather boots that had seen better days. What was left of his hair stood out in wispy clumps around the side of his head. But his small, dark eyes sparkled with life and mischief. And for some reason, every time Faith saw him she experienced a sort of soothing, reassuring feeling that all was right with the world.

Oggie stopped a few feet from Faith and the other two men. Slowly, he tipped back his grizzled head and gazed up at the turrets and towers of Montgomery House. "Whooeee. That's amazin'."

Faith laughed. "It is, isn't it?"

"Faith, girl, you sure you're gonna be happy runnin' Swan's Motel after livin' in a palace for half your life?"

Faith closed the short distance between herself and the old man. "I'll be happy." She planted a kiss on his wrinkled, stubbly cheek. "Just you wait and see."

Oggie squinted at her through those piercing black eyes. "You look worn-out."

She shifted back a step. "It's all the excitement of the move."

"Oh, is it?" Oggie seemed to peer at her even more closely than before.

"We gonna stand here all day?" Jared wanted to know.

Faith was glad for the interruption. She adored her old uncle, but sometimes he saw too much. "This way."

She led them into the kitchen, where she introduced them to Balthazar. Oggie plunked himself down at the table. "You three get to work. I'm a little hungry, myself." He grinned at Balthazar.

Balthazar turned to Faith. "Am I supposed to feed him?"

"Only if you want to."

Balthazar was already turning to the refrigerator as Faith led her cousin and Erik up the back stairs.

Over the years, Faith had gradually filled her living quarters with furniture of her own. So Erik and Jared set right to work, maneuvering her bed and sofa, easy chairs and end tables carefully down the two flights of stairs. Faith went up and down on her own, carrying boxes full of clothing and linens, books and knickknacks.

By her fourth trip down, she noticed that Regis and Ariel had joined Oggie at the table. Oggie was drinking coffee, eating what appeared to be a western omelet and regaling Price's parents with stories of his early years as a gambling man.

Ariel looked up. "Can we help, dear?"

"No. Enjoy yourselves. We're doing just fine."

"Where is Price?" Ariel wondered aloud. "He should meet your uncle and the others."

"Darling, he's gone out, remember?" Regis reminded her gently.

Ariel shoved her hair out of her eyes. "Oh, I don't know. So much coming and going around here. I just can't keep track of everyone anymore...."

Faith turned and left them. As she stowed the box she was carrying in the bed of Jared's pickup, she told herself that she would not be hurt if Price didn't return to say goodbye before she left. Really, it would probably be for the best if he stayed away. Having to see him one final time was only going to make this whole sad process all the more difficult.

She remembered her earrings, which were precious to her. But she didn't have to see Price to get them back. If nothing else, she could write from North Magdalene and ask him to mail them to her.

When she returned through the kitchen, Eli had joined the group at the table. He was explaining to Oggie all about how he had actually read ten whole books by himself and written a book report on each one. "That's why I'm a super reader, Mr. Jones."

Oggie grunted, shifted around in his chair and announced that he'd always admired a boy with a brain.

"So tell us more about this North Magdalene where our Faith is moving," Regis said as Faith headed for the stairs once more.

Oggie launched into a tale of the town he so loved.

The next time Faith entered the kitchen, Justine was there. She'd pulled up a chair between Oggie and Eli and was listening, rapt, as Oggie told how he'd come to North Magdalene and stolen his beloved, long-deceased wife, Bathsheba, from a cruel rich man named Rory Drury.

By a little before noon, everything was loaded up and ready to go. Ariel insisted that Faith and her relatives must be fed before they left. So lunch was served to all and sundry in the morning room.

Price appeared just as they sat down.

Longing, more intense and more painful than it had ever been, rose up in Faith at the sight of him. He wore a glove-soft suede sport coat and a black shirt and slacks. Faith thought that he had never looked more handsome.

Or more aloof.

He greeted them all, his distant smile skimming past Faith as though she hardly existed. Ariel introduced him to Oggie and Jared and Erik, then told him to take a seat. He said he'd love to, but he had too much work to do.

He started to go, then turned back, as if some minor thought had struck him. "Faith. I wonder if you could give me a moment before you leave. In the library?"

Her throat closed up and her heart pounded in her ears, yet somehow she managed to nod. "All right."

"After you've finished your lunch, of course."

"Yes. Of course."

He left. Faith picked up her fork and blindly attacked her pasta salad. After a moment or two, the buzz of conversation around the table started up again. Faith ate doggedly, barely tasting Balthazar's wonderful food. She didn't look up at her tablemates until she was certain that no one would be staring at her.

She was almost right. Everyone at the table seemed absorbed in talking to someone else. Everyone except Oggie. He was talking to Regis, but he met Faith's gaze when she dared to glance up. His wise, dark eyes held a speculative gleam. And then he winked at Faith and gave his full attention to Regis, who was lovingly describing his current invention.

Faith dropped her gaze to her plate again and saw that, somehow, she had done it; she had finished her lunch. She set her napkin on the table and pushed back her chair. "If you'll excuse me. I want to say goodbye to Parker. And see Price, too."

Ariel looked at Faith intently, but when she spoke, her tone was offhand. "Yes, dear. You go on now."

Faith climbed to the third floor first. She found Parker's door wide open.

He was sitting at his desk. "I was hoping you'd stop in to say goodbye."

She stood on the threshold and realized she wanted to cry. "Oh, Parker..."

Yesterday he'd surprised her with his concern and understanding. Now he did it again, this time by rising to his feet and holding out his arms. She ran to him. They held each other for a moment, and then she put her hands on his shoulders and looked up into his eyes. "Don't let too many more years go by, Parker. Life is out there waiting for you. You just have to...go out and meet it."

He actually smiled. "Like you?"

Price's image flickered into her mind. She blinked it away. "Yes. Like me."

Parker shrugged. "Hey. Who knows? Maybe I'll start with a visit to a certain motel in the foothills. What's the name of the place?"

"Right now, it's Swan's Motel. But it's going to be the Foothill Inn as soon as I get a new sign made. And you come see me. Anytime the mood strikes."

"I just might," he said.

Faith left him sitting at his desk, turning to the computer that provided most of his interaction with the world.

The hardest goodbye of all was next.

When Faith reached the doors to the library, she steadied herself with a few deep breaths. Then she knocked.

The familiar voice answered, "Come in."

She pushed the doors open and entered.

Price was standing at the big triple window on the east wall, looking out. Beyond the glass, the sun filtered through the leaves of the palms, casting spiky patterns of moving light and shadow onto the dense ground cover below.

"Sit down," he said, not turning.

If she sat, she was sure, her wobbly knees would never allow her to rise again. "Thanks. I'll stand."

He did turn then, focusing bleak eyes on her. The entire room, including the length of his desk, lay between them. "This is ridiculous."

He was right, of course. Her back was against the door. He stood at the window. They were as far apart as they could get without one of them actually leaving the room.

Faith drew herself up. She began walking toward the desk. He approached at the same time, so they ended up facing off across the width of polished mahogany and the bank of computers and phones.

He seemed to be studying her face. "Are you...all right?" His voice was rough and low.

She managed a quick nod.

He looked down at the yellow legal pad on his desk, then back up. "I wish you hadn't run off like that."

She swallowed and lifted her chin. "I know. I'm sorry. I just, um..."

A look of real pain crossed his face. He waved his left hand. "Never mind. It's all right." He was looking at the yellow pad again, as if he'd scribbled something important there and now couldn't read his own writing.

Then he reached in a pocket. He pulled out her earrings and extended them across the desk, between two of the computer screens. She stepped forward and took them, her fingers brushing over his palm, then stepped back immediately. He dropped his arm.

She couldn't help thinking of Annette Leclaire. Poor Price. Women were always leaving their earrings around for him to return.

She knew he was watching her, though she wasn't quite meeting his eyes. His next words took her breath away.

"Don't go."

The chair was right behind her. She sank into it. And then she waited. For him to grant her some small shred of hope. For him to say that, with time, there might be love. Maybe marriage.

And children. Oh, she did want children.

But she wouldn't have asked him to go that far right then. Right then, all she wanted was *Maybe, if you stay...*

But he said nothing more.

She was the one who broke the spell of silence. "I can't stay, Price. I meant what I said the other night. I want... love and marriage." She dared to say it all. "I want children."

He looked away at that, back out the window, at the absurdly bright day. "I'll never marry again." They were the words she had known he would say. Still, they seemed to drive into her heart like the sharpest of nails. "And as for children..." He didn't finish. There was no need to.

Faith stood. Her legs weren't wobbly anymore. She felt strong, suddenly. Strong enough to do what had to be done. "I know." Her tone was gentle. "I was there, remember? I know what you went through. I know it's... your life. And your decision, if you're determined to live it as a single man.

But I can't stay here, not anymore. It's just not enough for me. It hasn't been for a while now. And after the other night, I'm positive that it would never be enough again. Please understand.''

He met her glance. She saw resignation in his eyes. ''I guess there's not a hell of a lot more to say then, is there?''

''Nothing. Except goodbye.''

Chapter Eight

North Magdalene, California, lay tucked in a bend of highway 49, less than half an hour's drive out of Nevada City. At the height of the gold rush, the town had boasted over three thousand souls. But in the past century or so, the population had never seemed to get much over 225.

That February day when Faith came to claim her motel, the sun shone down on North Magdalene as clear and bright as it had on Sausalito. But North Magdalene, being farther north and well above sea level, looked slightly forlorn in the dead of winter, even on a sunny day.

Snow from recent storms was melting now. It dripped off the eaves of the covered sidewalks and lay in dirty piles next to the curbs. The maples that lined Main Street were bare, their naked limbs stark against the pale blue sky.

Of course, the blanket of evergreens that cloaked the surrounding hills remained unchanged in any season, and helped to soften everything a little. All a person had to do was look up, at the rise and roll of the higher land, with its soaring stands of pine and fir, to feel a little better about the world.

Swan's Motel stood at the foot of Main Street. It consisted of a pair of two-story shoebox-shaped buildings set perpendicular to the road. The office and the manager's apartment, which would be Faith's new home, had been stuck on the street end of one of the shoeboxes, like an afterthought. Between the two buildings lay a tarred parking lot, its surface riddled with cracks.

Faith turned her Trooper beneath the small porte cochere that projected off the front of the office. She switched off the engine and climbed from the driver's seat. Once on her feet, she put her hands at the small of her back and stretched a little.

Okay, she thought, so it's not much.

But a town the size of North Magdalene didn't exactly abound with business opportunities. And there were two wooded acres out in back, running roughly northward, which had been part of the deal. They would provide the space she needed for expansion. And when she added on, it wouldn't be with structures shaped like shoeboxes.

When Faith stepped into the office, the little bell over the door tinkled a cheerful warning to the manager inside. But Chuck Swan didn't hear it. He was fast asleep on the plaid couch next to the reception desk. At the sight of him lying there, Faith didn't know whether to grin or to groan.

She closed the door and then pulled it open again, hoping the repeated jangling of the bell would be enough to rouse him. No such luck. So she allowed Chuck to snore on undisturbed for a moment, while she glanced around at the knotty pine—paneled walls, the cobwebby corners and the chipped veneer racks of flyspecked tourist pamphlets.

A half-smoked cigarette still dangled from the lips of the stuffed deer's head above the check-in desk. When Faith was last here, right after Christmas, she'd specifically asked Chuck to take that poor dead animal's head down and dispose of it.

Oh, well, Faith told herself. Things could be worse. At least the awful chalk drawing of the motel's former owner, Chloe Swan, was gone. It had hung above where Chuck now slept, the first thing, next to the deer's head, that visitors saw. In the drawing, Chloe Swan had been looking over her shoulder, a sexy pout on her red lips and a dangerous gleam in her eyes.

Faith heard footsteps in the manager's apartment, the door to which stood open behind the desk. Jared appeared. Before they left Sausalito, Faith had given him a key that would open the apartment's two back doors.

"You want us to start bringing things in?"

"Yes. That would be great."

Jared retreated the way he had come.

On the couch, Chuck stirred. The bell hadn't bothered him, but the sound of voices apparently had. "Huh? What? Argh!" He sat up, saw Faith and blinked. "Oh." He ran a nervous hand back through his thinning hair. "It's you, Miz Jones."

Faith gave him a weary smile, "Yes, Chuck. It's me."

He was grinning, rather dazedly.

Faith said, "Chuck, you look tired."

"Well, as a matter of fact, Miz Jones, I'm bushed."

"How many of the rooms are occupied?"

"There's a couple in 203, and another couple in 106. And a single fella next door, in 101. It's all right there, in the register."

"Okay." Faith upped the wattage on her smile. "And...have you moved all of your things from the apartment?"

She was infinitely grateful when Chuck nodded. "You bet. Got the last of it out yesterday. It's why I'm so tired. I not only had to clear out my things, I had to look after the place until you came, so I slept on the couch here all night. It ain't real comfortable, I gotta tell you. And I'm pretty drowsy today.''

Faith was dreading the moment when she had to face that apartment. She'd seen it while Chuck was living there; the man was no housekeeper.

"Have you . . . found another job, as we discussed?"

He yawned hugely, showing that more than one molar was missing in back. "Yes, ma'am. I got me some prospects. Over in Reno. I'll be leavin' town in a week, and stayin' with my sister until then."

Faith decided not to ask what *prospects* he had. She was just happy that he was content to move on. Chuck seemed to be a nice man. But if she needed counter help, Faith planned to look elsewhere.

Still, she *was* grateful for the way he'd held down the fort. From her pocket, she took a check that she'd already made out to him. She handed it over. "I appreciate your keeping an eye on things, Chuck."

His tired eyes lit up. "Thank you kindly, ma'am."

"No problem." She could hear the men hauling her things in from out back. She wanted to get busy. "Good luck," she added.

Chuck dragged himself to his feet and headed for the door. He turned just before he went out. "Oh, I never did get up on the roof to check out that leak over 203 and 204. You might go and have a look at it as soon as you get the chance. And the lights have been acting up in 104 and 105. And you probably ought to call in a plumber about the toilet in 103. And there are a few problems with the heaters lately. They ain't all workin' like they used to."

Faith listened patiently to what sounded like an endless list of things that needed fixing. When Chuck finally fell silent, she thanked him again and sent him on his way.

Faith felt marginally better about the place when she stepped into the small front room immediately behind the office. It was knotty pine all the way. But it was empty of furniture. And it was clean.

She found out why when she reached the tiny kitchen in back and saw the old gateleg table and the two fancifully carved wooden chairs. The table and chairs were a set she had once admired in her sister Evie's store. On the table was a mason jar full of roses. A folded sheet of blue notepaper was propped against the jar.

I'll be back as soon as I close up my shop, the note read. Faith smiled at the pretty blue paper. Evie had been there. She'd cleaned the rooms where Faith would live and brought a beautiful housewarming gift, to make her feel welcome. And she'd be coming by around five, after her store, Wishbook, was closed for the day.

That was something to look forward to, something to push the blues away.

Faith heard sounds in the bedroom, which could be reached by going through the bathroom, or through a door that opened onto the small back parking lot. Jared and Erik were hard at work in there, setting up her bed. She had better get busy herself. With a determined smile on her face, she went out the kitchen's back door to start bringing in her things.

Evie arrived at five-thirty, having strolled over from her shop, a little farther up Main Street. As always, she looked like an angel. Her pale skin seemed to glow, her auburn hair shone, and her golden-brown eyes brimmed with warmth and love. Evie was the beauty of the family—and even more so in the past year and a half, since she'd met and married Erik Riggins.

The sisters embraced. Evie smelled of something fresh and old-fashioned. Lilacs, Faith thought, knowing that she herself smelled of dust and spray cleaner, since she'd just finished cleaning the reception area. After she helped the men unload her things, the office had been her number one priority; it was the first impression her guests would have of the Foothill Inn when they sought a room.

"I'll bet you're beat," Evie said. "Come with me, to my house. We'll get a hot meal into you."

It sounded wonderful, but Faith had to say no. She wouldn't start out her first night by leaving the front desk. And there were scores of boxes still waiting to be unpacked.

"Come on, sit down." Faith led Evie to the sofa. "Give me just a few minutes before you rush home."

The sisters talked for a little, and then Evie left. But she returned an hour later with her husband, her three stepchildren, and a picnic basket. They spread a blanket on the floor and shared the meal. For a few short hours, the small, shabby apartment echoed with laughter.

The next morning, early, Chuck Swan appeared to collect his cigarette-smoking stuffed deer head. Faith was inordinately happy to see the thing go.

Over the days that followed, Evie and the family were in and out all the time, eager to help if Faith needed a hand. Uncle Oggie dropped by often to regale her with a thousand and one stories of his forty-plus years in North Magdalene—and of all the years before that, as well.

And the Montgomerys wrote to her. Not Price, of course. But Ariel scribbled messages once or twice a week on fluorescent-green stationery. And little Eli wrote on lined paper. His words never stayed within the lines.

I am a super riter too, Faith. See wat I mean?

Parker wrote, as well. Short notes with little icons all over them that he must have printed from his computer. He said he was still thinking about that visit.

But in spite of the affectionate notes from those she'd left behind and the loving support of her family, Faith found her new life extraordinarily stressful.

Within a week of moving in, Faith began to understand that the motel was much worse than just run-down. She found, to her growing distress, that aside from new carpets, curtains and furniture throughout, the south building needed a new roof and the whole place needed plumbing and wiring repairs, a decent heating and air-conditioning system—and a whole new phone system, too. The phone lines were erratic, literally rotting inside the walls. Just bringing the place up to her strict standards of cleanliness was backbreaking work—work she did herself, in order to save money.

Within two weeks of leaving Sausalito, Faith was lying awake almost every night, obsessing on the limited amount that was left in her savings account and realizing she would have to borrow big-time to get all the work done. But how would she do that? She had so little equity in the place that she had nothing to borrow against.

A trip to a Grass Valley bank confirmed her fears. She'd need a cosigner to get the money to make all the repairs. And she didn't want anyone else being responsible for her debts. She wanted to earn what she had. On her own.

She should have checked out the investment more thoroughly, she could see that now. She hadn't taken the time to get professional estimates on what needed fixing and how much it was going to cost.

Maybe, in the final analysis, she simply hadn't wanted to know. Because then it would have been obvious that she couldn't afford this. She'd still be at Montgomery House, living out her days in the service of a wounded man who would never return her hopeless love.

Oggie came calling one morning, early, when Faith was feeling especially low. He coaxed the truth of her money problems out of her and then told her he'd be happy to lend her whatever she needed.

Faith said nothing for a moment after her uncle made the offer. She was thinking of how he lived with his only daughter, Delilah. And Faith was reasonably sure he was wearing the same threadbare shirt and grubby suspenders he'd worn on the day he came to help her move from Montgomery House. He barreled around in an ancient, rusted Cadillac Eldorado. Her disbelief that he could be much help with her finances must have shown on her face.

"Damn it, gal." Oggie was huffing; he clearly thought his dignity had been thoroughly impugned. "Just 'cause a man doesn't flaunt it is no guarantee he ain't got it. I'm a rich old coot, and don't you forget it." He leaned across her table and squinted at her. Hard. "Now how the hell much do you need?"

Faith shook her head. "No, Uncle Oggie. I'll find a way to do this on my own. It's just going to take awhile, that's all."

"Too much independence can give a woman wrinkles, you know that?"

But Faith kept shaking her head; she wouldn't take her uncle's money. Finally Oggie told her he was so offended, she was going to have to let him enjoy a cigar in her apartment before he'd be mollified. Though she hated the smell, Faith went to find an ashtray.

Then the bell rang out in front. She left her uncle happily stinking up her kitchen to go talk to the plumber about the toilet that kept overflowing in 103.

Things seemed to be getting worse by the day, yet Faith tried to stay positive. She often reminded herself that all her problems with the motel didn't leave a lot of time for mooning around missing Price. Even hardship had its blessings.

Back in Sausalito, Price had no tumbledown motel to distract him from the yawning chasm that seemed to have opened up in his life with Faith gone.

By the time she left, he'd accepted the fact that he was going to miss her. He just hadn't come to grips with how damn much.

He was miserable.

And he didn't handle misery well. It made him impossible to live with.

Justine was doing a beautiful job of filling Faith's shoes. But Price was curt with her. Somehow, it was like a knife turning inside him to see Justine doing the things that Faith used to do. To catch a glimpse of her winding the ormolu clock in the parlor, or carrying the flower arrangements through the rooms, or bending over the menus with Balthazar.

In the library, sometimes, when he was supposed to be working, he'd stare blindly at his Quotron and wonder why the hell he felt so completely betrayed. He was a reasonable man. He knew he had no right at all to feel the way he did. Yet knowing didn't help.

He took out his ridiculous, misplaced feelings of betrayal on anyone foolish enough to cross his path. Regis came to him with a new invention, and Price curtly told his father that patenting the silly thing would only be a waste of time. With great dignity, Regis informed his son that he was terribly sorry to have suggested that Price squander his *precious* time.

Another day, Ariel called him on the house line and asked him to come up and tell her what he thought of her new painting.

"Something just isn't right about it. I want you to look at it, Price. I want you to be thoroughly ruthless and tell me what you think."

He barked at her that he was working and had no time for her foolishness, then hung up. The line blinked again almost immediately.

Feeling like a heel, he picked it up. "Listen, Mother, I—"

Ariel interrupted his apology. "Lately, Price, you have been intolerably rude to just about everyone in this house. I suggest that you get a grip on yourself. And soon."

Before he could think of how to reply, the line went dead.

Part of his problem was insomnia, Price decided. He lay awake all night, thinking of Faith, and then was edgy and irritable all day. He began spending more time at his health club, working his body until sheer physical exhaustion seemed to promise he'd enjoy a good night's sleep for once. He never did.

Hog futures went up. Price had invested heavily, so he found himself significantly richer in the space of a day. It should have pleased him. He couldn't have cared less.

And then there was Parker, who seemed to be slowly emerging from the shell he'd built around himself two years before. Occasionally, now, Parker even came down and ate with the family. And Price knew his younger brother had made friends with Justine's boy. Ariel loved to prattle on about how Eli would end up a computer genius, with all that Parker was teaching him. Ariel swore that Parker really was coming out of the blue funk he'd lived in for so long. She just knew the day would come—and soon—when Parker would sit down at the grand piano once again and beautiful music would fill the house, just as it used to in the old days.

Price knew he should be incredibly grateful, to see his brother coming around at last.

But it was hard to be grateful. All he wanted was Faith. He wanted her back in his house, where she belonged.

And he wanted her in his bed.

They never should have spent that night together. He realized that now. Instead of satisfying his appetite for her, it had only served to whet it. Now there were intimate memories to taunt him in the darkest hours of the night. Visions of Faith, her eyes meeting his in bewildered desire, her sable hair tangled across a white pillow. The little cries she made when he was inside her. And her eager, awkward innocence, which somehow excited him more than the practiced caresses of any other lover he'd ever known.

Late one morning nearly three weeks after Faith had moved out, Ariel announced that she and Regis were going on a little trip.

They were sitting at the big table in the morning room. Price was taking a break after the early hours of trading. He looked up from the financial pages. "A trip where?"

Ariel brushed at the hair that lay over her eyes. "Oh, I think we'll wander down the coast. To Baja, maybe. Ensenada. Or all the way to Cabo San Lucas. Zoe is living there now." Zoe Webb was an artist friend of Ariel's. "Yes." Ariel traded a look with Regis, a look that made Price suspicious. "We'll just *feel* our way around, I think. Go where the mood takes us. Perhaps we'll even board the ferry for Puerto Vallarta."

From his cage, Sir Winston let out a loud guffaw.

"What is going on?" Price asked quietly.

"Why, nothing, dear. I just wanted you to know our plans. We'll be leaving tomorrow." Ariel sighed. "I had hoped Parker might join us. But he says he's not quite ready for a trip as of yet."

Price put down his paper. "Exactly how long a trip is this going to be?"

"I haven't the faintest idea. Weeks, perhaps. It depends. We'll be in touch, of course."

"You're leaving for *weeks,* out of nowhere like this?"

His mother sniffed. "Honestly, Price. It's not very pleasant around here lately. My work is suffering. I need a change of scene." She and Regis shared one of their mutually worshipful glances. "And your father has generously agreed to accompany me. I am a fortunate woman, when it comes to my mate—and I adore my younger son." She pursed her little rosebud of a mouth, then added stiffly, "And I love you, too, Price. But lately, you are driving me up the wall."

"Oh, come on, Mother. I'm not *that* bad."

"Yes, you are. You don't know. You don't realize. If we didn't love you so much, you wouldn't be that difficult to dislike."

"I really think you're being unfair to me."

"Well, of course you do. You *must* think that *I'm* the one who isn't fair. Because otherwise you'd have to take a long look at your behavior. And since you're a good man at heart, then you'd be forced to actually *do* something about your seething silences and your hair-trigger temper—and your desperate, depressing unhappiness."

Price knew then what she was up to. His mother was baiting him, pure and simple. Ariel wanted him to argue with her, to insist that he was neither seethingly silent nor desperately unhappy. Then she could start in on him about Faith. Which he had no intention of letting her do.

He gave her no opening, only reached for his newspaper again. "I hope you enjoy yourselves, Mother," he said coolly.

"We will. You can count on it."

* * *

Before they left Sausalito, Ariel stopped at the post office. Regis waited in the Range Rover, which she'd double-parked, for her to carry a large express-mail envelope inside and mail it off to Cabo San Lucas. The envelope contained postcards addressed to Price, each one already dated and scrawled with some little message about what a good time they were having. Zoe had agreed to send them, one each day, starting in a week, so that Price would believe his parents had actually gone where Ariel had said they'd be.

As Ariel started up the Range Rover, Regis cast her a doubtful look, "My angel, do you really think Price will fall for this?"

Ariel leaned back in the seat. "I don't know. And quite frankly, my dearest, I don't care."

"Then perhaps we should have simply told Price the truth, don't you think?"

"No. He might have tried to stop us. And you know how he is. So distressingly determined. We probably would have given in. No, this is the best way. I want to see Faith and visit that little town she loves so much. And that is exactly what I'm going to do." She put her hand on her husband's knee and squeezed. "Sit back, *querido,* and enjoy the ride." Behind them, someone leaned on a horn. Ariel blew her husband a kiss across the console and then put both hands on the wheel.

Three hours later, they pulled beneath the tiny porte cochere of the Foothill Inn. Ariel switched off the engine and gazed out the windshield at the two ugly buildings and the cracked parking lot. She turned to Regis, who was sitting very silent beside her. There was no need for words, really. She saw in his eyes a reflection of her own thoughts.

Poor, dear Faith. What can she have gotten herself into here?

But then the door to the office opened and the screen swung out. And there she was, dressed in jeans and a big red sweater, her hair coming loose from her bun, her eyes wide, her mouth just starting to smile. Ariel felt such a welling of affection for the girl that she forgot everything but how good it was to see that precious face again. Truly, Ariel realized right then, Faith Jones was the daughter she'd never had. That was why Montgomery House seemed so empty without her. When a daughter moved out, one's house was bound to seem empty for a while.

Faith clapped her hands and bounced over to the Range Rover, grabbing the handle of Ariel's door and pulling it wide. "Oh, I can't believe it." She held out her arms, and Ariel virtually fell into them. They hugged each other good and hard, and while they were doing it, Regis got out and came around to join them.

At last, Faith stood back. Her smile faded a little. "Does Price—?" She couldn't quite finish.

But she didn't really need to finish; Ariel understood. She shook her head. "We lied. We told him we were headed for Baja."

"Baja? But that would take days. Does that mean you'll stay awhile?"

"If you'll have us."

"There's nothing I'd like more." The light in Faith's eyes dimmed a little. "But, um, as you can see…" She swept out a hand, in a gesture that took in the ramshackle office, the run-down box-shaped buildings and the worn-out parking lot. "The accommodations aren't exactly what you're used to."

"The accommodations will suit us just fine, I think," Regis said. His voice, which had suddenly taken on a husky quality, sent a flicker of awareness along every one of Ariel's nerves. Ariel felt his arm slide around her waist. He drew her close, nuzzled her ear. "Remember, *mi amore,* our early years, our footloose, fancy-free life?"

Ariel shivered in delight. She remembered. In detail. Ah, how could she ever forget . . . ?

Regis pulled her nearer still and whispered something thoroughly scandalous in her ear. Ariel felt the familiar, delicious heat of burgeoning desire. She smiled at Faith. "We'll need a room, dear. Right away."

Regis and Ariel remained in North Magdalene for a little over a week. They were introduced to a bevy of cousins and their various spouses and offspring. Of course, they met Faith's younger sister, Evie, and Evie's three lovely stepchildren.

Regis played poker nightly at the Jones family's saloon, which was whimsically known as the Hole in the Wall. And except for the nights when one Jones cousin or another asked them to dinner, they dined at the Jones family restaurant, the Mercantile Grill, which was adjacent to the Hole in the Wall. The food there was excellent. Olivia Roper, trained in France, was the chef.

Olivia, whose father was *the* Lawrence Larrabee of Larrabee Brewing Company, was married to Jack Roper, who, it turned out, was Oggie's one illegitimate son. Apparently Jack had grown up not even knowing Oggie. But then, a few years ago, by accident, Olivia herself had led Jack here, where he'd found his family at last. Oggie and Jack had been united. Jack and Olivia had married. And now they were busy living happily ever after amid the family Jack hadn't even known he had.

Yes, the Joneses were a delightful clan, Ariel decided. She adored every one of them. She wished Price would hurry up and realize how much he loved Faith, so that Ariel and Regis would have an excuse to spend more time in such a charming town.

But, alas, as things stood now, they couldn't stay forever. The accommodations were fun at first, but too primitive to be enjoyable over an extended period of time. And Faith was in trouble. Even the most casual observer could see that her little business venture was falling down around her ears.

The third day of their visit, Ariel tried to offer a little financial help. But Faith wouldn't hear of it.

Thus, as each day passed, it became more obvious to Ariel that she and Regis must return home soon—if only to inform their overbearing son of exactly what Faith was suffering. Of course, the day they left, Faith took Ariel aside and asked her not to mention anything about her new life to Price, should Price learn the truth of where they'd actually been.

Ariel kissed Faith's soft cheek and swore she wouldn't say a word. Mentally, as she made the vow, she kept her fingers crossed. Really, Faith should know by now that Ariel was an artist. And artists were not governed by the same rules as ordinary people.

At home, Justine greeted them at the door with the news that Price wished to speak with them right away.

"Does he know?" Ariel whispered. Of course, Justine had been in on the whole thing all along.

"Yes," Justine replied. "I think he knew the first day. He went up to your rooms and snooped around in your drawers, I believe."

"Whatever for?"

"Checking to see if you took your summer clothes, would be my guess."

"Which we didn't."

"Exactly. He questioned me."

"You poor dear."

Justine grinned. "I didn't break. He talked to Parker—and got nothing from him, either."

"Then how—?"

"He managed to reach Zoe, down in Baja."

"He didn't—"

"Yes. Completely intimidated the poor woman. She told him what she knew, which wasn't enough, since you never told Zoe where you were really going."

"How did you find out he spoke with Zoe?"

"He told me. The *second* time he called me into the library and demanded to know where you'd disappeared to."

"And you still didn't tell him?"

Justine shook her head, but said no more. Right then, Regis cleared his throat. Ariel knew it for the warning sound it was.

"Welcome home, Mother. Father."

Ariel turned. Price was standing in the wide doorway that led to the front parlor. She granted him a thoroughly insouciant smile. "Hello, dear."

Price didn't smile back. "I'd like a few words with you both."

"Certainly." She turned to Justine again. "Is Mary around today?" At Justine's nod, she asked, "Would you have her bring in our things from the car?"

"Thirsty?" Price asked as soon as his parents were seated in the parlor. "After your long drive back *up the coast?*"

His mother and his father exchanged one of those telling glances they were so fond of sharing. "I'd love a Rob Roy," Ariel said.

Regis thought a moment. "I'll have Cutty on the rocks."

"And if you have something to say to us," Ariel advised in her best lady-of-the-manor tone, "then come out with it."

Price took his time mixing the drinks. When he handed them to his parents, he asked quite calmly, "Where have you *really* been for the last week?"

Ariel sipped her drink. "Heavenly," she declared. Then she added, without a trace of remorse, "We've been to North Magdalene, for a visit with Faith."

Just hearing that name scraped his nerve endings raw, but Price had his pride. He masked what he felt beneath a carefully reasonable tone. "Why did you lie about it?"

Ariel took another dainty sip of her Rob Roy. Then she sighed. "Price. Who can say how you'll react lately? I wouldn't have put it past you to try to stop us, if we had told you what we planned."

"That's ridiculous."

"Well." Ariel brushed her hair away with one hand and waved her drink with the other. "It's all water over the dam now. We've been and returned and you have found us out." She feigned an apologetic expression. "We are sorry to have deceived you. Truly. I hope you'll find it in your heart to forgive us."

"Yes," Regis said. "Let's forgive and forget. All right, son?"

Price looked from one to the other of them. Now that they were here and he could pump them for the information he wanted, the fact that they'd deceived him seemed to lose its significance. They were eccentric, but they were also adults. Where they went was their business.

"Price, please?" Ariel begged prettily.

Price shrugged. "All right."

"Oh, thank you, dear."

"Don't overplay it, Mother."

"I'm sure I don't know what you mean."

"Just tell me how she is."

"You mean—?"

"You know very well who I mean. How is she?"

Another speaking glance passed between his father and his mother. Then Ariel announced, in the gushy tones she usually reserved for art openings, "It was wonderful to see her."

"That tells me nothing."

Ariel turned to Regis. "It's too bad, isn't it, how *exhausted* she is?"

Regis nodded. "Those deep circles under her eyes. So worrying."

Ariel looked at Price. "And, of course, she wouldn't mention a thing about her problems to us. But that motel is a disaster. There's no other word for it. Run-down, with bad plumbing. And leaky."

"Leaky?"

"Yes. The roof leaks. In several places. A few of the rooms have watermarks, like giant Rorschach tests, on the ceilings. It's a bit eerie, actually. To lie in one of the horrible lumpy beds and watch the stain spreading, taking on new and terrifying dimensions."

"You're exaggerating."

Ariel fiddled with her hair some more. "Maybe. We all know I've never been prone to understatement." She set her glass on a marble-topped side table. "And Faith does have some wonderful restoration plans. Eventually, she wants to add more units on the acreage behind the existing buildings."

"She told me that."

Ariel did some more sighing. "Too bad she's so stubborn."

"Why?"

"She needs money. It's obvious. But her uncle Oggie confided in us that she wouldn't take a cent from him. And when *I* tried to offer, she didn't even let me get started before she was telling me no." Ariel laid a fond hand on Regis's arm. Regis met her gaze. Her smile returned, and her eyes grew bright. "Oh, but we did have a lovely time, didn't we, my dearest heart?"

"Fabulous."

She turned her smile on Price. "Oh, Price. It's such a charming little town. I can see why Faith fell in love with it. And her family is wonderful. Such . . . *vivid* people. Do you remember Erik? You met him briefly the day Faith moved. He's Faith's sister's husband. A housepainter. But he does landscapes in his spare time. Erik works in oils. His paintings are stunning. Such sweep and grandeur. They almost seem as if there is . . . magic in them. I've been thinking of talking to Maurice over at the gallery about him. And you know the famous horror novelist, Lucas Drury? Well, he's married to one of Oggie's granddaughters. Can you believe it? It is such a small world. Oh, and that Oggie is a pure delight. He lives with his only daughter, Delilah, who is married to a man named Sam, and—"

Price wanted to talk about Faith, not about her family, most of whom he'd never even met. He asked, "You say Faith looks tired?"

"*Exhausted* was the word I used."

"Wrung out," Regis elaborated.

"You think she's running short of money?"

Regis looked at Ariel. They shook their heads in unison. Then Ariel said solemnly, "We're *positive* she's running short of money."

"Did she mention wanting to come home?"

There was a silence. Price didn't realize his gaffe until his mother raised one sleek, pale eyebrow.

"Why, Price. I imagine she believes that she is home."

He cleared his throat. "Well, of course. Yes. What I meant was—"

"Never mind, dear." Ariel sounded infuriatingly smug. "Your father and I understand." She rose from the sofa. "Now. It's been a hellish drive. Traffic was beastly. I think these two old folks need a little nap." She held down a hand for Regis, who rose to stand beside her. "We'll just go up now and tell Parker we're back." She put her arm through her husband's. "And after that, we shall retreat to our rooms until dinnertime."

Price had a thousand more questions to ask. But he knew very well that his mother had said all she intended to say. He watched them go, arms wrapped around each other, on their way to greet their younger son and then to seek their bed.

The next morning, Price told his parents that he would be gone for the next few days.

Ariel lifted an eyebrow at him. "And just where are you headed off to, may I ask?"

"No," Price said, "you may not."

His mother only smiled.

Chapter Nine

Faith stood looking down at the burst pipe beneath the bathroom sink in room 104. She'd turned off the water as soon as she discovered the disaster, but by then plenty of damage had been done. The floor of the unit was soaked through.

Her plumber, who stood beside her with his trusty crescent wrench in hand, spoke up. "Look, Miz Jones, these pipes were never the best quality. And now they're old. They're gonna go on you, one by one. Unless you replace 'em."

Faith kept her gaze on the separated section of pipe. She was afraid that if she looked into the kind eyes of the plumber, she just might burst into tears. "I understand," she said. "Can you patch it up, though, for now?"

The plumber let out a long breath. "Sure, Miz Jones. You're the boss."

She made herself look at him then, and she made herself smile. "Thanks."

"S'all right."

Wearily Faith left the bathroom. She trudged through the puddles of standing water in the main room, looking straight ahead, not letting herself think of how disgustingly squishy the wet carpet felt beneath her tennis shoes. She didn't allow herself a single glance at the baseboards, either. And she refused to ponder how much leakage there had been into 105 next door. Firmly she told herself that it could have been worse. It could have been room 204 where the pipe had burst. Right now, water could be running down into the walls of all the units in this building.

The water on the floor was seeping into her shoes. Now *there* was something she could afford to think about. She could ponder how she'd change into clean socks and dry shoes as soon as she reached her apartment. Clean socks and dry shoes, she had. It was money she was short of. And as soon as she paid the plumber for fixing that pipe, she'd be even shorter than before.

Faith stepped out the door of room 104. Beyond the protection provided by the balcony of the upper floor, rain fell steadily, making a gray veil between the two buildings.

That was another thing she was going to have to deal with: how to dry out the room behind her, when the weatherman had predicted rain for the next three days straight. Maybe she should just rename the place Waterworld. It would certainly fit the other building, where the leaks in the ceilings on the upper floor grew worse every day, in spite of the patch job her cousin Patrick, Oggie's third son, had done for her a couple of weeks before.

Faith looked for her housekeeping cart and spotted it down in front of 106, right where she'd left it when she noticed the water pouring out from under the sill of the room behind her. With a sigh, Faith trotted down to the cart and pushed it through the door of 106, which she then locked with a key from the retractable ring latched to one of the belt hooks on her jeans. Now, if the rain started driving sideways beneath the balcony before she got back to the cart, her towels and room supplies would remain dry.

Trying to tell herself that she'd just averted one disaster, at least—albeit a minor one—Faith turned toward the parking lot again. That was when she saw the Jaguar. It was pulling to a stop beneath the porte cochere in front of the office.

"Price." The word escaped her lips on a groan.

The rain kept falling, making everything misty. But not misty enough. The car was pointed in Faith's direction. The windshield, in the shadow of the porte cochere, reflected only darkness.

What could he see? Had he spotted her already, cringing here in front of room 106, shivering in her soaking tennies and frayed jeans and tattered old gray sweatshirt?

The door on the driver's side opened. Price emerged from the car, tall and broad-shouldered, his hair impossibly dark and rich-looking, even on such a gray day. He shut the door and then stood there, unmoving, staring right at her through the wet curtain of the rain.

Well, one question was answered. He *had* already seen her.

Faith lifted her chin and stepped out into the downpour. By the time she made it beneath the porte cochere, where he waited, her sweatshirt was clinging to her shoulders and the strands of her hair that had escaped her bun were plastered to her cheeks and nape.

They regarded each other. Faith's heart seemed to be trying to beat itself right out of her chest. And yet, at the same time, she felt numb, in her hands and feet and at the very surface of her skin. As if her blood weren't making it to all the parts of her body.

Four weeks and a day since she'd last seen him. Not that long, really. It only *seemed* like forever.

Her hungry gaze took in every inch of him, from his shining black hair to his Tony Lama snakeskin boots. He wore one of those beautiful cashmere sweaters of his, with an attractively rumpled corduroy jacket thrown over it, along with a pair of ordinary khakis. He looked like what he was: a man who could afford the best. A man who had enough confidence to wear whatever he pleased—and wear it well. Her arms ached to reach for him.

At the same time, it occurred to her that the money he'd spent on his sweater and boots would have paid for about half of the new roof she needed on the south building.

He spoke first, whispering her name. "Faith." The one word seemed to carry a thousand meanings. There was greeting in it. And rebuke.

She felt his gaze running over her, the same way hers was over him. It came to her then: He *had* missed her.

And he wanted her—even in an old sweatshirt, with her hair dripping wet.

This hunger she'd borne alone for so long was a mutual hunger now.

Faith ordered her heart to slow down. She took even, deep breaths. And she said, in a voice that she tried her best to make uncompromising, "Why are you here, Price?"

His gaze moved over her face, hot and full of a yearning she knew so very well. It was her own yearning, after all, given back to her—at last.

As she accepted the power of his desire, her old, foolish hopes were born all over again. Could it be? Had he come here to tell her he'd changed his mind? That he was willing to let go of the past? That for her sake he would give love a try one more time?

"I know you're in trouble, Faith. I've come to help."

She stared at him, absorbing those words. *Help,* he had said. He had come to help.

Not for love. Not even for desire.

Faith knew who had told him of her troubles. "Ariel promised she wouldn't say anything."

"My mother's an artist. She makes her own rules."

A burst of anger shot through Faith, then faded as quickly as it had come, leaving her feeling drained, shivering. Ariel was Ariel, after all; she'd always considered herself above the rules that governed mere mortals—very much like her elder son.

"Let's go inside," Price said.

Faith stood her ground. "Let's not."

"Don't be childish. You need to change into something dry."

She wrapped her arms around herself to stop the shivering, and leveled her most uncompromising look on him. "Go away, Price. Don't come back."

He didn't move. "You need help. And you're too damn proud to take it. Somebody's got to get through to you about this. And I guess it's going to have to be me."

A slightly crazed burst of laughter escaped her before she could stop it. She composed herself, then sneered, "Do you know anything about roofs, Price? I could really use a roofer. Or an electrician. Or a plumber who works at minimum wage."

"What you could use," he said calmly, "is a large loan at a reasonable interest rate."

She was shaking her head before the words were even out of his mouth. "No. Forget it. No way."

"Faith . . ."

She was already turning for the office door. "Go back to Montgomery House, Price. I'm busy. My feet are wet. I want to change my shoes."

"Faith, listen . . ."

She pulled open the screen, pushed the door inward and marched inside, to the tinkling of the little visitor bell overhead.

Price was right behind her. "I'm ready to invest in this motel."

She kept walking, headed for the open door behind the check-in desk. "Absolutely not. I won't take your charity."

"It's not charity."

She stepped up to the door of her apartment, then turned on him, blocking his way into her private space.

He stopped at the outer edge of the check-in desk and regarded her measuringly. "I know you, Faith. You'll make a go of it if you get half the chance. I'm offering you that chance."

"My family's already offered. So has your mother. I turned them all down."

"They weren't offering a business arrangement. I am. I'll make a straightforward investment of capital here. And I'll turn a neat profit after you get on your feet."

Frustrated, knowing he was likely to end up breaking her down by the sheer force of his will, Faith folded her arms over her chest and looked away from him. "I just want you to go."

"Look at me, Faith."

She stared at the rack of tourist pamphlets, the worn plaid sofa, the nearly blank check-in book that lay open on the desk—anywhere but at him.

"Faith."

She caught her lower lip between her teeth.

"Faith. Please."

Slowly she dropped her arms and met his eyes.

"You're going to make it."

All her troubles came back to her. The plumbing. The wiring. The roof. "You don't know...."

His voice was firm. "All you need is a little help. I'll give you that help. And I'll make money from it in the end. Everybody wins."

For a quarter of a second, she almost believed him. And then she remembered that he was the last person in the world she could afford to come to any sort of an arrangement with—business or otherwise. He was never going to marry. And as long as she had to deal with him, she would never learn to stop loving him.

"Faith." His voice was tender. "It's really so simple."

"It's not. Oh, please, Price. You know that it's not."

His eyes were telling her things. Secret things. Forbidden things. "It's . . . something I can do. For you."

Rather than make a life with me. Rather than love me, she thought.

"Let me do it."

"No."

The finality of the word gave him pause. He put his hands in his pockets and shifted from one boot to the other, looking away. When he faced her again, his jaw was set. "All right. I'd like a room, then."

Faith drooped against the door jamb. "Oh, Price. Stop it. Give up. Go back home."

"No. Give me a room."

"But *why?* I've already told you—"

He cut her off with a sweeping gesture of his left hand. "This is what you want, isn't it? A life here. A business here."

"Yes. So what?"

"So I'm not leaving until I'm sure you'll have what you want."

"There's nothing you can do. Nothing I can let you do."

"That's not true. That's stubborn pride talking."

"You're wasting your time, Price."

"I'll be the judge of that."

They were deadlocked. Faith considered her options and decided that she was perfectly within her rights simply to refuse him a room. She started to tell him that.

He didn't let her get the words out. "If you send me away, I'll go looking for that peculiar uncle of yours."

She frowned. "Whatever for?"

"He seemed like an interesting old guy. And from what my mother told me, he's tried to loan you money, too. It's obvious he really cares about you. Maybe I can get him to plead my case for me."

Faith thought of Oggie, who saw too much and understood too well. If Oggie got involved in this, Faith would never hear the end of it.

And there was more, something Price couldn't know at this point: Oggie was a zealot when it came to romance. As the old sweetheart loved to tell anyone who'd listen, he had been instrumental in uniting each and every one of his children with their mates. To hear him tell it, his record was unblemished when it came to getting lovers together for their walk down the aisle.

Well, with Price, Oggie would be doomed to failure. But that probably wouldn't stop him from trying. And *that,* Faith decided, she could do without.

With a small sigh of defeat, she pushed away from the door jamb. Price backed up—careful, as he'd been since his arrival, not to get too near her. Faith suppressed another sigh. She knew what he was up to; by keeping his distance, he could convince himself that his motives in this were completely honorable.

She snared a key from the wall rack behind the desk. "Here. Room 206. Upstairs in back, the other building, across the parking lot." And as far away from me as I can get you, she added silently.

Price looked at the key in her outstretched hand. "Don't try any tricks."

She dropped the key on the desk. "What is that supposed to mean?"

"Ariel said all the beds were lumpy, so I guess I'm going to have to put up with that. But I'd like a room where the heater and the lights are dependable. And the ceiling doesn't leak."

She made a little humphing sound. "Around here, that's asking a lot."

"You won't get rid of me by making me uncomfortable."

She gave him a look of pure disdain. "This is not Montgomery House, Price. I don't run around here making sure that the flowers are fresh in all the rooms. By your standards, you are going to be uncomfortable, whether the roof leaks on you or not." She shoved the keys closer to him. "Go ahead. It's dry and warm and the lights still work. Or at least they did as of yesterday morning, when I last cleaned it."

He scooped up the key. "I'd like to pay in advance." She saw the light in his eyes before he added, "Say, for six months."

Another ploy to help her out with her finances. She wasn't going for it. "Oh, please. Try it a week at a time. See how much you *enjoy* it first."

"Faith." He had the audacity to assume a wounded look. "You never used to be this sarcastic."

She said nothing, just slanted him a long-suffering look.

Now, he dared to grin. "I know, I know. Hardship has made you this way. Let me put some money into this place. You'd be surprised how a little money will improve your attitude."

"No, thanks." She pointed to the register. "Sign here. Cash, check or credit card?"

He signed where she pointed and flipped out a gold card. She gave it a single glance. "Visa or MasterCard."

"You really should take American Express, Faith. All the best places do."

She looked him right in the eye. "Don't push it, Price. Maybe you'll learn that I really have changed—in a number of very unpleasant ways."

He was grinning again. "Sounds intriguing."

"Visa or Master?"

He gave her another card, and she ran it through the machine. "Here," she said. He scrawled his name. She tore out his copy and handed it over. "Do enjoy your stay with us."

"Thank you. I will."

Even nature seemed to bend to Price Montgomery's will. As soon as he'd checked into his room, the rain stopped and the sky cleared. Faith saw him stroll past the office, the sun making his hair shine like a raven's wing. Though she knew she shouldn't, she went to the window and watched him as he headed up Main toward the center of town. Even from the back, she decided with a slightly pained little moan, he was just about the best-looking man she'd ever seen.

She caught herself just as he reached North Magdalene Grocery. She would not stand here at the window, mooning over her former employer, all afternoon; she had work to do. Dressed in another old sweatshirt and dry shoes, she went to finish cleaning the rooms and to see how the plumber was getting along.

Three hours later, near five, the plumber had left with more of Faith's money. She'd borrowed an industrial vacuum cleaner from her cousin Patrick and vacuumed the standing water out of 104. She'd also found three old box fans in the back of the cleaning closet and set them strategically around on the floor. The fans were going full-blast, doing their best to dry things out.

She was checking a single man into room 106 when she saw Price go by the window again. He was carrying several shopping bags.

Resolutely she turned her attention back to where it belonged: her customer, a Mr. D. L. Billings. She flashed Mr. Billings a blindingly bright smile and handed over his receipt and room key. "Enjoy your stay."

Mr. Billings grunted, as if in disbelief, and left to claim his room. Once he was gone, Faith set the desk bell in plain sight, then turned for her apartment. It had been a gruesome day. She was going to brew a pot of tea and put her feet up for a while. As always in the daytime, she left the door to her front room open, so that she would be able to hear if anyone came in.

She was in the kitchen filling the kettle when the bell jingled over the outside door. She set the kettle on the burner, turned it on, started for the office—and met Price halfway there, in the middle of her front room.

He was carrying a small box and wearing a sheepish grin. "I brought you a housewarming present."

Her heart turned over. "Price," she said. "Don't."

"Oh, come on." He pretended total innocence, no mean feat for a man of his sophistication. "I chose it just for you. You have to see." He strolled right over to her sofa and took a seat, setting the box on her coffee table in front of him. Then he sat back and looked around. "This is charming. Honestly."

She did her best to suppress the flush of pleasure that swept through her at the compliment. Actually, the apartment did have its own rather rustic appeal. The furniture was all good-quality, pieces she'd collected over the years she lived at Montgomery House. In the weeks since she'd moved in, she'd managed to steal a few hours from the never-ending demands of her motel to run up tieback curtains in a blue-and-white print and trim them with eyelet ruffles.

She'd even re-covered a few throw pillows to match. Her own pictures, a few of them Ariel's vivid watercolors, hung on the walls, masking some of the never-ending knotty pine. In the bathroom, someone had even installed an antique clawfoot tub, probably because it was cheap. But cheap or not, it added a nice touch of whimsy to the place. And best of all, the office and apartment were a one-story add-on, built about twenty years after the rest of the motel. That meant she had her own roof, one that didn't leak. Also, the appliances, heater and electricity hadn't given her any trouble as of yet. The plumbing even seemed all right.

"Aren't you going to show me around?"

Faith knew it was of the utmost importance that she give him no openings at all. "No. You'd better go."

"Don't you want to see what I bought you?" Instead of waiting for her answer, he went on, as if she were dying to hear. "I've been all over town."

"That must have taken at least ten minutes."

He shook a finger at her. "Watch that attitude."

"Price—"

"I met several of your relatives."

"How lovely for you."

"It was great, to tell the truth. I had a terrific time. I walked by the garage. There's a sign over the door to the parts shop that says Patrick Jones, Proprietor. One of your cousins, right?"

"Right. And I mean it. You have to go now, because I—"

"Then I stopped in at your sister's store. She was there. I introduced myself. She's a beautiful woman. And a nice person, too, I think."

"Yes. Price—"

"It's odd, isn't it, all those years you worked for me and I never met your sister?"

"Why would you have met her? I was your housekeeper, remember?"

He ignored that. "But, you know, I think I remember meeting the other one. The one with all the curly red hair."

"You met Nevada?"

"I think so. A few years ago. It was an April morning. And she was sitting at the kitchen table, with you. You were laughing over something, and you stopped when I came in the room."

Faith vaguely remembered the incident he was talking about. Nevada had stayed the night on her way from Phoenix, where she lived, to somewhere up the coast, in Washington or Oregon.

"There's a family resemblance, with all three of you," Price was saying. "But you were right when you said that you're all really different."

"Yes. We are. And, Price, I want you to—"

"Right. I was telling you about my day. I bought some antique bottles from your sister. And a side table. For the morning room."

"That's nice, but—"

"Evie's keeping the table for me. Until I leave."

"I don't think I'm getting through to you about—"

"And then I wandered on down the street. I went into Lily's. The café?"

"I know what Lily's is. But—"

"I had a beer and talked to the waitress and a few of the customers. They all know who *you* are."

"Well, of course. It's a very small town. And it's time that you—"

"They think you're in trouble, and any one of them could have told you it was going to take some major renovations to get this place back in shape. But you just didn't ask around. You were in some kind of big rush, they all agreed, to find yourself a business here and start running it. And everyone says that your family should have stopped you. But then, they wanted you here, of course. And the word is that they had planned to step in and help you anyway, so it would have worked out all right. But you're much too proud for your own good. Everyone says so. You won't take money even from your family. Your family is very worried. A woman named Linda Lou Beardsly told me—"

She managed to cut in then. "Linda Lou Beardsly is a gossip. She has a very big mouth. Like a lot of people in this town. And I'm not interested in—"

Price shook his head and looked reproachful. "It's just honest concern from people who care about you."

"Spare me."

"But let's not talk about all that, if it depresses you."

"Thank you."

"I'll tell you about the rest of my tour."

"No, thank you."

"But there's so much more. Before I had that beer at the café, I went to Santino's Barber, Beauty and Variety. Bought a lot of things there for which I honestly have no use at all. And then I stopped in at Fletcher Gold Sales—run by the husband of your cousin Delilah."

"Sam. Delilah's husband is named Sam. And, Price, you have to—"

"Sam. Yes. Now, *that's* an interesting store. All those pickaxes and gold pans. Sam even sells dredging equipment. And jewelry and nuggets. And art. Landscapes painted by your sister's husband. And wood sculptures that I understand Sam carves himself."

"Yes, Sam is very talented. And if you—"

"Which brings me to your housewarming gift."

"No. Price. I—"

Before she could finish protesting, he opened the box and lifted out a wood carving of a little brown bird. It was plump, with a slender bill. Its tiny round head was thrown back, and its beak was open in fervent song.

"Oh!" Faith said softly. Entranced, she stepped nearer and leaned down so that she could admire the wonderful detail of the carving: the shape of the wide eyes, the ruffled indentations of the feathers, the absolutely adorable positioning of the wings, so tight to the body, but sticking out a bit above the pointed tailfeathers.

"It's a house wren," Price said. "But they don't live in houses here in the West."

"They don't?"

"Uh-uh. They nest in tree cavities. Abandoned woodpecker holes. Can you believe it? Sam told me all about them." He held the tiny treasure out to her. "Come on. Take it. Think of that big check you didn't take. And the gold watch. It had twelve good diamonds, one for each hour, that watch."

"I didn't want it."

"I know. You told me. But you want this. I knew you would. The minute I saw it."

"Oh, Price." She looked in his eyes, over the perfect little head of the precious bird. "If I take it..."

"You love it. It's written all over your face."

"You would think I was weakening. About the rest."

"No, I wouldn't. You're a woman of steel. Ask anyone at Lily's Café."

She started to reach for it.

He whispered, "Have dinner with me tonight. At the Mercantile Grill."

She dropped her reaching hand and jumped back. "Price. You promised."

He only smiled. "I promised nothing." He set the tiny figure on the coffee table, where it went on singing its ardent imaginary song.

In the kitchen, the kettle started to whistle. "Your water's boiling."

"I know. I—"

"Tea? Is that what you're brewing back there?"

"Yes, I—"

"Are you going to offer me some?"

"Price, I—"

He stood. "Never mind. I have to go look at all the things I bought, anyway, and try to figure out what in hell I'm going to do with them." He slid out from behind the coffee table and headed for the door.

Holding herself very still, pressing her lips together hard, Faith watched him go. Somehow, she had to keep herself from calling him back and throwing herself at him and telling him to forget dinner, she'd nibble on him instead.

She heard the bell tinkle over the outer door as he went out. Only then did she allow herself to move. With a sigh that should have been relief, but was actually profound disappointment, she turned for the kitchen and the now screaming teakettle.

Evie dropped by a few minutes later, after closing up her store for the night. She marched into Faith's front room and closed the door to the office behind her.

"He was in to see me," Evie said.

"I know. He told me all about it."

"Are you all right?"

Faith shrugged. "Last time I checked, I still had a pulse."

"That tea looks wonderful."

"Get yourself a cup."

Evie went to the kitchen and returned with a cup and saucer and sat down next to her sister on the couch. She poured herself some tea and sipped it gratefully before she said another word.

Then she set down her cup and turned to Faith. "You know, I really liked him. He's a very warm and friendly man."

"Of course he is. Or he can be, when he wants to. I didn't say he was a monster. I wouldn't feel the way I do about him if he was."

"He cares for you, Faith."

"Reading minds again?"

Evie stiffened. She never like to be reminded of her special gifts. "I don't read minds. That's all behind me now."

Faith relented. "Sorry. I'm on edge." She touched her sister's arm. "Forgive me?"

"Of course."

"Thanks."

"But you won't get me off the subject. What's he here for, Faith, if not because he cares for you?"

Faith shook her head. "Well, he *is* here because he cares for me."

"I knew it."

"But not the way I want him to care."

"I'm lost again."

"He wants to lend me money. He says he won't go away until I take it."

"Money," Evie echoed softly. "Money, and that's all?"

"Yes. No..." A little carelessly, Faith set down her own cup. It clattered against the saucer.

"Faith, I don't get it. Yes or no?"

Faith rubbed her tired eyes. "He's telling himself it's only money, that he just wants to see that I'll be all right, and then he'll leave. But I think if I fell into bed with him in the meantime, he wouldn't fight it too hard."

Evie's pretty brows drew together. "I don't understand."

Faith looked at Evie fondly. "Of course you don't. You have Erik. He loves you and you love him, so you got married."

Now Evie was smiling. "It works for us."

"I know. And it would work for me, too. But not for Price."

"But *why?*"

"I told you. He's determined not to get married again."

"Because he lost his child and his first wife."

"Right."

"But we all suffer losses. And then we have to pick up our hearts and learn to love again."

"Tell Price that."

Evie scrunched up her beautiful nose. "Do you think he'd listen?"

"No way."

"Well, then." Evie sipped more tea. "If he's not willing to commit to you—" now Evie sounded just a little bit prim "—he should let you go."

"No argument."

Evie set down her cup. "But then, on the other hand, maybe he just needs more time. Maybe you should—"

"Evie. Let it be, all right? Price and I know where we stand. I want marriage. He doesn't. We're on two different sides of a very big gap."

"So then, take his money and he'll go away."

"No. I won't do that."

"Then let someone else help you. I could—"

"Stop."

"Faith, you are so stubborn."

"Here. Have some more tea."

Price dined alone at the Mercantile Grill both that night and the two nights after it. The food was excellent, as Ariel had promised it would be.

Each night, after he ate, he went next door to the Hole in the Wall Saloon. He had a few drinks and played cards for a while.

The first night he went to the saloon, Oggie Jones was there, too. The old man was cordial and charming, in his rough way. But more than once Price looked up from the cards in his hand to find that the fellow was watching him, an odd gleam in his small, dark eyes. It made Price uncomfortable, but he shrugged off the feeling and went on with his game.

An old man's strange looks didn't bother him. He was here for a purpose, and he knew he would succeed.

He was getting to Faith. She'd taken his housewarming gift, after all. And even if she wouldn't go out to eat with him when he asked her, she couldn't seem to keep herself from getting involved in the conversations he kept striking up with her.

And he struck them up every chance he got. The morning after his first night there, he went down to the office a little before nine. He asked Faith to join him for breakfast at Lily's. She refused. But he managed to keep her there, hovering behind the check-in desk, talking for a good five minutes about nothing in particular.

It was the same in the afternoon. He just happened to run into her while she was pushing her cleaning cart around. He asked for an extra towel or two. She promised she'd take care of it. They talked about the rain that had started up again around noon. And about the flood she'd had in room 104. He got her to show him the damage. He helped her move the fans around. Then he said something that made her laugh.

That was when she caught herself. He watched her expression turn wary as she realized she was letting herself get too friendly with him. He got out while he was still ahead.

He stopped in at the office on his way out to dinner and asked her to accompany him. She said no. But he turned and looked back after he went out the door. She was there, in the window, watching after him. He waved. She quickly ducked out of sight.

It was more of the same the next day. She accepted none of his invitations, but she lingered to talk to him, always catching herself in the end and telling him she had to get back to work.

By late the third night, as he lay in his lumpy bed and listened to the rain drumming hard on the roof, he found himself thinking that it wouldn't be long now before Faith gave in. She'd accept the loan she needed so desperately, and he wouldn't have to worry about her anymore. He could return to Montgomery House, secure in the knowledge that she would be just fine.

But then again, maybe he wouldn't leave right away. There was no rush, really. He was enjoying himself here, in spite of the constant rain and the crude accommodations.

He liked being near Faith; that was the truth of it. He was...accustomed to being near her. She had run his house for all those years, after all. It was going to take him awhile, he supposed, to get used to the idea that she had her own life now, a life totally separate from him and his needs.

But then again, maybe, in the end, her leaving Montgomery House had been the best thing. Now, once she accepted the money she needed to fix this place up, she would be totally self-sufficient. He'd no longer have to deal with that nagging sense of responsibility toward her that he'd naturally felt while she was in his employ.

They were two grown adults. Neither of them was committed to anyone else. The blunt truth was, he could see no reason why they shouldn't become lovers again.

Of course, Faith wanted marriage. Price knew that. And children. And he wouldn't be the man to give her those things. But still, she desired him; he saw that in those big brown eyes every time she looked at him.

And, sweet heaven, *he* wanted *her*....

He might as well be realistic about this. It was going to take awhile for this thing between them to run its course. And he couldn't see why they shouldn't enjoy that time. She could visit him at Montgomery House frequently. He knew she loved it there, and his family would be thrilled to have her back, even temporarily.

And he wanted to go places with her. He and Marisa used to enjoy cruises and long vacations in the Bahamas and on Maui. And then, when Danny came along, they'd taken trips a little closer to home: to Disneyland and the Grand Canyon. But later, with both his wife and child gone, the idea of traveling had held no appeal.

But to travel with Faith. Yes. She could hire someone dependable to keep an eye on things here, and he would show her Venice and London and Rome.

He chuckled to himself. She'd be reluctant to go with him, at first. She was so damn proud and independent. And this place of hers was never going to bring in the kind of money that would allow her to get out and see what the rest of the world had to offer. But, given time, he was certain he could convince her to let him spoil her a little.

She'd worked hard all her life. She should learn to enjoy herself before she even thought about settling down. As soon as she got things under control here in North Magdalene, she deserved a little time just for pleasure. Time to let down that silky hair and have some fun for a change. With him.

Price fell asleep smiling, lulled by the pleasurable direction of his thoughts and the steady beating of the rain on the roof.

Chapter Ten

By late Friday afternoon, the third day of Price's visit, Faith was beginning to wonder how she was going to go on.

The Foothill Inn was a wreck.

The big storm the night before had saturated the roof of the south building. All the ceilings on the upper floor there actually had a slightly bowed look to them now, as if they just might disintegrate and drop, in waterlogged chunks, to the floor. Feeling guilty about bothering her cousin again, Faith dialed Patrick's number. He came right over and went up on the roof to do what he could, though the rain was still coming down. When he left, he said he hoped that would help, but added that Faith needed to get that new roof as soon as the weather gave her a chance.

And the roof she would end up buying instead of new beds in all the units was far from her only concern. The heater in room 105 of the other building, always undependable, had stopped working altogether. Faith suspected the problem might have something to do with the burst pipe and the ensuing flood that had occurred in the room next door to it. But the man who'd stayed in 105 hadn't cared *why* the heater didn't work. He'd thought he was coming down with something from sleeping in the cold and damp. Faith had told him how sorry she was and refunded his money.

Then there were the phones. The ones in the north building, where the flood had been, were acting more strangely than ever. Price told her on his way out to breakfast that he'd tried to call her the night before and gotten nothing but dead air after he dialed 0.

Faith apologized to him for the inconvenience.

"Don't you want to know why I called?"

"Not particularly."

He only grinned and said he'd bring her back a doughnut from Lily's; maybe that would improve her mood.

Shortly after that, Mr. Tottly, in 204, called.

"This is the fourth time I dialed 0," Mr. Tottly said. "The other three times I got no ring, no dial tone, no nothing."

Faith apologized to him and asked him what she could do for him.

"I'm starving. Where's the best place to eat breakfast around here?"

She told him about Lily's.

When she hung up, she called the phone company. They said someone would be over by 11:00 a.m.

The telephone repairman was there before ten. He left an hour and a half later, having handed her a hefty bill and told her there really wasn't much he could do. The problem was inside the building. Full replacement of interior phone lines was required.

Around two, Faith gave a Mrs. Miranda Banks the key to room 106. Mrs. Banks entered the room, flicked on the light switch—and heard a loud popping sound, followed by nothing. The light did not go on. She tried the other lights in the room; they didn't work, either. Nor did the TV.

Mrs. Banks returned to the office, where Faith was already receiving a call from Mr. Tottly in 204. No, Mr. Tottly told Faith, he'd had no problem with the phone this time. But his electricity had just gone out.

After checking the circuit breakers and finding no problem there, Faith called an electrician, who arrived an hour later. Three hours after that, at 5:15, he came to talk to her in the office.

"Sorry, lady," he said. "But you got no lights in that building."

Faith asked him why.

The electrician shook his head and told her that she needed new wiring in all six units; he handed her an estimate of how much that would cost. Faith saw that it was in the thousands and quickly set the thing aside.

The electrician was already on his way out the door. "But what *happened?*" Faith called after him.

He muttered something about water in the walls and a major overload on an already worn-out system. And then he was gone.

Fifteen minutes later, Faith actually had to turn away a customer. Except for the three units on the bottom floor of the south building, all her rooms were now uninhabitable. And the three good rooms were already occupied, one by a couple who intended to stay the weekend, the other two by the relocated Mr. Tottly and Mrs. Banks.

After she turned away the customer, Faith stood behind the desk, muttering to herself, staring blindly at the guest register. She was trying to avoid looking at the electrician's estimate, which sat on the desk next to the bill from the phone repairman.

Right then, Price came in the outside door. She heard the bell jingle. She looked up. And there he was. It came to her immediately that he must be here to complain about the lights—which were not going to be fixed anytime soon.

He'd want another room. And she had no room to give him. One more unsolvable problem in a day of endless aggravation.

And why did he have to look so excruciatingly handsome? Today, he wore black jeans and a soft black shirt. His denim jacket was beautifully faded, displaying a thousand subtle shadings of blue. But it was his alligator-skin belt that drew the eye. Sleek and chocolate brown, it boasted a silver buckle.

Faith wondered, as she had more than once since he'd invaded her home and her life, what he could possibly see in *her*. He looked as if he came from another world altogether than the one she inhabited, a world where the lights didn't dare go out and all the phones were cellular, where roofs never leaked and pipes never burst.

He strolled up to the desk and rested an elbow on it. "Hate to tell you, Faith, but my lights are out."

Faith closed her eyes and sucked in one long, deep breath. Then she opened them and met his gaze.

His brow furrowed; real concern moved in his eyes. "Hey. What is it?"

Faith couldn't take it. She just could not deal with it.

Without uttering a word, she turned on her heel and made for the door to her apartment.

Price slipped around the side of the desk and caught her arm.

Faith froze. It was the first time he'd put a hand on her since their one beautiful night.

"Come on, Faith. Tell me. What is it?" His voice was tender, his grip warm and firm through the sweater she wore.

She loved him.

And she was just so tired....

He gave a little tug, and she landed against his hard, strong chest. She breathed in the expensive scent of him.

Muscular arms curled around her. It felt so *good*. To lean on him.

His lips brushed her hair, at the temple, where the little wild curls were always escaping. ''Tell me.''

''Oh, Price...''

''On second thought, don't talk.''

''But I—''

''Shh...'' He held her even closer.

And she let him. Because it just plain felt *good*. It felt absolutely terrific, as a matter of fact. She burrowed her head against his shoulder and wished she could just stand there forever, cradled in his arms.

And then she reminded herself that she was headed for big trouble if she didn't get a grip here. She stiffened her spine, put her hands on his chest and lifted her head.

But that was a mistake, because it put her mouth in exactly the right position for kissing.

Price was not a man to waste a perfect opportunity. His mouth came down and met hers.

''Oh...'' Faith said with a sigh.

He kissed the word right off her lips.

And she didn't even try to turn away. On the contrary, she lifted her mouth eagerly and let him go on kissing her.

Now this, she thought greedily, was living. Her endless, insurmountable problems seemed to melt away, like winter snow off the roof on a sunny day. They might have been back in that beautiful suite at Tower on the Bay, instead of standing behind the counter of Faith's wreck of a motel.

Price lifted his head and looked into her eyes.

She saw how he wanted her. And, oh, how *she* wanted *him*. Looking in his eyes, it was so easy to forget all the reasons she shouldn't get near him. Looking in his eyes, all that mattered was how much she'd missed him, how she longed for his touch.

"Remember, Faith? Remember how it was?" He pressed himself closer. She felt the evidence of his desire.

All she could do was nod.

He made a low noise in his throat and lowered his mouth to hers once more. Faith realized dimly that she probably should be protesting. But somehow, in the space of mere minutes, he had managed to lay claim to all her senses. Reality had retreated; it was far, far away.

Price's hands roamed her back, and his tongue claimed her mouth. He pressed her so close...

It was heaven. And what fool would want to leave heaven? Especially when reality was such a grim place. Faith hoped she never had to go back there.

With a little moan that sounded like surrender, Faith gave herself up to Price's embrace. She clutched his strong shoulders and pressed herself tightly against him and ignored all the warning bells going off in her mind.

Price cupped her face. He shoved his fingers in her hair, which was pulled back, as usual, and anchored in a knot at her nape. He moaned against her lips, an impatient sound. And then he went to work pulling out hairpins. She felt the loosening as the pins gave way. She even heard a tiny pinging sound as one of them hit the floor.

Then Price was smiling against her mouth. "There. Better." He combed the long waves with his fingers, stroking them lovingly, so that the strands fell smoothly over her shoulders.

He kissed his way over her cheek to her ear. "Call your cousin, Patrick," he whispered huskily.

Faith really wasn't thinking too clearly right then. "Call Patrick?" she murmured, wondering what Patrick had to do with anything.

"It's his oldest girl, Teresa, who watches the desk for you when you have to go out, right?"

"How did you know that?"

"I know everything I need to know when it comes to you. Call Teresa. She can watch the desk tonight. We're going out."

"Going out?"

"Yes."

But Faith couldn't possibly do that. She tried to tell him. "I don't—"

He bit her earlobe, very lightly. "You need a break."

She shivered in delight, then tried to get control of herself. "No, I—"

"Yes." He found her mouth again and kissed her some more—to silence her, she knew. And it worked. She stopped protesting and went boneless all over again. When her mind was total mush, he broke the kiss, barely, and said against her softly parted lips, "You deserve a night off, Faith. Come on."

"I can't—"

"You can."

"But I—"

He muttered a low curse and took her mouth again. For a long time.

And then they started moving. Faith realized, vaguely, that he was walking her backward as he kissed her.

She didn't put up much resistance. Well, none at all, actually. She even stepped up when her foot hit the riser that led into her apartment. He urged her inside, kissing her the whole way, and pulled the door shut behind them. Once they had both crossed the threshold, he turned the lock.

Faith heard the lock engage—and she didn't make a murmur of protest. It just felt too wonderful, to have his mouth on hers, working the magic he worked so well. She twined her arms around his neck and returned the glorious kiss with all of her heart.

Somehow, they kissed their way through her living room, into the kitchen, on through the bathroom and into her bedroom.

He was undressing her by then. And she wasn't fighting it. Not one bit. He took her tunic-length sweater by the hem and guided it over her hips, her waist, her rib cage—then right over her head. Then he threw it somewhere beyond her left shoulder. She heard it land with a soft plop on a chair. His hands cupped her breasts, over her bra. He moaned into her mouth. And then he reached around her, found the clasp and unhooked it.

The bra went the way of the sweater. He sighed, and so did she, as her breasts filled his hands. He caressed the twin mounds, teasing the nipples to hard little peaks by rubbing them between his thumbs and forefingers.

And then he broke the kiss they'd shared all the way through her apartment. He nibbled down her neck and over her collarbone. And then his mouth found her breast.

Faith was far gone by then. She held his head and offered herself up to him, all thought of protesting now utterly flown away. His mouth closed over her nipple. He sucked hard and long. In her belly, heat coiled and yearning bloomed.

She heard little mewling noises of hunger and delight and knew they were her own. And she didn't care. Not in the least. Something had broken in her. Her will to resist was destroyed. She was all sensation. And grateful to be so.

She wanted to touch him, to feel his naked body against hers. The mewling sounds more urgent, she pulled at his lovely, soft denim jacket, pushing it from his shoulders, tossing it away. She unbuttoned his shirt, her fingers nimble, deft with desire. Within seconds, the shirt, too, was gone.

At last, sighing, she touched his chest, stroked the silken trail of hair that curled out around his little nipples and down his solar plexus to his alligator belt. It was so good to touch him, to feel once more the beautiful, lean, sculpted musculature of him.

Price grabbed her close again, nuzzling for her breast, finding it, latching on. Faith cried aloud as his hand slid down, unsnapping her jeans, seeking the heart of her.

He groaned in triumph when he touched her. She was so wet, and her readiness seemed to drive him on. She pushed herself against his hand, lifted her breasts to his hungry mouth.

And then he raised his head. He looked in her eyes as he went on working that magic down below.

She felt herself cresting.

"Yes, Faith. Yes..."

And she hit the peak right then, standing there, riding his hand. She shuddered and cried out. He held her steady with one hand while he went on driving her crazy with the other. And through all of it, through that entire, never-ending, intimate explosion, he watched her face.

Faith had barely stopped quivering when he began tugging at her jeans, shoving them down. When they caught on her tennis shoes, he pushed her back to the bed, knelt before her, and pulled off her shoes and socks, then finished dragging down her jeans and her panties, tossing them out of the way.

Naked, she reached for him. He backed away, smiling, and slowly stood. Watching her, he got out of his own boots and socks and then unbuckled the beautiful belt and slithered it off and away. He stripped down the black jeans along with his briefs. She gasped at the sight of him, standing before her, so exactly as she remembered. All that was male.

She reached up. "Please, Price. Come to me."

He smiled then, his gaze all over her, knowing, possessive. Outside, it was growing dark. He reached over, holding her gaze, and turned on the small lamp beside the bed. "There," he said. "I can see you now. I want to see you, Faith. Always."

Perhaps she should have been shy. Or embarrassed. But she wasn't. What was there to be shy about? Her flesh was his flesh. There had never been any other man for her. And the first time, that time at the Tower, she had taken him inside her and felt as if she had been born to have him there.

It was no different now. They were here. Naked, together. All her protests were as nothing. She would spare them both the exercise of them.

He glanced toward the chair by the bed.

"What?" she asked.

"My jacket."

"Over there." She pointed at the foot of the bed, where the jacket had fallen when she pushed it from his shoulders. He went to it and scooped it up. She watched, wondering what he was after, enjoying the sight of his body in motion.

He felt in the breast pocket and came out with three foil packets. Then he dropped the jacket where he'd found it and returned to her side.

He was still holding the packets—and still watching her. "Are you angry?"

"No."

She moved aside just a little. The bed gave as he sat down beside her and set the packets on the table, close by.

She took his hand and gave a tug. They both moved up and scooted around, so that they were side by side, sitting up against the headboard, surrounded by the throw pillows Faith had made herself.

Once they were settled, he searched her face. "I bought those today." He gestured with his head toward the table where he'd set the contraceptives. "There's a machine, in the men's room at the Hole in the Wall. Evidently, even in North Magdalene, someone's got sense enough to think safe sex is advisable. I bought those—and several more—from that machine."

"When?"

"This morning, as soon as the place opened. Last night I admitted to myself that I wasn't only here to help out with your finances. I decided I'd carry some with me at all times, not miss my chance for this, if it came along."

She couldn't quite look at him. "Well, your chance came along pretty quickly, didn't it?"

He whispered, "You *are* angry."

"No." She met his eyes again, brought his hand to her lips and kissed the back of it. "I'm not. I always try not to be a hypocrite. We're here. This is happening. We're both better off being honest about it. And responsible."

Price wrapped his fingers around hers and pulled her closer. He kissed the tip of her nose.

Then he let go of her hand and began caressing her, idly, as if he had all the time in the world to make her body sing with delight. Faith shivered a little, in pleasure, and in appreciation. She'd already found fulfillment; he had not. The proof of how much he wanted her was right there. All she had to do was look down to see it. Yet he seemed in no rush to claim his own gratification.

He trailed a finger up her arm and over the curve of her shoulder. He traced her collarbone, stroked her neck, caressed the line of her jaw, the shell of her ear.

Slowly, he forked his fingers through her hair, then drew his hand out and away from her face, taking the long strands with him. He made a fist. "Like silk," he said as the strands poured over his knuckles. Slowly, he opened his fist, drew the strands out even more, so that he could bring the ends to his mouth.

"I've missed you," he breathed against her hair.

Tenderness was a sweet ache all through her. She wanted to know that everything was all right for him at home. "Is everything working out, with Justine?"

He was stroking her hair again. "Justine is doing a great job. But she's just not you. No one is."

She reached out and cupped her hand around his head. "I hope you haven't been too hard on her."

He tipped his head back, into her touch. "I have. I've been terrible. To everyone."

She massaged his nape, where the hair was trimmed short and blunt. "You'll have to do better."

He looked at her again, his eyes lazy, warm, full of what was going to happen, of what he would do to her—and she to him.

"I will," he said solemnly. "I'll do better. I promise."

"Good."

"You'll help me. Won't you?"

Faith said nothing. What was there to say?

He moved then, so swiftly it took her breath away. He pushed her down and stretched out beside her and covered her mouth with his. His tongue learned the inside of her mouth all over again, as he stroked her hair and her shoulders, her breasts, and the long line of her waist and hip.

Faith returned touch for touch. And when he reached for the condom, she helped him to slide it on. He moved between her thighs and slowly pressed himself home.

Faith welcomed him. There were a thousand and one reasons why she shouldn't be doing this. And each reason meant nothing right then. For the first time in over a month, she was exactly where she wanted to be: held close in Price Montgomery's arms.

Chapter Eleven

They didn't leave Faith's bed until after seven. And then they showered together behind the wraparound shower curtain, in the old clawfoot tub that crouched in the middle of Faith's bathroom.

Faith told him she was sorry, but the electricity in his room would probably be out for a while. And she had no other room to give him.

He was slowly and thoroughly soaping her breasts at the time. "I guess I'll just have to sleep here, with you," he said.

She groaned, but more because of the silken feel of the soap on her skin and the sweet, hot sliding of his knowing hands than because of anything he'd said. "It's a small town. People will talk."

"We'll be discreet." He rubbed his palms against her nipples. She groaned again. He went on, his voice gruff but his attitude studiously offhand. "I'll go on renting my room.'' He chuckled. ''I need a place to store all the stuff I keep buying, anyway.''

He slid around behind her, so that his body no longer blocked the shower spray. He pressed himself against her back, which elicited a small gasp from her. Then he insinuated his hands under her arms, so that he could cup and lift her breasts. The water beat on them, hot and delicious, washing the lather away, down her belly and over her thighs.

Faith leaned back into his embrace, sighing. She felt glorious. Her whole body seemed to hum with life and energy. It was a wonderful feeling.

And yet, beneath the haze of lazy desire, a small voice kept whispering warnings.

This is foolish, and you know it. Nothing can come of it. It's bound to end badly. . . .

And some contrary part of her argued right back: *There are worse things than a bad ending to a beautiful love affair.*

Faith wondered what was happening to her. She really was changing. Sometimes, she didn't know herself anymore. For so long, she'd been quiet, well-behaved Faith, who dedicated her life to the care of others, who never dated, never planned to marry.

And then one day, after years of working at Montgomery House, she had realized that she was in love with her boss.

But her love hadn't changed anything, not really. Outwardly her life remained the same, though in her heart she lived in quiet hopelessness, worshipping Price from afar.

But then Evie had found Erik. Faith had seen her sister's happiness. And she'd started to think that quiet hopelessness wasn't such a great way to live. She'd wanted a new life, so she'd created one.

And she was making a complete mess of it.

But even if her business venture was nothing short of a disaster, her other dream remained. She was thirty-five. Not young, but certainly not old. She still hoped that someday she might meet a nice man, might marry, have a family....

"Stop it," Price growled in her ear.

"Hmm?"

"Stop thinking. Just...let it be." He locked his arms around her waist and kissed her hair, right beneath the thick knot she'd anchored high on her head to try to keep it as dry as she could in the shower.

She thought that if they were going to go on with this, she should at least tell him of her love.

But then again, she could see no point in telling him. It would do no real good—except, perhaps, to drive him away sooner than he would otherwise go.

Cautiously, she asked, "How long are you planning to stay, Price?"

He nuzzled her ear. "As long as I have to. Until you see reason."

"See reason about what?"

"The financial backing you need."

"I won't take your money."

"Then I may never leave." He licked water off her neck; she shivered at the teasing stroke of his tongue against her skin. "Hmm... That's a thought. I'll stay forever."

But she knew that he wouldn't. This moment was such a frail thing—and all the more precious for its fragility.

He nipped her earlobe. "Or maybe you could close things up here. Come home to Montgomery House with me for a while. For a visit."

She made herself refuse him on that score. "No, Price. That's not possible."

His hands slid lower, down over her rib cage. "Fine. Whatever. Just kiss me." He turned her and took her mouth. She felt his readiness again, against her belly. And she knew that she was ready, too. She dared to reach down, to touch him. He gasped and stifled a cry.

Then he took her by the shoulders and pushed her away. "Price?"

He shoved back the shower curtain and climbed from the tub, dripping wet.

"Price!"

"Don't move. I'll be right back."

He returned right away, wearing a condom. He got back in the tub and sat on the edge. "Come here." He tugged on her hand.

Faith went to him without hesitation. She took him inside her, wrapped her legs around his waist. They began to move together once again, toward the white-hot center of mutual ecstasy.

His mouth found her breast. It was a feeling like no other. He filled her and devoured her at the same time. She had no idea where her body ended and his began.

Her head dropped back, into the shower spray. Water ran in her eyes, drenched her piled-up hair. Faith didn't care one bit. She felt herself rising, reaching....

Price urged her on. She went where he bade her, past the boundaries of sensation. Into the realm of pure bliss.

Finally, around eight-thirty, when they'd managed to get into their clothes at last and Faith had dried her hair, Price decided that they were going out to eat. At the Mercantile Grill.

By then, he didn't have much trouble convincing Faith to leave the motel. There were no rooms to rent, anyway. The No Vacancy sign was already sitting in the window. All she had to do was call all her guests in their rooms to say she'd be out for an hour or two and let them know where she could be reached in case of an emergency.

Price called ahead and spoke with Eden, Jared's wife, who ran the Grill as she ran the Hole in the Wall. Eden promised to save them a nice table for two, in a private corner.

Jared's wife even came over to greet them when they sat down. A tall, pretty woman with long legs and strawberry-blond hair, Eden Jones was well along in expecting her second child. She said how good it was to see Faith. And Faith agreed that she didn't get out enough. The motel really kept her busy.

"But I see Price has talked you into getting out at last," Eden said, and looked at Price quite fondly, as if she'd known him all her life.

Faith hid a smile. Price was a domineering man, but he could be as charming as Ariel when he put his mind to it. More than once in the past few days, Faith had been forced to listen to people telling her what a generous, big-spending hunk of a guy Price Montgomery was. From the way people reacted to him, it appeared he'd succeeded in befriending the entire town of North Magdalene.

Price grinned at Eden. "What's good?"

"Everything," Eden said. "But my personal favorite is the prawns in coconut batter. Ask the waitress about it when she comes."

Price said he'd do just that. Eden patted each of them on the shoulder and then waddled away. Faith watched her go, suppressing the little surge of longing that rose up in her, longing to be happily married, with a baby on the way....

But then Price took her hand across the table. His eyes were so bright. She realized he looked the happiest she'd seen him in years. Her love was a warm glow all through her. She decided right then that she was going to stop thinking of the future for now. She was going to enjoy herself. Enjoy *him,* and the pleasure he seemed, miraculously, to find in simply being with her.

The waitress came. They ordered the prawns, which were delicious, just as Eden had promised.

After dinner, they went next door to the Hole in the Wall. Faith nursed a vodka tonic and tried playing pool, which was cause for a lot of good-natured teasing from Price, as well as from Jared, who was working behind the bar. She seemed to have an alarming ability to sink the eight ball— every time she took a shot.

Everyone seemed glad to see her. They behaved as if they were genuinely happy that she'd finally decided to get out and have a good time. She should have done this sooner, Faith could see that now. What was the point of living in a small town full of friends and family, if you never got out and enjoyed being with them?

Faith spotted Uncle Oggie across the room. He waved. It occurred to Faith that she hadn't seen much of him in the past few days—since Price had come to town, as a matter of fact. Which was probably just as well. The last thing she needed right now was North Magdalene's resident matchmaker nosing around in her life, asking questions about the future, when the future was something she couldn't really afford to think about.

It was well past midnight when Faith and Price ran back to the Foothill Inn through the rain. He insisted on stopping at his room to grab a toothbrush and a few clothes, as well as more little foil packets.

In her apartment, they proceeded directly to her bedroom, where they eagerly engaged in the task of undressing each other once again.

Faith woke the next morning with Price beside her. He was still sleeping, on his stomach, his face turned away from her. She smiled tenderly, reminded of that other morning, at Tower on the Bay.

She had run away then.

She would not run now. Whether that was progress or capitulation, she didn't know. And really, at the moment, she didn't much care.

Price turned his head and opened one sleepy eye. "'Lo."

"Good morning."

Beneath the covers, his hand traced a heart on her thigh. "I'm hungry."

"Want pancakes?"

"Uh-uh. Just you . . ."

For the next week, Faith and Price were virtually inseparable.

Faith's business limped along on its three usable units. She put off deciding what to do about all the needed repairs. The truth was, her real life was on hold.

She cleaned her three units and watched the counter most of the time. But her heart wasn't in it. All she thought about was Price. She lived to wake beside him in the morning, and to fall asleep in his arms at night.

Nevada, Faith's older sister, came for a short visit in the middle of the week. Nevada stayed with Evie, but the three sisters did spend Wednesday evening together. Price went to the Hole in the Wall for entertainment, so that they could have some time alone.

They sat in Faith's living room. Nevada had brought a nice bottle of merlot, which she and Faith shared. Evie drank herbal tea.

Nevada asked how the motel business was going. Faith rolled her eyes and ticked off a few of her problems. Nevada immediately offered to lend Faith some money.

"You're wasting your breath," Evie said with a sigh. "She won't take money from anyone. We've all tried."

Nevada laughed her husky laugh and told Faith that pride wasn't going to fix her roof. "And what about that Price?

Hunk city, huh? I always had a feeling there was something going on between you two. It's a sexy situation.''

"Oh, please," Faith groaned.

"No. I'm dead serious. The housekeeper and the lord of the manor..."

"I'm not his housekeeper anymore."

"Great. Now you're equals. That puts a whole new, delicious spin on things. Do I hear wedding bells in the near future?''

Faith shook her head. "No." She tried to sound cheerful. "You don't."

Nevada tossed her tumbling red curls. "Oh, well. Marriage isn't everything." She made a face at Evie. "No matter what our baby sister thinks." Then she looked at Faith again. "Want to talk to a professional about this relationship of yours?''

The "professional" in question was Nevada herself, of course. Since she spent five afternoons a week advising the lovelorn in Phoenix, she considered herself an expert in matters of the heart.

Nevada sighed when Faith took too long to answer. "You *don't* want to talk about it."

"Right." Faith lifted her wineglass. "But how about you? Any romance in your life?''

"Me?" Nevada put on a look of total disbelief. "Forget it. You know me. The original independent woman. I tell people how to handle their love lives, but I never get involved myself. I require objectivity to be really good at giving advice.''

"Right," Faith said. "Have some more wine."

Nevada held out her glass for a refill. At the other end of the couch, Evie moved to pour herself a little more tea.

"Look at her," Nevada muttered in feigned disgust. "She was always the prettiest one. And she always glowed. But now she's positively luminous. It's not fair."

"She's happy," Faith said tenderly.

Evie sat back with her filled teacup. She was blushing.

Faith knew at that moment that Evie had news of some kind. So did Nevada, who demanded, "All right. What's happened?"

Evie started to drink from the cup, then set it aside. "Well . . ."

"Come on. We can sense it. There's something."

An absolutely beatific smile lit Evie's face. "Well, I'm. . ."

"Come on, Evie. Tell."

"I'm going to have a baby."

There was a moment of absolute silence. And then Nevada let out a whoop. She leaped off the couch and grabbed Evie in a tight embrace. "Oh, honey. This is incredible! I can't believe it!"

"Me neither," Evie laughed. "But it's true."

Faith sat on the couch, watching her sisters. For her, the moment was bittersweet. She wanted what Evie had—a good marriage and children. She was going to have to talk to Price. And soon.

"Faith?" Evie was looking at her. "Everything okay?"

"Yes. Of course." Faith rose from the couch and went to join in the hugging and congratulating.

The next two days were happy ones.

Price stayed close. Except for his occasional forays into the local shops to buy more things he didn't need, it seemed to Faith, he was always at her side. He actually started making himself useful around the motel, pitching in with the vacuuming and with making up the beds. Faith told him that if he played his cards right, he might have a future as a maid. He grabbed her and pushed her down on the bed he'd been making and tickled her until she yelped that she took it back, he'd make a *lousy* maid. Somewhat mollified, he let her go.

Once or twice, she tried to broach the subject of what was in her heart. But something always stopped her. He would start kissing her, or the bell would jingle over the door out in front. She'd let it go, for a better time.

They took turns fixing meals. Faith did breakfast. Price was great at slapping sandwiches together. Thursday night, Faith made pot roast.

Friday, Price decided that they'd have a real night out. Teresa came over and watched the desk, and they drove down to Nevada City, for dinner and a show.

When they returned, after they sent Teresa on home, Faith and Price retired to their favorite place: bed.

But they didn't stay there. Price wanted to try some of the other furniture. So they loved each other in the easy chair in the corner for a while, then progressed to the living room and experimented with the sofa.

"Cramped, but functional," Price declared it, once they were both lying limp, their arms and legs wrapped around each other, panting in satisfaction.

After that, Price wanted a bath. Together, of course. And he also wanted to use the pair of brandy snifters he'd bought at Evie's store a few days before. So he produced a bottle of Courvoisier, acquired just that evening during their visit to Nevada City. He poured the drinks and put them on a tray beside the clawfoot tub, which Faith was busy filling with hot water and bath salts.

Once they were settled in the steaming, scented water, they didn't even make a pretense of bathing. Price lay back against the tub and Faith lay back against Price. They reached for the snifters.

"Heaven," Price declared. He set the balloon glass aside after a sip and wrapped his arm around Faith's neck, settling his hand companionably on her shoulder.

Faith agreed with him. She'd been in heaven for a week. She never wanted to come back down to earth. She took a sip from her own glass, then set it down next to his.

Price nipped her earlobe. "I've been thinking."

"About what?"

He reached for his glass, sipped again, and put the glass down. "About how I'd like to stay here forever. But I can't. I've got a few things pending at home. I need to get back to them."

Faith was silent. Her conscience had just given her a nudge, as it had been doing more and more frequently since the other night, with Evie and Nevada. She and Price really did have to talk seriously about where they were going—if anywhere.

Price ran a finger along her collarbone. Tiny sparks of desire went off in its wake. He had his own ideas about where they were going. "Come home with me. Just for a little while. We'll get someone to handle things here."

Faith closed her eyes. Who could they get? And how could she leave, with the roof collapsing in half of the place and a blackout in the other? "I can't, Price."

His hand strayed lower, beneath the bath-salt bubbles. He cupped her breast. "You can." His mouth was at her ear, whispering his temptations. "You've got to get real here. Close this place up. And start arranging for all the repairs you need. Do it the way I suggested at the beginning—all at once."

"I don't have the money."

"Money's no problem. You know that."

"I won't take your money, Price."

His hand, which had been stroking her arm, went still. Then he reached for his brandy again.

Faith knew that he would push her no further right then. They'd drink their brandy and soak lazily for a while. Then they'd get out and dry each other off, perhaps make love one more time. And then they'd wrap themselves around each other and go to sleep.

Tomorrow, or the next day, Price would try again to get her to come home with him. She'd put him off.

They couldn't go on in this lovely limbo forever. They had to make some real decisions.

Faith kept waiting for the right time to talk about it. But somehow the right time just never seemed to come.

Which meant, she reluctantly decided, that this very moment was as good a time as any.

She reached for her own glass and took a fortifying sip that burned a trail of false courage all the way down into her belly. Then she set the glass back on the tray. "Price..."

Was it the tone of her voice? She didn't know, but he seemed to sense, just from the way she said his name, that she was going to bring up a subject he didn't want to discuss.

"What?" His tone was not encouraging.

Oh, she couldn't do it. It was just too difficult. Especially like this, lying here naked in the tub after making love on different pieces of her furniture for half the night.

But she couldn't put it off anymore, either. He had to know what was in her heart. And *she* had to know if there was any hope for them.

And to do what she had to do, she needed a little distance—a little distance, and a towel.

She gathered her legs up under her.

"Faith?"

She stood.

"Where are you going?"

She turned to face him. "I...need a towel."

He looked up at her. She watched his eyes change as he took in her nakedness and the bubbles from the bath salts that were streaming down her breasts and belly. Faith knew she wasn't beautiful. But sometimes, when Price looked at her, she felt that she was.

He reached up, put his hand on her thigh. "Come back down here."

Her legs went weak. She wanted nothing so much as to obey his command. He would love her again. With his body. Even if he wouldn't give her his heart.

Faith bit her bottom lip, not enough to hurt too much, just enough to stiffen her resolve. She brushed Price's hand gently aside and climbed from the tub. Her robe hung on the back of the door to the bedroom. She padded to it, took it down and shoved her arms into the sleeves. She didn't turn to face him again until she'd tied the sash around her waist.

By then, he'd picked up his snifter once more. Blue eyes regarded her over the rim. After he drank, he set the glass aside. He waited.

Faith still had no idea how to go about this. She'd kept everything inside for so long. It just didn't want to come out now.

She closed her eyes and wrapped her arms around herself, the task before her seeming to grow more insurmountable by the second.

"Damn it, Faith."

She opened her eyes and looked at him. He was climbing from the tub, tender frustration in his eyes. He was coming for her. He would touch her. And she would never say what she had to say.

She pushed the words out before he could stop her. "I...I love you."

It sounded awful, ragged and low.

Price sank back into the tub again. Water sloshed over the rim.

"Price?"

He didn't speak.

"I love you, Price." Still he said nothing. Desperation seized her. She hugged herself harder. "Did you hear me? I said—"

"I heard." The words were flat.

"Well, then, I..." She sucked in a breath. She couldn't stop now. She had to get it all out. What she wanted. And the question. What she had to know. "I want to get married, Price. To you."

She waited. The silence was endless.

"Will you marry me, Price?" The question came out shrill. As foolish and desperate as she felt.

He went on looking at her, his face completely unreadable.

She couldn't stand it. She turned around and headed for the bedroom. But when she got there, she didn't know what to do next. Throw open the back door and run out into the night? Toss herself down on the bed and burst into tears?

Since both of those options seemed absurdly melodramatic, she sank slowly onto the side of the bed, folded her hands in her lap and wished she could disappear, just fade away to nothing, right there where she sat.

"Faith."

She looked up and saw him standing in the doorway to the bathroom. He'd wrapped a towel around his waist. Water glistened on his chest and on his powerful shoulders. He was so impossibly handsome. Her wounded, distant love.

"I thought you understood. I told you before you left Sausalito that I was never going to marry again." He sounded regretful, but resolved.

And that made her angry. She straightened her shoulders. "So? People do change their minds. Look at me. I was never going to make love with you again. I knew it would be foolish. But here I am. In bed with you every night."

"What we have is special."

"Yes. It is. But it's going nowhere."

"So? Why does it have to go anywhere? Why can't we just be grateful for the moment?"

"I already told you. Because I want more."

"Look—"

"No. *You* look. I mean it, Price. For me, there does have to be more."

He swore under his breath, then threw up a hand. "There's no point in this." He started to turn.

Faith shot off the bed and caught his arm before he could escape her. "We have to talk about it."

He looked down at her fingers where they dug into his skin, then up into her eyes. "There's nothing to say."

Faith knew she was getting nowhere. With a sigh, she released him. "All right, then."

He must have thought she was seeing things his way. Because he turned fully toward her. "Good." A knowing smile curved his lips.

She stepped back. "I want you to leave, please."

His smile froze. "What?"

"I want you to get dressed and go. I want marriage and a family, and you don't. And that's the end of it."

He stared as if he couldn't believe what she'd said. But then he nodded. "All right. I'll go." He brushed around her and went to her bureau, which lately held as many of his clothes as it did hers. He fumbled in a drawer and came up with a set of black sweats. Tossing his towel aside, he yanked the pants and shirt on. Then he shoved the drawer shut.

He turned to her. And all the energy seemed to go out of him. He slumped back against the bureau. "Why are we doing this? I don't want to go."

She wanted to cry. "Oh, Price..."

He began to walk toward her. "It's too strong, this thing between us. You won't kill it, just by sending me away."

She put up a hand. "Stay back."

He stopped where he was. "Faith..."

"No. I want...more than this, as beautiful as this has been. I want a whole lifetime. With you. And as long as I settle for less, less is what I'm going to get."

"Be reasonable." His voice had turned velvety, coaxing, soft. And he was advancing on her once more. "It can be almost the same as marriage. We'll be together, just like we are now. There won't be anyone else for me. And whatever you want, you can have. I'll see to it." He was right before her. Tenderly, he clasped her arms. "I swear to you."

She refused to be appeased. "Anything I want, I can have?"

"Yes."

"Do you mean money, Price? You already offered me money, remember? I turned you down."

He clutched her arms tighter. "Faith. Don't do this."

She looked up at him defiantly. "I want to know, if not money, then what? How about *children?* Can we have children, even if we can't get married?"

"Stop it."

"No. I can't do that, Price. It's always...forbidden, to talk about this. But I've lived in your house. I've seen it all. I remember the ladies. All the nice, smooth, sophisticated ladies. The Annette Leclaires you've been with—since you gave up on loving the way you really want to love. Since you made that terrible promise to a dead little boy five years ago."

That did it. He let go of her arms and stepped back.

"You know what I'm talking about, Price."

"Don't..." He backed away.

Now she was the one advancing on him. "I'm talking about that promise you made on that last night you got so drunk. You cried that night."

"Stop—"

"Do you remember?" She backed him as far as she could, until his calves met the easy chair where he'd made love to her earlier. "Do you remember that night, Price?"

He glared at her. And then he sighed. "All right."

"All right, what?"

"All right, yes. I remember."

"Do you remember that I held you while you cried?"

He dropped heavily into the chair. "Yeah."

She gazed down at him. "And then I helped you to bed."

He looked away. "Is this really necessary?"

"Yes. I helped you to bed."

"I don't remember . . . how I got to bed."

"I do."

"What the hell does it matter, how I got to bed?"

"It doesn't. It was what happened on the way there. That's what matters."

He looked up at her. And then he looked away again.

She felt like some kind of heartless monster, throwing all of this in his face.

She returned to the edge of the bed and sat down. "All right. If you want me to stop, I will."

He rubbed at his temples. "No. You're right. I know it. Go ahead. Say it."

"You're sure?"

"Hell. No, I'm not sure. But go ahead anyway. Say it all. Get it out."

She folded her hands together and looked down at them, remembering, conjuring up that night.

When she spoke, her voice was low. "I had your arm over my shoulder and you were a dead weight, more asleep than awake. But somehow, I got you out of the library and on the way up the stairs. One step at a time, we were managing. Kind of staggering along."

She glanced up. But he wouldn't meet her eyes. So she looked at her folded hands again. "We got about halfway up. Then you caught your foot on the riser somehow, and we fell against the stair rail. We were all tangled up together, and I had to pry myself off of you and then try to get you upright again. I grabbed your hand and started to pull and you squinted up at me. You said, 'Faith? S'that you?'"

Price shifted in the chair. She looked at him in time to see him put a hand over his eyes.

She went on, staring into the middle distance, picturing that night just as it had been. "You looked so lost and sad, saying my name. Reaching out for something to hold on to, when so much of what you'd loved was gone forever. And something . . . happened inside me. Right then, when you looked at me. Like a light switching on. A hot, painful light. Blinding me."

He was looking at her now. "What are you saying?"

She saw herself, on the stair that night, just as she'd been then, a quiet, capable woman whose whole world was suddenly changed—and yet remained exactly the same.

"I thought, 'I'm in love with him. With Price. With my boss. After all these years. It can't be. . . .'"

Price spoke again, his voice barely a whisper. "You . . . loved me? You loved me *then?*"

A painful laugh escaped her. "Yes."

"But I never—"

"Of course you didn't. I never intended you to know. From that first moment, when I knew how I felt about you, I started to practice hiding it. You said, 'Faith? S'that you?' and I said, 'Yes, Price. It's Faith. Come on. Time for bed.' I was amazed at how calm and unruffled I sounded. I got your arm over my shoulder again, and off we went, stumbling upward.

"You hung on to me, barely able to stay upright. But agreeable. Obedient as a child. You started mumbling to yourself. But I hardly heard you. I was thinking how strange it was. On the outside, nothing had changed. I was still the loyal housekeeper, trying to get my boss up to his bed. But in my mind, everything was different. I kept going over what was happening inside me. I kept thinking that I loved you. *Loved you.* You kept on mumbling. I kept thinking that it was impossible, it couldn't be. But it was. *I loved you.*

"And then, right then, when we reached the top of the stairs, I actually *heard* those words you kept muttering over and over to yourself, like some kind of prayer."

Faith took in a breath. Then she asked softly, "Do you remember those words, Price? Do you remember the promise you made?"

He didn't answer. But he didn't try to stop her, either.

She finished it. "You were saying, 'I'll never have another little boy, Danny. I swear to you, Danny. I'll never get married and I'll never kill another little boy.'"

Price closed his eyes, bowed his head. His hand, which rested on the arm of the chair, was bunched tightly in a fist. Faith ached for him, as she had on that long-ago night, when she learned that she loved him and heard his terrible vow.

She slid from the bed and went to kneel beside his chair. "Your parents are so in love it's embarrassing sometimes. You grew up with them, seeing every day what love can be. And for a while, I know, what you and Marisa had was good. I think a loving marriage is everything to a man like you. That's what you made all your money for, what your huge, safe, beautiful house is for. And if you really wanted to punish yourself, if you really wanted to cut the heart and soul right out of your life, the best way to do it would be to deny yourself what matters most to you—marriage and children."

Faith put her hand over his. He pulled away. He kept his eyes closed, his head down.

"Price. Please. You have to stop blaming yourself. It really wasn't your fault."

His head shot up then. He looked at her. His eyes were hard with a bottomless self-loathing.

Faith felt the tears well up. They spilled over and made wet trails down her cheeks. She didn't bother to wipe them away. They were tears for him. "Oh, Price..."

He spoke then. "I blame myself because I *was* at fault."

"No."

"Yes. Danny was sick, and Marisa knew it. She knew it was bad. But I told her she was overreacting. And by the time even *I* admitted how bad it was, it was too damn late. She never forgave me. And she was right not to forgive me. I killed Danny."

"But all the doctors said—"

Before she could finish, he shoved himself out of the chair and stalked away from her. He turned back only when he was on the other side of the room. "I don't give a damn what the doctors said. If we had taken him in earlier, it might have made a difference. But we didn't. He died."

"You did the best you could, Price."

"And it damn sure wasn't good enough."

"And so you'll punish yourself for the rest of your life, is that it?"

"No, I just won't—"

She finished for him. "Marry or have children."

They looked at each other across a distance of perhaps twelve feet. It might have been a thousand miles.

Faith stood from beside the chair. "We're right back where we started."

He let out a long breath. "I know. But I still want you. I can't see my life without you." He seemed almost angry about it. "Maybe it will be all right."

Faith shook her head. "No. We both know it won't."

"So what the hell do we do?"

"Oh, Price."

"Just say it. Just tell me."

"You have to leave me, Price. You have to let me try to get over you."

Price stared at her. She watched as acceptance came into his eyes. Foolishly, she wanted to cry out against it, though it was the very thing she'd begged him for.

He asked, "Will you please take the damn money you need?"

She started to shake her head again, but then stopped herself. Until she was on her feet financially, he would always feel responsible for her. She was going to have to let him help her with this. "All right. I'll take that loan."

"Just let it be a gift. Please?"

"I can't do that."

He raked a hand through his hair. And then he sighed. "Okay. A loan. Since you insist."

"I do."

He looked down at his bare feet and then up at her again. "I'll get some shoes on and get out of here. It won't kill me to spend one night in a room without lights."

Chapter Twelve

The next morning, Price rang the outside bell at a little after eight.

"We need to get this money thing handled," he said when Faith let him in.

"Of course." She pointed at the stacks of his clothes that she'd set on the office sofa. "Let's take your things out first."

Together, they carried out the piles of clothing and put them in his car, which was already packed with his suitcases and a number of bulging shopping bags.

Then she led him back into her kitchen and poured him some coffee. He blew on it and sipped. Faith turned away, stared out the window over the sink at the back parking lot and beyond, to a small section of the road that led out of town, toward Nevada City.

"How much do you think you're going to need?"

She made herself face him and then told him how much.

"I'm going to add another ten thousand to it, just to be safe."

"That's way too much. I won't need it, really."

He shrugged. "Take it. For insurance. It'll come back to me eventually, anyway. Unless you'd rather I just cosigned for you. That would be fine with me."

"If you cosigned, you'd never make a cent off the deal."

"It doesn't matter."

"It does to me."

He looked so tired. "All right. We'll stick with the original plan." He quoted a monthly payment and an interest rate. "Is that all right?"

"The payments are small."

"You can pay two a month, if you want to."

"The rate's awfully low."

The ghost of a smile haunted his mouth then. "If you don't stop complaining, I'll make it even lower. Then how will you feel?"

She tried to answer his smile. "Okay. It sounds really great. Thank you."

"You're welcome." His eyes ran over her.

Desire rose in her belly, curling languidly, like smoke from a buried fire. She backed up against the sink.

He drank some more coffee. "I'll have the papers drawn up. You should get them in a few days."

"Yes. That will be fine."

"I'll send you a check, as soon as I receive the papers."

"Sounds great."

"And will you let me kiss you? One more time."

"Yes, of course, I..." She felt her cheeks turning pink as what he had just asked sank in. "Oh, Price..."

He stood. "I really am leaving. You saw that my things are in the car." His expression turned rueful. "What I could manage to fit, anyway. I did buy a lot of stuff. I'll send a truck for the rest of it. Have your sister get someone to bring over the furniture I bought from her. Put it in my room until the truck arrives."

"Fine." She swallowed. "That sounds fine."

He took a step closer.

"Oh, don't. Please..." She pressed herself harder against the counter rim.

He reached in a back pocket and took out his room key. "Give me your hand. Come on. This won't hurt."

Slowly, she stretched out her arm.

His fingers, so warm and firm, closed around her wrist. He dropped the key into her palm and folded her fingers over it. "There." She pulled her hand away, but he held her eyes. "Do you know, when I first realized I wanted you, I thought maybe there was something wrong with me?"

She stared at him, having no idea what to say.

But she didn't need to say anything. He was still talking. "I was so used to not wanting. I'd been numb for years. Going through the motions. With all those...sophisticated ladies, as you called them. But then I saw you. Really *saw* you. For the first time. It was a few days after that opening of Ariel's, when you finally cornered me in my office and told me you were leaving in two weeks, no matter what. Do you remember that day?"

"Yes. But, Price, I don't think we should—"

"Shh... I'm almost out of here. I swear. All I'm saying is, I realized I wanted you and I thought I had a damn hormone problem."

"Oh, Price..."

"I still think I have a damn hormone problem, if you want to know the truth. All I want to do is make love with you."

"Why are you telling me this?"

He chuckled. "Because I just have no shame about it. Even after all the ugly truths, after last night. I keep thinking that nothing matters but having you. That everything will be all right, if I can just get you into bed."

"But it won't be all right. You have to know that."

"I know." He shrugged. "I guess. Hell. I spent all that money on psychiatrists for Parker. Maybe I should have spent some time talking to them myself." He put a finger beneath her chin and made her look at him. "You're not saying anything." He put his hand on the side of her cheek. "Faith? Talk to me."

The scent of him swam around her, and she could feel the heat of his body, so close . . .

"You have to go, Price. Please."

"My kiss?"

"All right." She closed her eyes and lifted her mouth.

His lips brushed hers, so lightly, so sweetly. "Goodbye, Faith."

"Goodbye, Price."

She kept her eyes closed as he left. She was afraid that if she opened them and saw him walking away, she wouldn't be able to bear it. She'd chase after him, throw herself on him, beg him to stay.

The door between her apartment and the office was still open. Faintly, far away, she heard his car start up. She turned slowly and looked out the kitchen window again. She saw the Jaguar, too briefly, as it passed through the little patch of highway that could be seen from where she stood.

The key he'd given her was still clutched in her hand. And she could still feel the imprint of his fingers on her wrist, his gentle touch beneath her chin, across her cheek. Her lips burned where his had brushed them. She tried to absorb the fact that this was the last time she would feel these things. But her mind refused to take that in quite yet.

Faith set the key on the counter. Then she went to the coffeepot and poured herself a fresh cup. She carried the coffee into the living room and sat on the couch.

Before her, on the coffee table, was the house wren Sam Fletcher had carved, still singing its ardent imaginary song.

Faith's song, however, had ended. It had been so beautiful. And so heartbreakingly brief.

Not more than five minutes later, the outside bell jangled. Faith started to get up.

But then she realized who it was.

"Faith? Gal? Where the hell did you get off to?"

"In here, Uncle Oggie."

He was standing just inside the door to the parking lot, and he caught sight of her on the couch. "Got coffee?"

She stood. "You bet. Come on in and I'll get you a cup."

"Lots of —"

"Sugar. I remember." She went to pour it for him.

When she returned, Oggie was lowering himself into her big blue easy chair. She set the coffee on the side table at his elbow while he fussed with propping his cane against the opposite chair arm. Finally, he was settled. He took the cup and had that first long sip.

Then he sighed. "Just what I needed. Thanks."

"Anytime."

He set the cup on the table again. "So. He's gone, eh?"

She blinked. "How did you know?"

"An old man has his ways. Did he take care of your money problems?"

"Oh, Uncle Oggie."

"Come on. I'm family. You can tell me."

She looked down at her folded hands and confessed softly, "Yes. He did. I'll be just fine now."

"Oh, will you?"

Faith looked up. "Sometimes, Uncle Oggie, you ask uncomfortable questions."

"I know. I'm a pain in the . . . neck." He leaned forward and squinted at her. "Are you really gonna be all right?"

"Yes. I am. Eventually."

He sat back, picked up his cup. "Not him, though."

"What do you mean?"

He drank. "You know."

And she did.

Oggie made a noise in his throat as he set his cup down again. "I don't know what it is about some men, gal. With some of them it takes nothin' less than an act of God for them to reach out and take the love they need."

Faith felt the tears rising. She swallowed them down. "I know, Uncle Oggie. Believe me. I know."

The first thing Price saw when he went in the front door at Montgomery House was that little boy of Justine's. He was flying a paper airplane in the foyer, laughing and making vrooming sounds.

Price thought immediately of Danny. Danny had only been three when he died. He'd never gotten old enough to make himself a paper airplane and go vrooming around the foyer with it.

Price gave the kid a look. The boy snatched his airplane from the air and vanished from sight.

"Price, dear. You're home!" His mother came drifting toward him, wearing a diaphanous, tentlike thing with swirling colors so bright that she resembled a floating bowl of rainbow sherbet. She threw her arms around him, enveloping him in the scent of Tabu, and kissed him on the cheek. Then she stood back. "Now. Where's Faith?"

After running the gauntlet of his mother's endless questions, Price locked himself in the library for most of the day. He tried to concentrate on getting things in order, preparing for Monday, when he'd get down to work again.

But the columns of numbers blurred before his eyes. All he saw was Faith's smile, her big brown eyes, her adorable overbite, the flush of pleasure and desire that pinkened her cheeks whenever he touched her.

The longing to return to her was already killing him. But he would never act on it. She would settle for no less than a lifetime. And he had already made a promise that would last that long. A promise to Danny's memory. He didn't deserve another family; he would never have one. And Faith was going to get the chance he couldn't give himself.

That night, he hardly slept. And when he did drop off, he dreamed of Faith.

And of Danny, smiling, laughing his baby laugh, reaching out his chubby little hands.

Then, later, sometime near dawn, he had a nightmare.

In some dark place, Price was wandering. And he could hear Danny calling, "Daddy! Daddy! Help me, Daddy!"

But no matter how fast he ran, how frantically he searched, he couldn't find his child. He woke from that one in a cold sweat, sure he'd never sleep again.

But he must have. Because he woke once more, disoriented, just as dawn began to bleach the sky. He looked at the clock: 6:35. Cursing, he threw back the covers and pulled on a pair of slacks and a sweater and started for the library. The stock market opened at nine eastern time, which meant six o'clock on the West Coast. Serious trading would already be well under way.

He was halfway down the stairs when he remembered that today was Sunday. He was hurrying to work when there was no work to do.

He stopped and turned and started to climb again. Then he changed his mind. He just didn't feel like going back to his empty bed. He went down again, headed for the kitchen. He'd turn on the coffee Balthazar would have left ready to brew. And when it was finished, he'd sit in the morning room and drink the stuff and wait for Justine to bring him his *Chronicle*.

In the kitchen, he went to the counter and pushed the brew button. Then, not even bothering to turn on a light that would banish the early-morning shadows, Price leaned on his elbows and watched the pot. Feeling vague and fuzzy and not really all there, he stared at the green light that showed the thing was working and waited for the little sucking sound that meant the water was being dripped onto the grounds.

He heard the childish voice just as the steam began to rise from the reservoir. It was coming from the morning room.

"Shh... Nice kitty. Pretty kitty. Be nice." There was a hiss and an angry growl.

Great, Price thought. Justine's kid.

He didn't want to deal with any kid this morning. He would have to get rid of him.

"Ouch!" the kid cried. "Don't scratch me...."

Price straightened as the child went on talking to what was obviously a cat—though there were no cats that Price knew of in his house. "It's okay, kitty. I'm gonna ask my mom if I can keep you. You'll like it here. I'll take care of you...."

Price went to the arch that led into the morning room and flicked on the light there.

From beneath the big central table, he heard a small gasp. And a feline yowl.

Price stepped down into the morning room and dropped to a crouch. He looked under the table. There, through a welter of chair legs, he caught sight of the kid. He sat cross-legged, wearing a pair of red pajamas, his eyes as wide as saucers as he stared back at Price. In his arms, he held a squirming, scruffy-looking ball of gray fur.

"Where did that cat come from?" Price demanded.

The boy winced at Price's harsh tone. But then he lifted his little chin. "I found him. Outside."

"Get rid of him."

"But—"

The kitten gave another loud yowl. Sharp little claws found their mark. Eli cried out. The cat sprang from his arms, darted through the barrier of chair legs, and ran out the back door, which was open just a crack.

The boy clutched his arm, over the angry red welts that the cat had inflicted. "You scared him."

In the corner, Sir Winston flapped his wings, making an agitated sound.

Price opened his mouth to tell the kid to get lost.

And that was when it happened.

The floor lurched.

Everything lurched.

It was a kind of snakelike, rippling sensation. As if the whole world were a whip abruptly cracked by a skilled and furious hand.

"What the—?" Price dropped to all fours, trying to steady himself.

But there was no stability to be found. The lurch had broken something free. The earth, all at once, had come alive. It began to shake, making a sound that was like distant thunder, rolling closer, taking over the world.

Sir Winston's cage went over. The bird screamed in outrage.

From overhead came a thunderous cracking sound. Windows exploded outward, shattering into a thousand madly tinkling shards. Huge decorative pots skittered like pebbles across the room, the plants they held shivering and twitching, as if in some manic wind. Chairs and other small pieces of furniture rolled and danced over the buckling floor.

Sir Winston screamed again. Black wings took flight out a broken window.

And beneath the table, which was bouncing around as if the big turned legs were made of rubber rather than carved hardwood, Eli started to uncurl.

The little fool! He was going to bolt out from under the only possible protection in the room....

Muttering a low curse, Price dived for the child, just as the ceiling and the story above came crashing down on top of them.

Chapter Thirteen

In North Magdalene, Faith was sitting at her kitchen table, eating her breakfast of cornflakes and milk topped with sliced banana, when her phone rang. She went to the end of the small counter and picked it up.

Her uncle spoke before Faith even got a greeting out of her mouth. "They just had a good-size shaker out there in the Bay Area."

"What?"

"Earthquake. In the Bay Area."

"When?"

"Now." Her uncle made a snorting sound. "Gal. Just turn on your TV. And I'll be right over."

"Yes. Of course." Faith hung up and rushed to the living room.

The networks had already started their emergency coverage. It had happened at 6:49 a.m., less than half an hour before. Early reports from seismologists said it was centered on the Peninsula, in the mountains just above Half Moon Bay. They said it was a 6.6 or 6.7 on the Richter scale, smaller than the Loma Prieta quake of '89.

A few disaster shots were already in: cars buried in rubble, a collapsed overpass, people standing around in bathrobes, looking shocked and lost, in front of houses whose facades had caved in. So far, a single fire, from a burst gas main, had been reported, between the Presidio and Golden Gate Park. But the announcers said fire fighters were on the scene and the wind was low.

"And before seven on a Sunday morning is far from the worst time of day to suffer an earthquake," one of the anchormen said. "People are home, the streets and freeways are relatively deserted . . ."

Her cornflakes growing soggy in the other room, Faith sat on the edge of the couch and watched, telling herself that it wasn't so bad. Not as bad as '89. And in '89, the damage at Montgomery House had been confined to a couple of toppled breakfronts and some broken windows. Sausalito was on firm ground, not landfill, like so much of the Marina district, which had fared so badly in the earlier quake.

It would be all right. There was no need for her to call or anything. The phone lines were probably down right now, anyway. And if the phones *were* working, she had no right to tie up the lines just to ease her own mind. . . .

"M-Mr. Montgomery?" The small voice was hushed, hollow with a breath-held kind of terror.

Price pulled the boy a little closer, but gently. So gently. The small, warm body meant everything right then. Another human being. In this dark place. He whispered, "I'm here, Eli. I've got you."

He felt the boy sigh.

They sat for a moment, not speaking. Price squinted into the thick darkness. He hadn't put on his watch in his rush to get downstairs, so he had no way to tell how long they'd been here.

A while, he was sure. Twenty minutes, perhaps half an hour. Time he'd spent rocking the child and whispering reassuring things that were probably lies: that they were safe, that they would be all right.

To a limited extent, he supposed, his lies were truth. The table had protected them. They were both still alive.

The air was thick, choked with masonry dust. In his arms, Eli coughed.

The small, sharp sound disturbed the careful balance of the rubble packed so tightly all around them. A few chunks of masonry slid down; one hit Price sharply in the small of the back. The table creaked in protest at the minuscule shifting of its load.

Eli whimpered.

Price put his mouth very close to the boy's ear. "It's okay," he breathed. "Just stay still. Try not to make any loud sounds. Talk in a whisper. We'll be all right."

The small body shook with shock and fear. "M-Mr. Montgomery... I'm so scared...."

Price hugged the boy more tightly. "I know. So am I. But we're not hurt, are we?"

"I'm not."

"Me neither. And soon, I'm sure, help will come."

"But how will they know where we are? My mom was in the bathroom taking her shower when I snuck out of bed. She doesn't know... where I went."

"They'll find us," Price said, with more assurance than he felt.

"But what if everyone's all buried just like us?"

"They're not."

"But how do you *know?*"

He didn't, but he wasn't telling the kid that. He explained, "The morning room and the floor above it just weren't attached well enough to the rest of the building, that's all. And as soon as the earthquake separated them, there was nothing to hold the ceiling up. It's a special situation. The rest of the house should be fine.''

"Fine?''

"Fine.''

The boy was silent. His shivering seemed a little less. There was more shifting and settling around them. Price felt the boy start to cough—then hold it back.

"Mr. Montgomery?''

"Look. Just call me Price.''

"Okay. Um, how long do you think it will be? Until they find us?''

"I don't know.''

"Like hours?''

"I don't know.''

"But...''

"Look. I just don't know.''

"Oh.'' There was a world of worry and disappointment in that single sound. "And we have to just sit here?''

"I don't know.''

"Well. What *do* you know?''

"Hell.''

"You swore.'' It was an accusation.

"I'm sorry.''

"It's all right.''

"Look.''

"What?''

"In a while, after we're...more relaxed, maybe we'll explore a little.''

"Explore?''

"Yes. We'll check this place out. Very carefully. We'll see if there's a way we can dig *ourselves* out of here.''

The boy considered that idea, then decided, "That would be good, wouldn't it? To dig ourselves out. Maybe we could be heroes then. They'd put us on TV."

"I'd just settle for getting out of here, myself."

There was a small sigh. "Me too..." The boy's head relaxed against Price's shoulder.

In the moments of silence that followed, Price pondered all the things he didn't know: how much debris surrounded them, how strong the table was, what the odds were that an aftershock would start a slide that would fill in their little cave and crush them alive. How the rest of his family had fared...

Price's leg was going to sleep. He shifted a little.

The boy moved, too, getting himself more comfortable. Then, hesitantly, he asked, "Do you, um, think my cat's okay?"

"*Your* cat?"

"Well, he's going to be my cat. I just know my mom would let me have him. I would feed him and take care of him. She wouldn't have to worry about him at all."

"Right."

"I mean it. I *would* take care of him."

"Okay, okay."

A silence, then "Well. Do you? Think he's all right?"

"Sure he is," Price said, as if he actually knew what he was talking about. "That cat is just fine."

After fifteen more minutes of buried cars and shell-shocked faces, Faith couldn't take it. She went back to the kitchen and dialed the familiar number.

She heard two rings, and then a recorded voice told her to try her call another time. She hung up just as Oggie arrived.

He hobbled into the kitchen. "What do you think?"

"I don't know what to think. I called and couldn't get through. And there's been no mention at all of Sausalito and how bad it is there."

"Got coffee?"

"You bet."

"Pour me a cup, will you?" The old man was already turning toward the big blue chair in the living room.

Faith started to reach for a mug, then paused for a moment and stared out the window that had provided her that final view of Price's Jaguar yesterday, when she'd sent him out of her life forever.

It will be all right, she told herself. The Loma Prieta was a much larger quake than this one.

The odds of Price or his family being hurt had to be minimal....

"M-Mr. Montgomery?"

"Price."

"Oh, yeah. Price?"

"I'm listening."

"I wish it wasn't so dark."

"Me too."

They'd just spent several minutes "exploring" their cave—feeling around in the dark for a possible way out. They'd found none. To all intents and purposes, they seemed to be buried alive.

The boy in Price's arms took in a big breath and asked as he let it out, "Are we gonna die?"

Price felt his throat close up. What the hell could he say to a question like that? "I, um, don't know, Eli."

This time the child didn't comment on all the things Price didn't know. Price didn't like that. It meant the kid was getting scared again, too scared to argue. He decided he'd better try a little reassurance. "The table's strong. And we'll stay very still, won't we, and keep our voices quiet?"

"Yeah. Yeah, okay." The small body relaxed against Price once more. Eli let out a careful breath of air. "Mrs. Curry died."

Now who the hell was that? "Mrs. Curry?"

"She was a real nice lady. In the house before this house." The small whisper went on, "You know, where my mom worked before. Mrs. Curry was very old. She had lots of wrinkles. But they were nice wrinkles. Like from smiling, you know?"

Price made a noise of understanding.

It was all the encouragement Eli needed to go on. "But my daddy wasn't old when he died. He was young. For a grown-up." Eli laid his small hand on Price's arm. "Did you know that my daddy died?"

The boy's hand was so small. And soft. And warm. *God. Don't let him die here.* Price realized he was praying. *He's so little. Let him have a damn life....*

"Price? Did you hear me?"

"I... Yes. Your mother told me. I was sorry to hear it."

The boy shifted around a little. He moved his legs, wiggled his arms. When he spoke again, it was with a sigh. "My mommy says all people die. She said that we, my mommy and me, we have to go on living. My daddy would have wanted that, she said." There it was, that small hand on his forearm again. The small head was turned, looking back at him. He could feel warm breath across his cheek. But it was too dark. Their eyes couldn't meet.

"So anyway," Eli whispered, "I think we better not die under here, Mr. Montgomery. 'Cause my daddy wouldn't like it."

Price had to swallow. "I... I think that's a good idea, Eli."

"Mr. Montgomery?"

"Price."

"Price, right. Are you okay? Your voice sounds kinda funny."

"I'm fine." Price swallowed again. And then, with an eerie mixture of horror and relief, he heard himself say, "I...I had a little boy like you."

"You did?" The small voice was eager.

"Umm-hmm."

"What happened to him?"

Price thought, *Stop talking about it.* But he didn't stop. "He died."

"Oh." Eli thought about that. "I bet you miss him lots."

Through the darkness, Price saw Danny, sitting in the antique carved high chair they used to pull right up to the formal dining room table. Marisa was trying to feed him green peas. Danny blew on the spoon. The peas rolled off and bounced around on the high-chair tray. Danny chortled in delight and clapped his pudgy hands....

That was the thing about Danny. He'd been so damned *alive....*

"Price? Do you miss him?"

The image faded. "I do miss him," Price made himself admit aloud. "Lots."

"So," Eli said. "You have to go on living, too, huh?"

Surreptitiously Price swiped a hand across his damp eyes. "Excuse me?"

"Like me and my mom. You know. Because your little boy would have wanted that."

"He would have—?"

An aftershock hit. The earth growled and mumbled. Eli let out a small, terrified yelp, then somehow managed to squirm around and bury his head against Price's shoulder.

Price cradled him, close and sure, as the table creaked and shuddered and the rubble around them seemed to creep inexorably closer.

When it finally stopped, they were still safe in their dark little cave. But it was a smaller cave than before.

"Price?"

"Um?"

"We're still alive."

"Yes."

Price realized that he was glad. So damn glad.

It occurred to him that death happened. And that no man had the power to stop it when it came.

But not to *live* every moment of life in the meantime. That would be the truly unforgivable thing....

Before him, superimposed on the darkness, he saw Faith, in that last moment before he had left her, her sweet face tipped up, her lashes like fans against her cheeks as she closed her eyes for his final kiss. As usual, wisps of shiny brown hair had been curling around her temples, having escaped the plain knot at the back of her head.

God, how that woman could love.

And what a damn fool he'd been . . .

The small body in his arms stirred again. "Price?"

"I'm here."

"What was his name? Your little boy?"

Price moved just a little, readjusting Eli against his chest. "Danny. His name was Danny."

"Did you ever tell him stories?"

"Yes, I did."

"What kind of stories?"

"I, um . . . *Jack and the Beanstalk,* I think. And stories about Paul Bunyan and Babe, the blue ox."

"I know both of those. But it's okay. I could hear them again."

"Eli. I haven't told a story in a long time."

"It's okay." The whisper was full of trust and expectancy. "You can do it."

Price closed his eyes, which changed nothing. It was dark whether they were open or not. Then, hesitantly, he began, "Once upon a time, there was a boy named Jack . . ."

It was only one shot, but Faith saw it.

An aerial view of Sausalito. And there, near the top of the hills, Montgomery House.

"Look!" She pointed at the screen. "There! That's it! Montgomery House!"

Oggie leaned forward in the chair. "It looks like—"

"The morning room!" Faith leaped from the couch. "What happened to the morning room?"

The helicopter bearing the camera moved on, back toward the Golden Gate Bridge. But the grim image was already burned in Faith's brain. The morning room was completely gone, and the roof of the floor above it sat like a hat on a pile of pulverized debris.

Oggie was looking at her.

Faith marched into the kitchen and tried the Sausalito number again. Again she was advised to call at another time.

She went back to the living room.

"Well?" Oggie asked.

"The phones are still out."

"What're you gonna do?"

She smoothed her hair back with a nervous hand. "What *can* I do, really?"

Oggie shrugged. "Nothin' that I can see."

"The Bay Bridge is closed. And the Golden Gate. They're not letting anybody in except emergency crews. I have to be realistic."

"Right. Realistic. But the Richmond-San Rafael Bridge is still open, I do believe. . . ."

"But everyone's probably all right, don't you think? I mean, what's the likelihood that there was anyone in the morning room or on the floor above it when the earth quake happened?''

''Not large?''

''Not *that* large. It *was* early. On a Sunday.''

''Probably nothing to worry about then, right?''

''But that's the first place they all go. On Sunday morning. When they get up, you know?''

''Well, since you say it, I guess I know now.''

Faith went to the couch and tried to sit down.

She couldn't do it. ''It's insane. There's nothing I can do.''

''Right. Nothing you can—''

''But I can't just sit here.''

''I can understand that.''

''I . . . I have to go there. I have to go to them.''

Oggie reached for his cane. ''Fine. I'm ready.''

''Oh, Uncle Oggie, I can't ask you to—''

''You sure as hell can. And whether you ask me or not I'm goin'. I wouldn't miss this for the world.''

''Price! Eli!''

The boy in his arms stirred. ''Price?'' The excited whisper brimmed with hope.

He rested his chin on the small, dusty head. ''They're looking for us.''

Above them and several yards away, Price heard boards being shifted.

''Price!''

''Eli!''

One of the voices sounded like Justine's. And the other Price could have sworn, belonged to his brother. More voices joined the chorus. Ariel's. And Regis's, too.

Price closed his eyes. Praying again. He'd turn into a praying fool before this was over. This time it was a prayer of gratitude. Everyone in the house was alive.

So far.

"We have to answer them," Eli whispered.

Price thought of the precariousness of their cave. How much more rubble would shouting dislodge? And would the damn table withstand the strain?

"I suppose we have to chance it," Price said.

"Now?"

"Now."

They threw back their heads in unison and yelled as loud as they could.

"Here!"

"We're here!"

"Help, we're under here!"

The table started to shake. Above them, something shifted, and they heard a scraping sound.

The man and the boy fell silent. Price didn't know he was holding his breath until he heard his brother call.

"We heard you! Sit tight! We'll get you out!"

Chapter Fourteen

Since Oggie insisted on driving, they took his Eldorado "Wouldn't drive nothin' else," he told Faith with pride.

Oggie had something of a lead foot, but Faith didn' complain. She wanted to get there fast, anyway. They race down highway 80 at well over the speed limit. But traffi thickened and slowed them down as they neared the belea guered Bay Area.

Oggie brought them in from above, across the endles Richmond–San Rafael Bridge. As the old man had pre dicted, the bridge was open, though traffic was bumper-to bumper all the way across. They got on Highway 101 on th other side, then had to detour off the highway in Cor Madera for some reason Faith never did understand. Ogg drove with one hand most of the time, fiddling with the ra dio dial, trying to get a station with decent coverage of th earthquake. He didn't have much luck.

"Need me a new radio, I'm afraid," he muttered more than once.

Fortunately, except for the failing radio, the ancient Cadillac ran like a dream.

They crossed the finger of bay to Marin City without incident. And at last, they were there. On Bridgeway in Sausalito, passing the Marin ship area, the docks that housed stately yachts and floating software companies. The damage from the earthquake didn't appear too bad, though Oggie dodged bricks in the street and traffic crawled.

All the streetlights were out. A few buildings, she noticed, looked not quite right somehow—their facades had massive cracks now, or decorative masonry had chipped and broken off. There were a lot of shattered windows. And already, in many places, yellow caution tape had been strung. All over, people were at work cleaning up the mess.

Faith told Oggie where to turn to start the climb into the hills. There, on narrow, winding streets amid thick, green trees, the damage was even harder to gauge. Most of the houses seemed intact. But only a closer look would let her know for sure.

And Faith had no time for a closer look. By then, five hours had passed since they'd left North Magdalene. All she wanted was to find out whether Price and his family were okay.

At last they reached the gravel drive that would take them to the house. Faith could see its tall towers and bays, standing proud against the cloudless sky.

Oggie drove them right to the kitchen door. As they approached, they saw a lot of men, climbing all over what was left of the morning room wing. Some of the men wore hard hats and sturdy rescue gear. But there were others in cutoffs and T-shirts and running shoes, pitching in to do what they could. The screams of chain saws filled the air.

Dread settled in Faith's stomach, like a hard ball of ice. Why would all these men be here right now, when there were so many emergencies all over the Bay Area? Unless there was someone trapped under there . . .

Oggie pulled the car to a stop. Faith spotted Ariel, not ten feet away, in a torn pair of linen slacks and a dirty lime green silk shirt. Ariel turned at the sound of the car. Her face was smudged with soot and crisscrossed with scratches. Her hair—as always—was hanging in her eyes.

Faith jumped from the car. Ariel's exhausted face lit up. She shoved the hair out of her eyes and started running, her arms outstretched.

"Oh, my dear!" Ariel cried. "I cannot tell you. We need you so. I'm so grateful you've come."

Her nostrils filled with the smell of Tabu and dust, Faith wrapped her own arms around Price's mother and held on for dear life.

Then Ariel pulled back.

Faith searched the older woman's face. "Who is it? Who's under there?"

"Price and Eli."

"Are they alive?"

"Yes, we think so."

Just then, the ground came alive; it rumbled and rolled. Faith grabbed Ariel again and prayed that the man and boy beneath the rubble would be all right when the shaking stopped.

At last, near dark, having removed the roof piece by piece with power saws, the rescue workers finally managed to clear away enough broken beams and plaster that the boy and the man had room to crawl through to safety.

Parker, in the center of the action, had just grabbed Eli and pulled him into his arms when once again an aftershock began. Parker clutched the child close as everyone waited for the shaking to stop.

As soon as the earth was still, Justine slogged through the rubble to reach her son. She held out her hungry arms. Parker handed the boy over.

Right then, the child looked down and saw that the small tunnel he'd just climbed through was gone.

He started shouting, "Price! Price!"

"Shh..." Justine murmured soothingly, "Settle down, they'll get him out."

Parker signaled to her to carry the boy out of there. She turned and stumbled away, her child begging frantically, "Mommy, where's Price? He has to get out. They have to get him out...."

The EMTs were waiting to look the boy over. They surrounded Justine and took Eli from her.

In the rubble, Parker was calling, "Price? Big brother, you still with me?"

He got no answer. Faith heard a strangled sob from behind her. She turned to meet Ariel's despairing violet eyes.

The women grabbed each other.

"Tell me he's going to be all right," Ariel whispered in Faith's ear. "Tell me. Tell me, please."

"He will," Faith replied through clenched teeth. "I promise he will."

Half an hour later, beneath an almost full moon, they pulled Price out, in one piece but unconscious. Faith was granted one quick glimpse of his frighteningly pale, dirty face, and then the paramedics were all over him, monitoring vital signs, strapping him to a gurney.

"Come on, gal," Oggie said, "get Ariel and Regis. And Parker, too. We'll follow the ambulance right to the hospital."

Quickly Faith collected the elder Montgomerys and herded them into the back seat of the Cadillac.

Then she turned to Parker, "Come on. Get in."

"Naw. I'll take Mom's Range Rover, I think. So we'll have another car if anyone wants to go home."

Faith looked him over. His Def Leppard T-shirt was ripped in several places. His long hair had plaster in it. His face was filthy, and his high-tops were covered with dust.

Love welled in her, pure and strong. "Are you sure you're ready for this?"

Parker threw back his head and laughed at the big, pale moon. "Hell. After today, I'm ready for just about anything. And about time, too."

"Has your license expired?"

"Nope. It's still good. Barely."

"Drive carefully. There are people who count on you."

"I know. I'm one lucky guy."

Oggie was already gunning the engine, eager to move. "Come on, gal. That ambulance'll get away...."

Faith settled into her seat, and Parker shut the door.

The hospital was packed. There weren't enough rooms to go around. They put Price on a bed in a hallway, with an IV in his arm, and people in white coats came by periodically to pry open his closed eyes and check his pulse.

Faith was with him, around ten, when he woke. He groaned and slowly opened his eyes.

He blinked. "God. Am I dreaming?"

"Don't talk. I'll get a nurse or something."

He started to sit up, then settled back with another groan.

Faith flagged down a passing orderly, and within moments medical people were all over Price, checking his eyes and his pulse and his IV drip, scribbling notes to themselves. Then, as quickly as they'd descended, they left, threatening that they'd return soon.

Faith stayed back out of the way until Price was no longer surrounded by white coats. Then she cautiously drew near once more.

He smiled at her. A wobbly smile, but a smile nonetheless. "You're really here."

"Did you think I'd be able to stay away?"

He said nothing, just looked at her.

Faith thought of the others. "Your mother and father. And Parker..."

"What?"

"They'll kill me if I don't tell them you're awake. They went to find the cafeteria. To see about getting something to eat."

He was frowning. It looked as if it hurt him to do that. "*Parker's* here?"

"You bet."

His eyes clouded. "Eli?"

"He's fine. Or he will be, as soon as he finds out that *you're* all right." She put up both hands. "Stay right there."

"No problem."

She hurried down to the nurse's desk and asked them to page the Montgomerys in the cafeteria. They looked at her as if she'd lost her mind. The hospital was total chaos. They had better things to do than page people in the cafeteria.

Faith hurried back to Price's bedside. "They can't page them. I'll have to go get them."

"You're real," he said.

That gave her pause. "Huh?"

"Every time you leave, I get positive I only hallucinated you."

"No. I'm perfectly real. Listen, I'll just go and—"

His hand closed over her wrist. "No way. Stay with me."

"But—"

"Are all of them all right?"

"Yes. They're fine."

He sighed. "I thought so. But I wanted to be sure. And you don't have to go. They'll be back here soon enough."

"But don't you want me to—"

"No." His eyes drifted closed, but he didn't let go of her wrist.

Two nurses barreled past them, jostling Faith. And voices kept coming over the loudspeaker, calling doctors to different places of the hospital. A man in another bed, about four feet from the end of Price's, kept groaning and mumbling to himself.

"How long will you stick around?"

The sound of Price's voice surprised her; she'd assumed he'd drifted to sleep again. She looked and saw that he was watching her. "I, um, thought we could talk about that a little later, when you're feeling stronger."

"Later." He repeated the word as if it offended him.

"Yes."

He shook his head, then swore softly at the pain it caused him. "No. Let's talk now."

The man on the other bed mumbled something unintelligible. A little girl went by in a wheelchair, pushed by a man with a beard.

Faith ached to touch Price. So she reached out and smoothed his brow. He closed his eyes once more and released her wrist, his hand dropping to the sheet as if the effort of holding her there had tired him out.

"I've missed you so," she whispered.

His eyes popped open. "So how long will you stay?"

"Oh, Price..."

"How long?"

She gave up all pretense of evasion. She had made her decision, and he might as well know it. Still, the words came out haltingly. "I guess... indefinitely. If you want me to."

"Indefinitely..." He seemed to run the word through his mind, checking for flaws.

She thought she'd better explain a little further. She bent close, so that none of the people who kept rushing past his bed could hear. "I guess I just can't stay away from you, Price Montgomery. I...want to be beside you, on any terms...." Her face was turning red, she just knew it. She felt like ten kinds of fool.

He groped for her hand. She gave it to him. He brought it to his lips. The brushing caress set every nerve she had humming.

"Are you telling me you won't send me away again, even if I won't marry you? Even if there are no babies?"

The man on the bed a few feet away went on groaning and babbling to himself. And a voice on the PA system demanded that Dr. Valerian report to ER immediately. A woman walked by, sobbing, muttering to herself, "She's all right. They said she's going to be all right...."

Faith hardly heard any of it. She bit her lip and nodded, squeezing the hand that held hers. "I want every moment I can have with you. Life is too short. You're the one I love. And I'll be with you. Whether you'll marry me or not."

His eyes were so tender. "That's bull," he said.

Faith blinked and pulled back. "What?"

"It would last about two weeks. Then you'd be miserable again."

"No, I..."

"Faith. Come back here."

"But, I..."

"Don't argue with an injured man. Come on. Bend down close."

Cautiously she leaned near him once more.

"Closer."

She put her ear near his lips.

"Marry me," he whispered.

She was sure she hadn't heard right. She pulled back enough to gape at him. "What?"

"Marry me. As soon as I can get out of this place. Marry me . . . and we'll throw all those damn foil packets out the window of our honeymoon suite."

Faith had to remind herself to breathe. "Oh, Price. What are you saying?"

"That I love you, Faith. And that I want you to marry me. And I want to have babies with you. As many babies as . . . God will give us."

Her legs felt strange. She had to grip the bed rail. "What—? I can't— Are you—?"

Price chuckled. And then he groaned.

"What's the matter?"

"My head aches. Even my *hair* is in pain."

"I'll get the—"

"Forget it. Just kiss me."

"You're not in any condition for kissing."

"Bend down here."

"Price."

"No. I mean it. Down here. Now."

She cast a quick glance around. No one was looking at them. "I don't think we should . . ."

"Don't torture me. Kiss me."

"Price . . ."

"Don't you *want* to kiss me?"

"You know I do."

"Well, then?"

Carefully, mindful of his bruised and battered body and the IV drip, as well, she bent over and laid her mouth against his. It was not the most passionate kiss they'd ever shared. But it was certainly the sweetest.

When she looked up, the Montgomerys and Oggie were blocking the hallway. They were all grinning.

Eli, holding his mother's hand, had the widest smile of all.

Faith stepped back beside Oggie to let the others get near the bed.

"Think everythin's gonna be all right now, gal?" Oggie asked.

"I do, Uncle Oggie. I truly do."

"He gonna marry you now?"

"Yes. He is."

After a few moments, they joined the others, close to Price.

Price was asking about the house. Ariel said everything in it was now in pieces on the floors. But the building itself—not counting the morning room wing, of course—seemed fine.

Nevertheless, they planned to camp out on the grounds for a night or two, until the aftershocks tapered off and someone could be brought in to declare the place safe.

"Roughing it," Ariel said proudly. "Like everyone else in the Bay Area will be doing."

They shared what they knew of how others had fared. Several people had died. And more than one building had been completely destroyed. But all of the hospitals remained fully functional, if overcrowded. And the fires had been kept to a minimum, thanks to lack of wind and quick response by local fire fighters.

Soon enough, a nurse came up and said they couldn't all stay with the patient; they were blocking the hallway. It was agreed that everyone but Faith would retreat to a waiting room for a while.

As soon as the others were gone, Faith moved close. She took Price's hand.

"Go ahead, ask," he said.

"No. I know you're probably tired."

"I am. But I know it's driving you crazy, wanting to know."

"All right," she admitted. "Tell me. What happened, Price? What changed your mind?"

He mouthed a name. "Eli."

She repeated it. "Eli?"

Price nodded. "He told me that I had to get on with the job of living. That Danny would have wanted that."

"And you actually listened to him?"

He squeezed her hand. "Faith, when you're trapped in the dark under two stories of rubble, things you never understood before tend to become very clear." He tugged on her hand, so that she'd bend down again.

She held back a little. "You saved Eli's life, didn't you?"

He made a noise in his throat. "Hell. Maybe. It's impossible to say for sure, though."

Faith knew she was right, even though Price wasn't willing to come right out and admit it. She thought of Danny. And all the years that Price had blamed himself for Danny's death. Now he'd saved the life of another little boy. Maybe it didn't make up for the loss of Danny. But it seemed that it meant something. It made it possible for Price to forgive himself.

Or maybe it had just been the earthquake that did it. An act of God, as Uncle Oggie had said.

"Come back down here."

Faith was still marveling. "Eli's very bright. He's a super reader, you know?"

"Faith . . ."

"All right, all right." She bent close.

"I love you," he said.

Her heart took wing as her lips met his.

In another hallway, off the waiting room where he'd just left the Montgomerys, Oggie Jones chortled to himself. Yessiree, life was grand.

He pulled out a cigar.

"You can't smoke that in here!" a passing orderly told him huffily.

"All right, all right," Oggie said. "Show me to the door. It's time I headed on home, anyway. I've done what needed doing here."

Epilogue

Two weeks later, Faith and Price were married in the Community Church in North Magdalene. Parker was best man and Eli Clary was the ring-bearer. Since both Price and Faith considered Montgomery House their home, they returned there to live after all the necessary repairs had been completed.

Justine Clary, her son Eli, and Eli's gray cat, Shaker, moved to North Magdalene, where Justine took over the Foothill Inn.

Sir Winston seemed to have disappeared. But then, three months after the earthquake, Ariel was enjoying an outdoor show of her watercolors in Plaza de Vina Del Mar Park, right beyond the ferry docks. The black bird swooped down out of nowhere and landed on her head.

"How you been, baby?" Sir Winston inquired.

Ariel laughed and told him that she'd been just fine.

Eden Jones bore a second daughter, Diana, in June. Evie Riggins bore a son, Stephen, in October.

And on Easter Sunday, one year after Faith and Price were married, Faith went into labor with their first child. Oggie appeared out of nowhere only minutes after a little girl was born.

Oggie took one look at the tiny scrap of humanity and declared, "This here is Hope."

Though Price and Faith had been arguing about names for months, nobody argued with Oggie. They named the baby Hope.

* * * * *

*Watch for HONEYMOON HOTLINE,
the next installment in Christine Rimmer's
JONES GANG series, coming in November from
Silhouette Special Edition.*

The first book in the exciting new
Fortune's Children series is

HIRED HUSBAND

by *New York Times* bestselling writer
Rebecca Brandewyne

Beginning in July 1996
Only from Silhouette Books

Here's an exciting sneak preview....

Minneapolis, Minnesota

As Caroline Fortune wheeled her dark blue Volvo into the underground parking lot of the towering, glass-and-steel structure that housed the global headquarters of Fortune Cosmetics, she glanced anxiously at her gold Piaget wristwatch. An accident on the snowy freeway had caused rush-hour traffic to be a nightmare this morning. As a result, she was running late for her 9:00 a.m. meeting—and if there was one thing her grandmother, Kate Winfield Fortune, simply couldn't abide, it was slack, unprofessional behavior on the job. And lateness was the sign of a sloppy, disorganized schedule.

Involuntarily, Caroline shuddered at the thought of her grandmother's infamous wrath being unleashed upon her. The stern rebuke would be precise, apropos, scathing and delivered with coolly raised, condemnatory eyebrows and in icy tones of haughty grandeur that had in the past reduced many an executive—even the male ones—at Fortune Cosmetics not only to obsequious apologies, but even to tears. Caroline had seen it happen on more than one occasion, although, much to her gratitude and relief, she herself was seldom a target of her grandmother's anger. And she wouldn't be this morning, either, not if she could help it. That would be a disastrous way to start out the new year.

Grabbing her Louis Vuitton totebag and her black leather portfolio from the front passenger seat, Caroline stepped gracefully from the Volvo and slammed the door. The heels of her Maud Frizon pumps clicked briskly on the concrete floor as she hurried toward the bank of elevators that would take her up into the skyscraper owned by her family. As the elevator doors slid open, she rushed down the long, plushly carpeted corridors of one of the hushed upper floors toward the conference room.

By now Caroline had her portfolio open and was leafing through it as she hastened along, reviewing her notes she had prepared for her presentation. So she didn't see Dr. Nicolai Valkov until she literally ran right into him. Like her, he had his head bent over his own portfolio, not watching where he was going. As the two of them collided, both their portfolios and the papers inside went flying. At the unexpected impact, Caroline lost her balance, stumbled, and would have fallen had not Nick's strong, sure hands abruptly shot out, grabbing hold of her and pulling her to him to steady her. She gasped, startled and stricken, as she came up hard against his broad chest, lean hips and corded thighs, her face just inches from his own— as though they were lovers about to kiss.

Caroline had never been so close to Nick Valkov before, and, in that instant, she was acutely aware of him— not just as a fellow employee of Fortune Cosmetics but also as a man. Of how tall and ruggedly handsome he was, dressed in an elegant, pin-striped black suit cut in the European fashion, a crisp white shirt, a foulard tie and a pair of Cole Haan loafers. Of how dark his thick, glossy hair and his deep-set eyes framed by raven-wing brows were—so dark that they were almost black, despite the bright, fluorescent lights that blazed overhead. Of the whiteness of his straight teeth against his bronzed skin as a brazen, mocking grin slowly curved his wide, sensual mouth.

"Actually, I *was* hoping for a sweet roll this morning— but I daresay you would prove even tastier, Ms. Fortune," Nick drawled impertinently, his low, silky voice tinged with a faint accent born of the fact that Russian, not English, was his native language.

At his words, Caroline flushed painfully, embarrassed and annoyed. If there was one person she always attempted to avoid at Fortune Cosmetics, it was Nick Valkov. Following the breakup of the Soviet Union, he had emigrated to the United States, where her grandmother had hired him to direct the company's research and development department. Since that time, Nick had constantly demonstrated marked, traditional, Old World tendencies that had led Caroline to believe he not only had no use for equal rights but also would actually have been more than happy to turn back the clock several centuries where females were concerned. She thought his remark was typical of his attitude toward women: insolent, arrogant and domineering. Really, the man was simply insufferable!

Caroline couldn't imagine what had ever prompted her grandmother to hire him—and at a highly generous salary, too—except that Nick Valkov was considered one of the foremost chemists anywhere on the planet. Deep down inside Caroline knew that no matter how he behaved, Fortune Cosmetics was extremely lucky to have him. Still, that didn't give him the right to manhandle and insult her!

"I assure you that you would find me more bitter than a cup of the strongest black coffee, Dr. Valkov," she insisted, attempting without success to free her trembling body from his steely grip, while he continued to hold her so near that she could feel his heart beating steadily in his chest—and knew he must be equally able to feel the erratic hammering of her own.

"Oh, I'm willing to wager there's more sugar and cream to you than you let on, Ms. Fortune." To her utter mortification and outrage, she felt one of Nick's hands slide insidiously up her back and nape to her luxuriant mass of sable hair, done up in a stylish French twist.

"You know so much about fashion," he murmured, eyeing her assessingly, pointedly ignoring her indignation and efforts to escape from him. "So why do you always wear your hair like this . . . so tightly wrapped and severe? I've never seen it down. Still, that's the way it needs to be worn, you know . . . soft, loose, tangled about your face. As it is, your hair fairly cries out for a man to take the pins from it, so he can see how long it is. Does it fall past your shoulders?" He quirked one eyebrow inquisitively, a mocking half smile still twisting his lips, letting her know he was enjoying her obvious discomfiture. "You aren't going to tell me, are you? What a pity. Because my guess is that it does—and I'd like to know if I'm right. And these glasses." He indicated the large, square, tortoiseshell frames perched on her slender, classic nose. "I think you use them to hide behind more than you do to see. I'll bet you don't actually even need them at all."

Caroline felt the blush that had yet to leave her cheeks deepen, its heat seeming to spread throughout her entire quivering body. Damn the man! Why must he be so infuriatingly perceptive?

Because everything that Nick suspected was true.

* * * * *

To read more, don't miss
HIRED HUSBAND
by Rebecca Brandewyne,
Book One in the new
FORTUNE'S CHILDREN series,
beginning this month and available only from
Silhouette Books!

MILLION DOLLAR SWEEPSTAKES

Silhouette
SPECIAL EDITION ™

WONDERING WHAT EVER HAPPENED TO YOUR FAVORITE CHARACTERS...?

Silhouette Special Edition's
SPIN-OFF SPECTACULAR finally gives much-loved
characters their own story. Catch these exciting titles from
some of your favorite authors:

OF TEXAS LADIES, COWBOYS...AND BABIES: (August, SE #1045)
Jodi O'Donnell first introduced Reid and Glenna in DADDY WAS A COWBOY
(SR #1082). Now as Glenna begins her life anew—with Reid—she
discovers she's going to have a baby!

A FATHER'S GIFT: (August, SE #1046)
In the first book of GREAT EXPECTATIONS, a new miniseries from
Andrea Edwards, a tough cop becomes Mr. Mom when he moves back
in with the family he's never stopped loving.

DADDY OF THE HOUSE: (September, SE #1052)
Diana Whitney's new series PARENTHOOD begins with the story
of Cassie Scott—and she's expecting! And the perfect daddy is
Jack Merrill—who's already the father of matchmaking twins!

THE HUSBAND: (October, SE #1059)
The popular SMYTHESHIRE, MASSACHUSETTS series by Elizabeth August
comes to Special Edition in October!

Don't miss any of these wonderful titles, only for our readers—only from
Silhouette Special Edition.

Who can resist a Texan...or a Calloway?

This September, award-winning author
ANNETTE BROADRICK
returns to Texas, with a brand-new
story about the Calloways...

SONS ►OF◄ TEXAS

Rogues and Ranchers

CLINT: The brave leader. Used to keeping secrets.

CADE: The Lone Star Stud. Used to having women
fall at his feet...

MATT: The family guardian. Used to handling
trouble...

They must discover the identity of the mystery
woman with Calloway eyes—and uncover a
conspiracy that threatens their family....

Look for **SONS OF TEXAS:** Rogues and Ranchers
in September 1996!

Only from Silhouette...where passion lives.

SONSST

You're About to Become a *Privileged Woman*

Reap the rewards of fabulous free gifts and benefits with proofs-of-purchase from Silhouette and Harlequin books

Pages & Privileges™

It's our way of thanking you for buying our books at your favorite retail stores.

PROOF OF PURCHASE
SSE-PP159
Offer expires October 31, 1996

Pages & Privileges ™

**Harlequin and Silhouette—
the most privileged readers in the world!**

For more information about Harlequin and Silhouette's PAGES & PRIVILEGES program call the Pages & Privileges Benefits Desk: 1-503-794-2499

Silhouette®

SSE-PP159